'Here. Drink this,' Zan ordered.

The girl sighed, accepted the glass, then sipped.

Zan tossed back a glass of brandy himself before he turned to her. To his amazement his temper heated, rapid and out of control, then bubbled up to spill out in hard words. 'What were you thinking, madam, getting yourself trapped by an incoming tide? Did you not see what was happening?'

The soft summer blue of her gaze sharpened, as did her voice. 'No, I did not see. Or I would not have been trapped, would I?'

She had spirit. He'd give her that. Zan raised his brows as his irritation began to ebb. 'Now what do I do with you?'

'You do nothing with me.' Her eyes flashed. 'I am very grateful that you rescued me, of course, but I am perfectly capable of returning home on my own. You are at liberty to ride on your way.'

Zan simply stood and looked at her, torn between amusement and frustration. She sat and looked back at him, mutiny in her face.

And there it was. The sword of Damocles fell.

Anne O'Brien was born and has lived for most of her life in Yorkshire. There she taught history, before deciding to fulfil a lifetime ambition to write romantic historical fiction. She won a number of short story competitions until published for the first time by Mills & Boon. As well as writing, she finds time to enjoy gardening, cooking and watercolour painting. She now lives with her husband in an eighteenth-century cottage in the depths of the Welsh Marches.

You can find out about Anne's books and more at her website: www.anneobrien.co.uk

Recent novels by the same author:

THE DISGRACED MARCHIONESS*
THE OUTRAGEOUS DEBUTANTE*
THE ENIGMATIC RAKE*
CONQUERING KNIGHT, CAPTIVE LADY
CHOSEN FOR THE MARRIAGE BED
COMPROMISED MISS†

The Faringdon Scandals

†RAKE BEYOND REDEMPTION is
   connected to COMPROMISED MISS

and in MIRA® Books:

VIRGIN WIDOW

RAKE BEYOND REDEMPTION

Anne O'Brien

First published in Great Britain 2010
Large Print edition 2010
Harlequin Mills & Boon Limited,
Eton House, 18-24 Paradise Road, Richmond, Surrey TW9 1SR

ISBN: 978 0 263 21169 6

Harlequin Mills & Boon policy is to use papers that are natural, renewable and recyclable products and made from wood grown in sustainable forests. The logging and manufacturing process conform to the legal environmental regulations of the country of origin.

Printed and bound in Great Britain
by CPI Antony Rowe, Chippenham, Wiltshire

AUTHOR NOTE

COMPROMISED MISS ended with Luke and Harriette finding true happiness together. But two of the characters in COMPROMISED MISS, both of them dear to my heart, were left under a dark cloud. Marie-Claude de la Roche from France, young, unhappy, widowed with a small child to raise, might have been rescued from physical danger, but was now dependent on an unknown family in a new country. And then there was Alexander Ellerdine, unscrupulous rake and smuggler, his character ruined beyond redemption, guilty by his own admission of any number of terrible sins and cast off by his family.

Both were alone and, for different reasons, without hope.

Were they to remain so? I decided I could not abandon them, and RAKE BEYOND REDEMPTION came to be written. Marie-Claude needed a new life, and the chance of love to replace the one she had lost. Could it be with the disreputable rake Alexander Ellerdine? It would seem to be completely beyond belief with a man of Alexander's black and vicious reputation. How could the immoral villain of COMPROMISED MISS possibly be reinstated into Polite Society?

But perhaps…

Read on to discover how Alexander and Marie-Claude find their destiny together against all the odds. I'm certain you will love the grief and passion, the pain and the eventual fulfilment in their story as much as I enjoyed writing it.

To George, as ever, with love.

Chapter One

June 1818—Lydyard's Pride, a rambling manor house on the cliffs above the smuggling village of Old Wincomlee, Sussex

'How can you not be happy? What more can you possibly want from life than what you have? Considering everything, you should be deliriously content!'

Alone in her bedchamber overlooking the cliff top and endless succession of sprightly waves, Marie-Claude Hallaston, her French accent more pronounced than usual, raised her chin at her own sharp reprimand and continued to draw patterns with her fingertip on the grimy, salt-encrusted pane. Leaves and scrolls bloomed around her artistically executed initials, becoming more flamboyant as she replied with a cross frown, 'I really don't know what I want. I've no idea what's sunk my spirits, that's the problem.' She added another swirl of vegetation to the pattern on the glass, before regarding her begrimed finger with distaste.

Perhaps it was the remnants of the fever that had laid her low in the spring months and had robbed her of all her spirits, the reason she was now here at Lydyard's Pride, to enjoy the benefits of sea air and restore her to health. Perhaps. Or, Marie-Claude added with a sigh, 'Perhaps it's because I see myself as a widow for the rest of my life, wearing black, high-collared gowns and lace caps!'

And Marie-Claude breathed on the glass to obliterate the leaves before, rather wistfully, drawing the outline of a little heart.

Then impatiently swiped the heart away with the heel of her hand.

This was no good. Rather than simply standing at the window and looking at the view, wallowing in wretched self-pity, she'd go and walk off her megrims. At least here at Lydyard's Pride she had no need to take a maid or one of the servants to escort her. No one knew her here. No one would think her immodest or in need of a chaperon. Besides, as a widow of long standing—six years!— she had earned the right to do as she pleased.

On which note of defiance, Marie-Claude tied the

satin ribbons of a plain straw bonnet—very suitable for a walk along the cliffs—and put on a dark blue velvet spencer over her gown of celestial-blue silk with its intricate knots of ribbon and ruched hem— not suitable at all for striding along the beach, but what matter. She exchanged her silk pumps for a pair of ankle boots, stalwart but still elegant on her narrow feet, and set off down the steep path to the cove and the village of Old Wincomlee. The light breeze was gentle, the sun dipping towards the sea, glowing on an enticing patch of shingle at the base of the cliff where the inlet narrowed to the first row of cottages, turning the stones a soft pink in the light. Little waves, lace-edged, frilled on to the pebbles. That's where she would go with no one to please but herself.

Alone. Always alone, the voice whispered in her mind. The little racing waves repeated the phrase as they shushed on the pebbles. *Alone.*

Marie-Claude's hands stilled on the ivory handle of her parasol as she prepared to snap open the delicate silk and lace. Would she go to her grave, never again knowing the nearness of a man who was more than brother or friend to her? Would she never have a *lover*? It swept through her, a driving need, an intense heat that raced over her skin. Suddenly her throat was desert dry with a longing, a longing so strong to feel the touch of a man's hard mouth against hers. To shiver under the determined caress of experienced fingers. To know the slide of naked flesh against hers, slick and hot with desire. To know the possession of a man's urgent body…

Well! Marie-Claude swallowed. Her breathing was shallow, her cheeks flushed as she finally snapped the parasol open. Such wanton thoughts. She should be ashamed—but found it difficult to be so. Why should she not imagine a perfection of male beauty if she wished to? Even if she was a widow with a five-year-old son. With a little laugh at her impossible dreaming, she twirled the lace parasol so that the fringe danced, and as the sea and shingle beckoned, Marie-Claude strode out down the cliff path, well-worn and distinct for a lady who was neat of foot. Something would happen. Surely there was something in fate's hand waiting for her.

At the brisk pace she set herself, Marie-Claude was soon stepping on to the beach. The scrunch of shingle was loud beneath her feet, and made for heavy going, but she persisted until she was at the water's edge, where she lifted her face to the kiss of sun and salty air. Her hair would curl outrageously but she did not care, her mood revived. How Raoul, her son, at present with Luke and Harriette at The Venmore, would love this. One day she must bring him here. Picking up one of the flat pebbles, she threw it far out, dusting the sand from her fingers, momentarily wishing for a man at her side to teach her son such skills as stone-skimming—perhaps even her mythical lover, she thought wryly—but she would do it just as well.

Her mind more at ease with the pretty scene, Marie-Claude walked slowly along the water's edge, stepping back as the waves encroached and retreated, encroached again. The tide had turned, she realised. Not that she knew anything about tides.

'You don't know much about anything really,' Marie-Claude commented waspishly, then laughed as a pair of gulls wheeled and screamed overhead as if in reply. 'And you are undoubtedly a foolish woman!'

But her optimism had returned.

The sun was descending rapidly now towards the horizon, reminding Marie-Claude of the need to retrace her steps. She turned on her heel.

And froze with a little gasp of surprise. And trepidation. In front of her, between her feet and the cliff with its steep track, a fast-flowing channel of water had appeared. How careless she had been. Why had she not had the sense to take note of the path of the incoming sea? Any woman of wit would have done so! But it was no great matter after all. She spun round towards the village itself. So she would have to make her way up the inlet and into Old Wincomlee, past the old inn, the Silver Boat, then walk around the path on the top of the cliff. A long way, she sighed, but the evening was still fair, the light good.

Her optimism was short-lived. A thread of anxiety encircled her heart, and tightened at what she saw. An expanse of water, little waves chasing one after the other, stretched before her as well as at her side, fast running now, growing deeper by the second. Behind her the first little wave lapped at her boots.

Surrounded!

Mon Dieu! Marie-Claude took a breath and swallowed hard against the first leap of real fear. No point in being afraid. She'd lived through worse dangers than this in her life. She'd just have to brave the water. It wasn't too deep yet. No point at all in standing here, frozen in indecision.

Closing the parasol with fingers that did not quite tremble and tucking it beneath her arm, Marie-Claude hitched her skirts and stepped into the water, pushing herself forwards as it suddenly grew far deeper than she could have imagined. For a moment she considered retreating to the little island of shingle, but she knew she must not. Summoning all her courage, she forced herself to take another step and then another. Around her the waves were swirling, overlapping each other. Her boots, her skirts and petticoats were soaked and heavy. The stones beneath her feet sucked and slid, making progress slow and difficult. How had the sunny evening suddenly become so menacing, so threatening? Grasping her skirts tighter, Marie-Claude had to fight to stop panic anchoring her in her tracks.

The cottages of Old Wincomlee and the roof of the Silver Boat suddenly seemed an impossibly long way distant.

Ellerdine Manor: a manor house on the cliff top, a mile west of the smuggling village of Old Wincomlee

A cold sensation trickled through his chest. Alexander Ellerdine, at some half-seen, half-heard command, raised his head, pushed himself upright, hands tightening over the carved arms of his chair, then, with an impatient shrug and a flex of his fingers, allowed himself to settle back. The spaniel at his side subsided with a sigh.

'Just a goose walking over my grave, Bess.' The gentleman's voice was heavily sardonic as he stretched to run a light caress over the dog's ears. 'Nothing new in that!'

Shadows began to lengthen in the room as afternoon dipped into early evening. There were still long hours of daylight left to be enjoyed, but the corners of the shabby library in Ellerdine Manor where the sun no longer reached on this June evening were dark and sombre with neglect. Alexander Ellerdine sprawled in a well-worn Chippendale Windsor chair, booted feet crossed at the ankle on the desktop. Before him, leaving careless rings of liquid on a mess of scattered papers, stood a half-empty decanter of superior French brandy, courtesy of the Brotherhood of the Free Traders. In his hand was a half-empty glass of the deep amber liquor. Clearly the focus of his mind was far distant. He did not see the unkempt surroundings. The threadbare carpet, the faded curtains at the windows, the worn upholstery on a once-elegant set of spindle-legged chairs, the undusted leather-bound books that looked as if they had not been taken down from the shelves any time in the past decade—he did not notice them. Perhaps he was too used to the deficiencies of his library to note the depredations of time and lack of money. And of lack of interest.

Alexander Ellerdine. Gentleman, landowner, expert smuggler.

Wrecker.

A man with blood on his hands.

A man of ruthless energies and dangerous reputation.

Despite the dust and the worn furnishings, he made a striking impression. His home might be shabby, but he was not. Here was a man who had a care for appearances. His topboots were highly polished, his breeches well cut, his white shirt of good quality linen. If there was any carelessness it was the lack of a cravat, his shirt worn casually open at the neck to show his strong throat and the firm flesh of his chest. His hair, dark as to be almost black, was longer than was fashionable, curling against his collar, and disordered from the attentions of restless fingers. His eyes, set beneath similarly dark brows, were the deep blue of an angry, storm-whipped sea, hawk-like in their intensity. Even slouched as he was, it was clear that he was tall and rangy, not heavily built, but with a wiry athleticism that told of a life of action and strenuous activity. The hand gripped around the stem of the old glass was well moulded, fine-boned with long fingers, nails neatly pared. His face would have been formidably handsome, if it were not set in such sombre lines.

Suddenly, again, he turned his head, sharply, eyes and features arrested, at the echo of footsteps in the entrance hall. It was a breathtaking transformation.

There was the dark glamour. The breathtaking allure of wild good looks fired with animation. But then the gleam of anticipation was quenched, hooded beneath heavy lids as the sounds died away. Only his house-keeper, Mrs Shaw… Not the man he was half-expecting, Rackham or one of the other vicious minions of Captain D'Acre, commander of the smuggling gang out of Rottingdean. Not one of the Fly-By-Nights whose hold on the Free Trade along the Sussex coast was becoming more brutal by the month.

Alexander Ellerdine reached for the decanter to refill the glass as the house settled heavily around him, silent except for the creak of old timbers and the rattle of a loose pane of glass in the stiff breeze off the sea. Except that something—that same *something*—no more than a shiver of awareness, but still impossible to ignore, traced an uneasy path down his spine.

Irritated, Alexander lifted the decanter to pour another glass.

And froze, perfectly still. Hand outstretched. Listening. All senses suddenly stretched. Almost sniffing the air. Or sifting through the vibrations of some… What *was* it? That same slither of cold, now from his chest into his belly. A warning? Some presentiment of danger? There was the finger again—now of ice—scratching between his shoulder blades so that he inhaled sharply.

The spaniel at his side sat up.

'What is it, Bess?'

He stilled her with his hand, but the foreboding did not go away, rather an uncomfortable breath of misgiving tripped across his skin, settled in the marrow of his bones. As he would have been the first to admit, he was not a man given to anxieties over the unseen and the unknown. Alexander Ellerdine was not a superstitious man, but one who lived by his wits and his own resources. Confident and assured of his own skills, he had no truck with the smugglers' fears of long-drowned sailors come back to haunt them or the ghosts of murdered excise-men roaming the cliffs. Captain Rodmell, the Preventives' efficient and oh-so-capable Riding Officer and very much alive, was the greatest of his worries. But now in this empty room his flesh shivered. No idea what or why, Alexander tried to shrug it off, lifting the brandy to his lips.

But there was some *thing* that demanded his attention. Something was amiss. An urge to go and see for himself could not be shaken off and the longer he sat and debated, the stronger, more urgent the strange sense of fear grew…

That was it. Fear. A sense of mounting terror. As Alexander recognised the unusual emotion that jabbed beneath his ribs, he tossed back the rest of the brandy in the glass and pushed himself to his feet. Snatching up a well-cut riding-coat, he shrugged into it with casual but careless elegance. No doubt he was completely misguided and would find no reward for his efforts, but he'd saddle his mare and ride down to the harbour. Probably just a body of opportunistic excise-men lurking on the cliff on the unlikely off chance of tripping over a run of contraband. Alexander grinned with a feral show of teeth. No chance of that tonight, a night that would have a full moon and an abnormally high tide. Or perhaps Captain Rodmell of the Preventives was paying a passing visit to the inn, the Silver Boat, in Old Wincomlee. Nothing dangerous, nothing unusual in either occurrence. And yet…

He collected hat and riding whip, resigned to his journey. If there was nothing to warrant this irritating sense of danger, well, there was nothing lost, and besides… A faint smile curved his mouth. If he was in the mood he might chance a flirtation with Sally, who dispensed the ale with a provocative swing of her hips and a sharp tongue.

'What do you think, Bess? Should I tempt Sal into parting with a kiss or two? She's a lovely girl and not unwilling. And since no respectable woman would choose to tangle with the likes of me…'

The spaniel whined and licked his hand.

'Quite right, Bess. I'm beyond redemption. And what use do I have for a respectable woman? I've a tarnished name, no legitimate money and no prospects but the hangman's noose if I ever fall into Preventive Officer Rodmell's clutches with a cutter-load of contraband in my hands. Let's go and waste an hour looking for some danger that doesn't exist. And if she's of a mind, sample Sal's pretty lips.'

But a ripple of unease stirred the hairs on his forearms and made him shiver. As if some invisible sword of Damocles hovered over his life.

Alexander pushed his mare into an energetic walk along the cliff top, curbing her playful habits but letting her have enough of her head to make good progress. Skittish she might be, as were all females in his opinion, but she was sure-footed, allowing him to scan the scene before him. No one on the cliff path. No excise-men in sight. He, the horse and dog and the gulls seemed to be the only living creatures.

Kicking the mare into a trot, Bess following at his heels, he was soon at the edge of the village and slowed to wind through the lanes between the cottages. Quiet here too. A few children playing, voices raised in shouts and laughter. George Gadie's stout wife unpegging a line of washing. George, he presumed, with his son Gabriel, would be out with one of the fishing boats. He greeted Mistress Gadie with a lift of his hand and a preoccupied smile, but moved on. Dismounting in the courtyard, he looked in at the Silver Boat. Quiet as the grave. No one sampling the excellent stock of contraband. No Captain Rodmell sniffing out evidence of lawbreaking. Even Sam Babbercombe, the entirely sly and ruthless innkeeper who never passed up an opportunity to bring money into his pockets, was nowhere to be seen. Most likely sleeping off the effects of the last glass of brandy before emerging to fleece his evening customers.

Back outside, Alexander remounted. And frowned in indecision. There was nothing here to raise his hackles. So why did a hand still grip his heart? What made his belly churn, his throat dry? Clear sky, calm sea, the only boats in the bay the fishing smacks of the inhabitants of Old Wincomlee engaged in their legitimate business. Nothing to disturb him. No threat, no danger.

Down to the cove, the little harbour. There was *Venmore's Prize* anchored in the bay, sails neatly rolled and stashed. His cousin Harriette's vessel, not used as much now as she might once have been. A pity. A fine cutter even if not of the same quality as the ill-fated *Lydyard's Ghost*, fired by the Preventives in revenge for a successful contraband run that they failed to apprehend. Five years ago now, a night he did not care to think about.

Alexander's narrow-eyed scrutiny moved on. Next to the *Prize* was his own cutter. For a brief moment of sheer pleasure Alexander simply sat to admire her lines. The *Black Spectre*. Not the most cheerful of names, he thought with a wry amusement, but it had suited his mood at the time. She was a masterly vessel, riding the waves with spectacular ease, as swift and invisible on a dark night as the spectre he had named her. No outlay of money spared here, where a fast cutter to outrun the Preventives could be a matter of life or death.

He cast an experienced eye over the inlet and cove. High tide tonight, the water already racing in as it did through the deep channels worn over the years between the shingle. Not as an innocuous scene as might appear to the unwary or foolish who did not know they could be outflanked and surrounded within minutes. He looked lazily towards the distant headland where the first wave-edged inflow would now be showing.

And then he saw.

His heart gave a single heavy bound. His breath backed up in his lungs so that he had to drag in air.

A woman. Clearly in danger. Floundering through the water, skirts held ineffectually to try to prevent the drag of them in the rapidly rising swirl. She was already cut off from dry land. Soon she would be out of her depth entirely and overbalanced by the undertow. What the devil was she thinking? He cursed viciously, silently. This went far beyond foolish. This was suicidal!

Alexander did not hesitate. 'Stay!' he ordered the spaniel who promptly sank, chin to paws. And Alexander nudged the mare forwards into the water.

With hands and heels, keeping a tight hold on his own fear, Alexander persuaded the reluctant mare into the waves, urging her through the shallows, out on to the rapidly disappearing shingle until the water swirled knee-deep. The mare jibbed, but Alexander soothed with hands and voice, all the time keeping an eye on the floundering figure, skirts bunched in her hands, pressing determinedly forwards. She was not yet in any real danger, he estimated, but was having increasing difficulty in keeping her feet. Five minutes later and it would have been a different matter.

Not a woman, he decided as he took stock of the slight figure bracing herself against a larger wave. A mere girl, and a witless one at that! Didn't she know any better? Chancy tides were a matter of course at this time of year with the June surge, filling deep troughs and channels, leaving islands of shingle cut off from the shore, to be inundated when the only chance to escape from them was to swim. He'd wager his gold hunter that the girl—some empty-headed town girl in her fashionable gown and ribboned bonnet, even a damned parasol tucked beneath her arm!—couldn't swim.

Alexander drove the mare on. Not the best of animals for this—he'd rather have chosen one of his sturdy cobs—but she'd do the job well enough as long as the girl kept her nerve and didn't panic. The knot of fear began to ease.

He saw the moment she became aware of him. The moment she began to strive towards him, his fears flared once again into life.

'Stay there!' he shouted above the hush and slither of the shingle. 'Don't move! There's a deep channel in front of you. Just keep your footing. I'll come and get you.'

She froze.

At least, he acknowledged caustically, she had the sense to obey him.

Taking the path he knew to avoid the channel, Alexander manoeuvred the mare, conscious all the time that the water was fast rising above the girl's knees. Increasingly difficult to keep her footing, she swayed, almost overbalanced and in staggering abandoned the parasol, which was immediately swamped and sucked down into a watery grave. The seconds stretched out into what seemed endless minutes as the mare made headway. But then he was at her side—and not before time.

'Take my hand.' He leaned down, hand outstretched.

A brief impression of blue eyes, dark and wide with fear, fastened on his, lips white and tense, parting as she gasped for breath. Cheekbones stark under taut skin. Still the girl obeyed readily enough.

'Put your foot on mine and I'll lift you.'

'I can't…' A hint of panic.

'No choice. I can't lift you without some help from you. Not in this sea.' A rogue wave, higher than the rest, slapped against her, driving her against the mare's shoulder. He felt her nails dig into his hand. There was no time to be lost or they'd both be in difficulties. He could dismount and push her bodily into the saddle—if the mare could be guaranteed to stay still. Not the best idea…

Alexander tightened his hold around the girl's wrist, leaned to fix her eyes with his as if he would make her obey him through sheer strength of will. 'Lift your foot on to mine in the stirrup,' he ordered again forcefully. 'It's either that or drown. No place for misguided maidenly modesty here. Lift your foot, girl!'

A cold dose of common sense should do it.

It did. The girl grasped her skirts in one hand, placed her foot on his boot—'Now push up as I pull'—and he lifted her, catching her within his arm, turning her to sit before him, his arm around her waist to hold her secure. He turned the mare back to shore.

The girl sat quietly, rigidly in his arms. She shivered as the evening breeze cooled and her hands clenched, fingers digging into his forearms. Water dripped from her skirts to soak his breeches and boots. As the mare staggered momentarily, he heard her breath hitch, felt her muscles tense against him.

'Relax. You're safe now,' he said, concentrating on encouraging their mount. 'You'll not drown and I don't bite.'

He felt rather than saw her turn and lift her head to look up at his face. Her reply, sharp with an edge of authority, was not what he had expected.

'I never thought you would! Just get me to dry land.'

Where should he take her? Surprised by the edged reply, repressing a grin at the lack of thanks for saving the girl's life, Alexander considered the options. Not many really. He grimaced. Unless he wished to take advantage of the limitations of the Gadie household, it would have to be the Silver Boat. Not the place he would have chosen, for as an inn its hospitality had a finite quality. No comfort, no welcoming warmth, and even less sympathy to be found from Sam Babbercombe. But his rescued mermaid, skirts plastered to her legs, was now trembling from the breeze and her sodden garments and from shock. The Silver Boat it would have to be.

The mare ploughed on through the waves and shingle, the pull of the tide growing easier now with every step, and was soon on dry land. The spaniel greeted them with fuss and fierce barking. And Alexander was able at last to exhale slowly. For the first time since it had struck home like a punch of a fist, when he had been raising the glass of brandy in a toast to his professional liaison with Captain D'Acre of the Fly-By-Nights, he waited for the sharp apprehension to drain away. And leave him in peace.

He was irritated when it failed to do so; rather, the jittery awareness intensified.

So, he considered, thoroughly put out, directing the mare towards the inn, was this the cause of his strange premonition that something was wrong, that had demanded his immediate action? An unknown woman who had come to grief in the rising tide? But if it was, he felt no better for the problem being resolved. The danger was over, but his heart was thudding within his ribcage as if he had just unloaded a dozen barrels from the *Black Spectre* in a high sea. She was rescued and he would see that she was delivered safely to wherever she was staying—end of the problem—but he was conscious of every inch of her, the hard grip of her hands on his forearms, the fact that she had not relaxed at all, but sat as rigid and upright as if on a dining-room chair. Her hair blown into curls, brushed against his cheek. A momentary sensation. But every inch of his skin felt alive, sensitive. Aware of her.

Frowning, Alexander glanced down at the curve of her cheek, the fan of dark lashes. She was nothing to him. Simply a silly girl visiting the area, getting into difficulties because she hadn't the sense she was born with.

'You can let go of my sleeves now,' he remarked brusquely.

The girl shuddered, and did so, but remained as tense as before.

For the second time within the hour Alexander dismounted in the courtyard of the Silver Boat. He looked up, raising his arms.

'Slide down—you won't fall.'

He caught her as she obeyed and lifted her into his arms.

'I can walk. I am quite capable of...' Her voice caught on an intake of breath and she shuddered again, hard against him.

'I'm sure you can. But humour me.'

She was light enough. Alexander strode into the inn, shouldered open the door into an empty parlour. Drab, cold, dusty, but empty. He thought she would not want an audience of local fishermen when they returned from their expedition. Once inside, he stood her gently on her feet, then strode back to the door, raising his voice to echo down the corridor.

'Sal...bring some clean towels, if you will. And a bottle of brandy. Also bring—'

'I would prefer a cup of tea,' the voice behind him interrupted. Neat, precise, faintly accented.

'Not at the Silver Boat you wouldn't,' he replied, closing the door. 'There's been no tea brewed within these four walls in the past decade to my knowledge, although plenty's been hidden in the rafters over the years.' He saw a shiver run through her again. 'Sit down before you fall down.'

'I've lost my parasol,' she remarked inconsequentially, regarding her empty hands in some surprise.

'It's not the end of the world. I'll buy you another one. Sit down,' he repeated.

When she sank into one of the two chairs in the room, Alexander came to kneel before her.

'What...?' She didn't quite recoil from him, but not far off.

He didn't reply, curbing his impatience, but simply raised the hem of her ruined skirt. Ignoring when he felt her stiffen, he grasped her ankle and removed her ruined boot, first one foot, then the other. 'There, you need to dry your feet when the towels get here.' Then, catching her anxious glance, 'Don't worry. I've no designs on your virtue.'

'Oh…'

The inquisitive spaniel muscled in to sniff and lick the girl's feet. When she flinched back, Alexander nudged Bess away.

'Sorry. She's nosy, but won't harm you.'

For the first time a glimmer of a smile answered him. 'I don't mind dogs. It's just that—'

The door opened and brandy and towels arrived in the hands of a curious Sal. Alexander cast a glance at the girl he had just rescued, her hands clenched white fingered in her lap, and made a decision.

'Can you manage to make a pot of tea, Sal?'

'I'll try, Mr Ellerdine, sir.'

'And put these by the fire to dry, will you?' He handed over the girl's boots.

Although he had no real hope for the tea, he smiled encouragingly at Sal before shutting her and the spaniel out of the room. He considered the wisdom of drying the girl's feet for her. Then, after a close inspection of her, changed his mind. He handed her the grey, threadbare towel, liberally stained but the best the Silver Boat could manage.

'Here. Dry your feet.' It would give her something to do to occupy her mind and her hands, to remove the glassy terror that still glazed her eyes. Then he changed his mind again as she eyed the linen askance and seemed incapable of carrying out the simple task. He supposed he must take charge. Once more he knelt at her feet.

'Hold out your foot.'

She did so. 'I'm sorry. I'm not usually so helpless…'

'It's shock, that's all. Don't flinch—I'm going to remove your stockings.' He continued to talk inconsequentially, matter of factly as he began to perform the intimate task with impersonal fingers. 'You need to dry your feet, Madame Mermaid. My mother swore that damp feet brought on the ague. I don't know if she was ever proved right, but we'll not take it to chance. Lift your foot again…'

He doubted that his mother had ever expressed such practical advice in all her life, but that did not matter. He felt the muscles of the girl's feet and calves under his hands tense once more, but he unfastened her garters and rolled her stockings discreetly down to her ankles, drawing them from her feet, placing the sodden items neatly beside her. Her skin, he noted, was fine and soft against the calluses on his own palms, her feet slender and beautifully arched. She owned an elegant pair of ankles too, he thought with pure male appreciation. He forced himself to resist drawing his fingers from heel to instep to toes as he ignored the increased beat of his pulse in his throat when she flexed her foot in his grip. Instead, briskly, he applied the linen until her feet were dry and the colour returning.

'There. It's done.'

He raised his eyes to find her watching his every move. Somewhere in his deliberately businesslike ministrations, her fear had gone and her eyes were as clear and blue as the sea on a summer's day. Remarkable. It crossed his mind with an almost casual acceptance that he could fall and drown in them with no difficulty at all.

He had no wish to do any such thing.

'Thank you,' she said. 'You are kind...'

'I don't need your thanks.'

More abrupt than he had intended, disturbed by his reaction to her, Alexander pushed himself upright, picking up the jug to pour brandy with a heavy hand into the smeared glass. 'Here. Drink this.'

'I don't like brandy.'

'I don't care whether you like it or not. It will steady your nerves.'

The girl sighed, accepted the glass, sipped once,

twice, wincing at the burn of the liquor, then placed the glass on the table at her elbow whilst she untied the satin strings of her bonnet. Alexander tossed back a glass of brandy himself before he turned foursquare to look down at the girl—the lady, for certainly from her clothes and bearing she was of good family. To his amazement temper heated, rapid and out of control. A surge of anger that she should have endangered her life so wantonly. That she might have been swept to her death before he had even known her. For some inexplicable reason the thought balled into fury that he could not contain.

'What were you thinking, madam, getting yourself trapped by an incoming tide? You could have been swept out to sea if you'd fallen into one of the channels. The undertow of the tide is strong enough to drag you under. It's happened before to an unwary visitor. Did you not see what was happening?'

The soft summer-blue of her gaze sharpened, glints of fire, as did her voice. 'No, I did not see. Or I would not have been trapped, would I?'

'If I hadn't ridden into the village by chance, George Gadie would have been fishing your dead body out of the bay to deliver it to your grieving family.' The heat in his words shook him. How could he have been drying her feet one minute and berating her with un-reasonable fury the next? She did not deserve it.

'But thanks to you I'm not dead,' she snapped, matching temper with temper. 'Thank you for your help. I'm sorry to have been an inconvenience to you. I'll make sure it never happens again.'

'Then it will be a good lesson learned if you're to stay in this part of the world for long!'

'I'll heed your advice, sir.'

She had spirit, he'd give her that. Intrigued by her sharp defence, by the definite accent when under stress, Alexander raised his brows as his irritation began to ebb. The lady did not appear grateful at all. He felt the need to suppress a smile at the heat that had replaced the frozen terror.

'So we are in agreement, it seems. Now what do I do with you?'

'You do nothing with me.' Her eyes actually seemed to flash in the dim room. 'I am very grateful that you rescued me, of course, but I am perfectly capable of returning home on my own. You are at liberty to ride on your way about your own concerns. Now if you will give me back my shoes, which appear to have vanished in the direction of the kitchen…'

Alexander Ellerdine simply stood and looked at her, torn between amusement and frustration.

She sat and looked back at him, mutiny in her face.

And there it was. The sword of Damocles fell.

Chapter Two

Alexander looked, really looked at the girl—no, the woman, he realised—for the first time.

And he could not look away. His heart stopped for a breathless moment, before resuming with the heavy thump of a military drum.

Not as young as he had first thought, certainly older than her twentieth year, even if not by too many years; her slender figure and compact stature gave her a youthful air. She was extraordinarily pretty with fair hair now in a riot of curls from the wind and the damp, and those astonishing blue eyes. The blur of panic had definitely gone from them. They sparkled like sunlight on waves in a morning sea. Not classically beautiful, he noted dispassionately—her brows were too dark, her nose formidably straight and her chin had a hint of the masterful. Perhaps her lips were a little wide for her heart-shaped face—but that was not to her detriment. Now parted in what could only be a moment of baffled consternation to mirror his own, Alexander felt a precise urge to kiss those lips, to press his mouth against that exact spot where a charming indentation might hover in her cheek if she smiled.

At this moment, to his regret, she looked as if she had no intention of ever smiling at him.

He blinked, mentally ordering his thoughts back into line. To no avail. She was quite lovely and Alexander felt the pull of some intense, deep-seated connection between them. A bond that linked him to her whether he wished it or not. Fancifully he considered its existence, ephemeral but solid in his awareness. Like an arc of light that had managed to seep through the grime-caked windows. Or a tightening of a fist to take up the tension in a rope. Perhaps it was an invisible skein woven from the dusty air in the drab little room. He did not know. What he did know was that it was there between them. An entity that he could not shake off.

It was, the thought crept into his mind to overwhelm it with its novelty, as if he had been waiting for this moment, for this particular woman, all his life.

Again it took his breath and his heart stumbled on a beat.

Whilst Marie-Claude simply sat with her bonnet in her lap, her stockings at her feet, and surveyed the man who stood before her. An even greater shock to her than the threat of the incoming tide had been was that he seemed to be in the same grip of the same blinding discovery as she. It whispered over her skin. This man touched her heart, her mind. Her soul. How could this be? How could she feel this link to a complete stranger?

She took a difficult breath. It was as if all the air had been sucked out of the room so that she must struggle to fill her lungs. And yet there was a strange stillness, as in the eye of a storm. Still, silent, as if waiting for some momentous revelation.

Marie-Claude touched her tongue to her dry lips and raised her eyes to his, amazed at her boldness, only to see that he was looking at her as if she were a prize he would snatch up and carry off for his own possession. *She* would be his possession. It unnerved her, but did not distress her. Not at all.

She could not bear the silence that had fallen between them. 'Sir?'

'Tell me your name,' Alexander demanded softly.

'Marie-Claude.'

'Marie-Claude,' he repeated as if he had no choice but to do so. It was a sigh, a soft caress even to his own ears.

Nor did the lady show any sign of objecting to his crass lack of formality.

'Are you French?' he asked, searching for something to say. *Unnecessary, you fool*, he admonished. Of course she was, with her attractive accent.

'Yes, I am. But I have lived here in England for more than five years now.'

Her eyes were direct, forthright. She had recovered from her ordeal and delicate colour returned to her cheeks and lips. Those lips now curved beautifully, revealing the little hollow in her cheek. Alexander swallowed against the sudden power of heat in his blood, a treacherous warmth in his groin.

'Who are you?' she asked.

'My name is Alexander. People who know me call me Zan. You can do so if you wish.'

'Zan.' Could she believe this? Here she was, sitting without her shoes or her stockings in an inn parlour, alone with a man she had known but an hour, and she had agreed to call him by his given name? Ridiculous! Indiscreet! She had actually allowed him to remove her stockings! Marie-Claude felt her cheeks flush—but was compelled to use his name again.

'Zan—Mr Ellerdine, I think the girl called you.'

'Yes.'

With no timidity and considerable pleasure, she

allowed her eyes to travel over his face and figure. Far taller than she, he had a rangy, graceful stance that masked a degree of strength. She recalled how he had lifted her with ease, carried her. How he had controlled the mare when the animal had fought for her head in the waves. Encircled by his arms she had, even in her fear, been aware of the sleek muscles beneath the sleeve of his coat, the powerful thighs that had held her firm and safe.

Whilst his face… An arresting face. Strong features, all flat planes and stark edges, lean cheeks. As for age—some years over thirty, she considered. A handsome man even if he was intimidating. Patience would not come easily to a man with that proud nose, that firm jaw. His mouth was uncompromisingly stern. His eyes fierce under well-marked brows. And his hair—dark, longer than she was used to seeing in the fashionable haunts of Bond Street, falling into disordered waves. Her fingers itched to touch it. He was nothing like the smooth, fashionable, London gentlemen with nothing in his thoughts but the cut of his coat and the polished shine of his boots. There was an energy about him—a *spiritedness*—that lit the room. And also a distinct lawlessness in him… His speculative appraisal of her face and figure, a caress in itself, made her shiver.

Marie-Claude forced another breath into her lungs. 'Do you live here? In Old Wincomlee?'

'Nearby.'

'Then it is my good fortune that you had by chance ridden down to the bay. If you had not—'

'No…' Zan broke in. 'I think it is my good fortune.'

Zan stretched out his hand, palm up, not at all surprised when Marie-Claude instantly placed hers there. He lifted her slender fingers to his lips. Was this it? Was this the premonition, driving him with an urgency that he had not been able to cast aside, to be at the harbour at the exact time that she was in danger? He had been meant to save her. It had been meant that their paths should cross. Even when he had brought her to shore, the strange link had held fast, even when she was perfectly safe, so that he felt the need to carry her into the inn rather than leave her to her own devices. Was this desire to put her beyond all danger, to cherish her—was this driving force how it felt to fall in love?

No! It was a dousing of cold water, as if a wave had just broken over his head. Love was an emotion to be avoided at all costs.

But this woman spoke to him. Called to him. He could not deny it.

'I had to come down to the bay,' he admitted as much to himself as to her. 'I didn't know why, but now I do.'

Not understanding, Marie-Claude tilted her head, hoping he would continue, accepting when he did not. He did not have to explain. It was enough that he had been there, enough that he was here now with her. Since he still held her hand with no immediate intention of releasing her, Marie-Claude stood. In her bare feet she came only to his shoulder. It sent a jolt of delight through her. She had never felt so safe, so protected. Not that she needed protection, but sometimes a woman liked to feel the power and strength of a man...

He took a handkerchief from his pocket.

'What is it?'

'Nothing to disturb you.'

Gently he wiped a smear of drying sand from her cheek, from her jaw, and tucked a wayward curl behind her ear. Then couldn't resist stroking his fingers over that same cheek. Soft, smooth. Alluringly flushed. It took all his control not to kiss a path along the curve from her ear to that inviting mouth. To take those lips with his own. To feel them part and welcome him...

Of course he couldn't! Hell and damnation! What the devil was he thinking? Here was no tavern wench who would ask for and enjoy his attentions. This was a well-born lady, alone and unprotected, who deserved respect, courtesy. And here he was touching her face, kissing her hand, thinking—if truth was in it—of nothing but taking her to his bed, stripping away that pretty gown and making her body subject to his.

'I think you might have saved my life.' She broke into the private scene that had already driven his body into hard arousal. 'How can I ever repay you?'

'You don't have to.' It seemed that her being there with him in the inn parlour was all the reward he needed, enough to last him a lifetime. He thought he should tell her that, but all his habitual facility with words had deserted him.

'I don't think the tea will come,' she observed with a glimmer of a smile.

'No. I don't think it will.'

'I was at fault, not watching the tide, and I was not very gracious.'

'You could not have known. And you were afraid.' Still he held her hand in his, and Marie-Claude felt no urge to demand its return. She realised he was looking quizzically at her.

'What is it? More sand? I must look a positive wreck. As for my dress…' She looked down at the ruined flounces with a grimace.

'You are beautiful.'

A deliberate pronouncement that took her aback.

Cheeks aflame, Marie-Claude managed a soft
laugh. 'You flatter me.'

'No. I tell you the truth. And if you are going to
tell me that no man has ever told you that before, then
I would have to say that you lie. Or all the men of
your acquaintance have been either witless or blind.'

'Oh!' Marie-Claude, lost for words, felt the colour
in her cheeks deepen even further.

'I feel I have known you all my life. Why is that?'
Not wanting to know the answer, voice harsh with dis-
belief, Zan felt his hand tighten involuntarily around
Marie-Claude's fingers. By God, it was not what he
wanted! But he wanted her. He wanted her physically.
The heat of awareness throbbed through his blood.

'Yes. As I have known you all of *my* life too.'
Marie-Claude's breath caught at the blatant immo-
desty of her reply. She did not know this man. An
hour ago she had not even met him and all she knew
of him now was his name. Astonished at her
temerity, Marie-Claude snatched at the moment,
speaking the words her heart prompted. 'I don't
understand it—but I feel as if I have been waiting
for you. Waiting for you to step into my life. And
here you are.'

They stood and looked at each other, unable to
look away, his eyes dark and stormy, hers shadowed
with uncertainty.

How could she have dared to say that? Surely so forward, so presumptuous a female would put any well-bred man to flight. Or at least earn herself a damning put-down. Marie-Claude saw how the muscles in Zan's jaw tightened under some rigidly applied control. How austere he looked, how frighteningly stern. How could she have displayed her feelings so obviously? Suddenly swamped by doubt, Marie-Claude turned her face away. 'How immodest I seem to have become. How brazen you must think me…' Her words crumbled to dust as she felt her face flame once more, this time with embarrassment.

'No, never that,' Zan replied softly, his tone at odds with the taut desire in his loins. Her self-conscious bewilderment arrowed straight to Zan's heart. Circling her wrists, he placed her palms together, enfolding them within his own hands where they seemed, inexplicably, to belong. 'And not brazen at all. If you are immodest, then I seem to have lost all sense of honour as a gentleman. Do you…?'

Do you believe that a man can love a woman from the very first moment he sets his eyes on her? Can a man feel indivisibly bound to a woman he has never met before?

His dark brows snapped together. Well, he could hardly ask her that, could he? Only at the risk of her fleeing the room, no doubt shrieking accusations of seduction and debauchery. Had he in truth lost all sense of reality? Disgusted at his inexplicable lack of finesse, Zan controlled the urge to drag her against him, cover that lovely mouth with his. How had his response to this woman suddenly become so inexplicably complicated? Instead he fell back on brisk practicalities.

'I expect you're exhausted after your ordeal. Do you feel sufficiently recovered to go home?'

'Oh…yes.' Marie-Claude was perplexed. She could not read this man at all. One moment he looked at her as if he would snatch her up, the next he rejected her as if he found her distasteful. Obviously he regretted that first astonishing admission. Disappointment settled to fill the space around her heart, and she took her lead from him. 'Of course. I'm quite restored. It's no distance—an easy walk from here. If you will release my hands…'

Zan saw it, the light quenched from her eyes, her mouth settling in a solemn line, the corners tightly tucked in as if she would express no more confidences. That was not what he had intended at all. He experienced a protective urge to sweep her up and make her laugh. Make her admit again that she had been waiting for him to step into her life. But perhaps this was not the time or the place.

'I'll take you home,' he determined, yet kept possession of her hands. 'And I'll come tomorrow to ask if you're fully recovered. If you will allow it.'

'Yes. I would like that.'

When her face lit again in a smile, it ignited a flame in his heart. Without thought, without questioning his motives other than it was what he wished to do more than anything on earth, he bent his head and took her lips with his. Soft, inviting, at first the merest whisper of a caress. And the sweetness of her took him aback, flooding through his veins, awakening every male instinct. In reply his mouth changed from gentle invitation to dominant demand.

Marie-Claude knew she should resist, remonstrate—*what was she doing?*—but could not. The slide of that hard mouth over her lips, with such unexpected delicacy, stirred shivers over her skin. When the pressure deepened, when she felt the forceful sweep of his tongue over her lips, she did not hesitate but, her will shattered, she let them part against his shocking insistence. Her heart fluttered like a trapped bird.

Whilst Zan's blood raged. His body responded, his need hard against her as he held her fast. Whatever lay in wait for him in the uncertainties of his future, she was his. His mouth ravaged, his tongue tasted, seduced then plunged as her lips failed to withstand his assault. She was his, now, always. No one would stop him…

When he felt her sigh softly against his mouth he raised his head, drawn back into reality. His smile was a little twisted, but his hands still gripped firm.

'I suppose I must now listen to you condemn me for my ungallant conduct.'

But her eyes were glorious, sparkling with life. Her reply, her reaction, startled him.

'I liked it.' A twist of her hand to free it from his and she lifted it to touch his cheek with her fingertips. 'I should not, I dare say, but I did. My sister would say that no good can come of it. Do you suppose I shall regret it? I doubt it. Unless you are planning to seduce me, to steal my heart and break it.'

So she would flirt with him.

'You think I would seduce you?' An audacious lift of a brow. 'Do you think I am a libertine?'

'I don't know.'

'A rake?'

'I don't know that either.'

'If I was either, you should not be here alone in this room with me. Will you take the risk?'

'I must.' Marie-Claude smiled. 'I seem to have lost my will-power along with my wits.'

Zan inhaled sharply. 'Many hereabouts would say you'd be foolish to trust me.'

'You've given me no reason not to trust you. I would

have been regretful if you hadn't kissed me. Does that make me too forward again? I'm afraid it does.'

'It makes you a delight. It makes you all I've ever dreamt of in a woman—' What was he saying? Zan closed his mouth like a trap on any more revelations before the control of his thoughts and words broke entirely. 'Where are you staying? I presume you are visiting. Where do I take you home?'

'There's really no need.'

'I wish it.' Once again he pressed his lips to hers, all his senses overpowered by her instant response when she slid her hands around his neck, lacing her fingers in his hair to draw him closer. He groaned softly against her mouth. 'I don't want to let you go, but I must. Tell me where…'

'Not far. Take me to Lydyard's Pride.'

The Pride!

It was like the echoing clang, discordant and ill fated, of a death knell. The name was like an arctic blast to chill the heat in his blood to ice. Or perhaps it was a searing fire from the depths of hell to blast and destroy the flame of his desire.

Zan encircled Marie-Claude's wrists and pulled her hands slowly from around his neck, trying to ignore the skittering of her pulse. Why did it feel as if a bottomless black void had appeared before his feet? And equally in his chest where his heart had been?

Whilst Marie-Claude could only marvel at the effect of her words. This man who had kissed her with passion was now regarding her from a distance of his own making, with some species of stark horror.

What had she said?

'Lydyard's Pride?' Zan heard his voice, bleak as the cliffs in a winter's gale, dreading the reply.

'Yes. The house on the cliff…'

'I know where Lydyard's Pride is. What's your name—your full name?'

'I'm Marie-Claude Hallaston. I was Marie-Claude de la Roche before my marriage.'

Hallaston. Marriage.

Why hadn't he discovered this pertinent piece of information in the first place? It had never crossed his mind. His lips curled in cynical acknowledgement of this unexpected turn of the cards. So the gift from the hand of fate had all been a mischievous charade after all. Well, he had been taught a short hard lesson, had he not? It was as if he had been offered his heart's desire only to have it snatched away in some malicious game. Zan took a step back, his brows meeting in a black bar.

'Zan…?'

He took another step. When he could think, memory struck to fill in the gaps.

'Ah, yes. Of course. I should have known, I suppose. You're the widow of the noble Earl of Venmore's brother.'

'Yes. Captain Marcus Hallaston. He died in Spain.'

'I know.'

'Do you know the Hallaston family? And Harriette's family, the Lydyards? I suppose you must since you are a neighbour.'

'Yes.'

'I'm staying here for a few weeks.'

'I see.'

'Harriette and Luke are at The Venmore, but I—'

'I must take you home,' Zan interrupted. 'I've kept you here long enough.'

She was a Hallaston. Of all the families she could have been connected to. Striding to the door, he flung it open, raised his voice in the direction of the kitchen.

'Sal! Bring the lady's shoes. Now!'

When they arrived, Sal at a run, he took them with a brief word of thanks, handed them over.

'Put your shoes on.'

Not understanding, Marie-Claude simply did as she was ordered. What point in attempting an explanation when the man who had first saved her life and then had kissed her into mindless delight had inexplicably decided that he wanted nothing more to do with her? Without a word, spine straight against the humiliation, Marie-Claude took the little boots, then sat, just as rigidly, struggling with the soaked fabric to pull them on. They were, sadly, past redemption.

'Never mind.' Impatiently, Zan all but snatched the boots from her, tucking them with her stockings into his capacious pockets. 'Put your arms around my neck, Madame Mermaid.' When she obeyed because his sly mockery seemed to rob her of any will to do otherwise, he effortlessly lifted her and carried her out of the parlour.

'I can walk!' Flustered, mortified by her response to his nearness, hurt by his rejection of her, Marie-Claude pushed against his chest. 'There's no need for this! Put me down.'

'Not in bare feet you can't,' he responded, as cold as January.

Without further comment he carried her outside, where he boosted her into the saddle, then swung up behind her, immediately gathering up the reins and turning the mare's head in the direction of the Pride. His mouth curved in what was not a smile at this change in plan. Had he not intended to allow the mare to walk as slowly as she wished, to make her own way so that his time with the girl was stretched as far as possible? Now he kicked her into a canter, holding the Hallaston widow before him as impersonally as he might. Trying not to be aware of her warmth and closeness, the subtle perfume from her hair, the brush of her body against his. He clamped his mouth shut. There was nothing more to be said between them.

Thus a tension-filled, uncomfortable journey, until they reached the long drive to the Pride and Zan turned the mare in.

This was no good, Marie-Claude decided, trying to clear her thoughts. Did the baffling Mr Alexander Ellerdine intend to deposit her at the door without another word? Not if she had any influence on the outcome.

'Do you know Harriette and Luke well?' she asked against the wall of his silence, lifting her chin so she could see his face.

'Once I did.' His eyes were grimly fixed on the approaching house. 'But no longer. We're not on visiting terms.'

'Why not?'

'It's of no consequence.'

In other words, it's not your concern. Marie-Claude frowned as silence once more shrouded them. As she had suspected, when they arrived at the front sweep of steps, he swiftly dismounted, beckoned for her to slide down into his arms. Immediately he placed her on her feet on the bottom step. Returned her boots, her stockings into her hands. And without one word of ackowledgement or farewell turned away to remount.

Marie-Claude felt a return of her temper. Was he not going to explain? She would *force* him to explain!

'Will you not come in?' she invited with edged sweetness. A provocative lift of her brows, already knowing the reply. If he could taunt, so could she. 'Some refreshment, perhaps, after all your efforts on my behalf?'

He looked back over his shoulder, his reins tight in his fist. 'No.'

'And are you usually so ill mannered, Mr Ellerdine?'

'Not ill mannered, Madame Mermaid. Merely mistaken.'

'So you have decided you have not known me all your life after all.'

'Yes. So it seems.'

A cold whip of words. It was like fighting through an impenetrable mist. 'How capricious you have turned out to be, sir,' she observed, an intense regret cutting through her anger. And watched, startled, as her rebuke caused colour to slash across Zan's splendid cheekbones.

'Is Meggie here?' he demanded unexpectedly, facing her again.

'Yes. Why?'

'Tell Meggie what happened on the beach. She'll take care of you. Doubtless she'll tell you what you need to know about me—and take pleasure in doing so. Don't tell her you spent time in the Silver Boat with me, unchaperoned. And for God's sake don't tell her that I forced my attentions on you. It would be better for you if you did not.'

'Why should I not tell her? Besides, you didn't force yourself on me. As I recall, I enjoyed the experience as much as you did. As I *thought* you did!'

'Then you were as mistaken as I was.' And what a flat rebuttal that was; it robbed Marie-Claude of all speech for a moment. 'A word of advice, Madame Mermaid. You're far too innocent for your own good.' The edge in his voice was as keen as hammered steel. 'You should beware of believing what rakes and libertines in inn parlours tell you. They prey on the innocent and you were the perfect peach, ripe to fall into my hand. You were fortunate not to be further compromised.'

How unfair! How appallingly unfair! 'I did not *choose* to be in the inn parlour with you. You took me there, if you recall. And as for innocent! If you know anything of my past, as you seem to do, you would know that I am far from innocent and inexperienced in my knowledge of the evil that can drive some men. I didn't think you were a man without honour.'

'Then you lack judgement. You have no idea what sort of man I am.'

Marie-Claude's eyes flashed fire, her brows rose. It was impossible to believe that he could be so insulting, so deliberately wounding. Something had driven him into this fast retreat, this deliberate attack. Seeing a possible advantage, she pressed on to make the most of it. 'You didn't answer my question. Why should I not tell Meggie?'

Zan sneered. 'I wouldn't want to ruin your impeccable reputation, would I? If you value your good name, you'll keep your tongue between your pretty teeth.'

He had already turned back to his mare, gathering the reins. Marie-Claude made a last attempt to restore some normality to this situation, clutching at a final hope. 'Zan…I don't know why you would deny what was between us. Or lash at me with temper. Let me thank you—'

'No! I'll let you do nothing of the sort. Have you not been listening to me? Just forget the whole incident. It will be better for you if you do. As for my denial, put it down to indifference. You entertained me for a bare hour—nothing more.' His mouth twisted.

As Marie-Claude's eyes widened at this final un-bridled, *unforgivable* slight, with one long stride, Zan dropped the reins and was back to swoop and pinion her. Hands firmly cupping her shoulders, he pulled her hard against him. 'Or perhaps, in honesty, a little longer than an hour. No man could overlook or forget the sweetness of your kisses.' His mouth devoured hers, his tongue owned, a scrape of teeth along her soft lips. Yet even as she resisted the assault, the sheer insolence of him, her senses absorbed the thrill.

Zan thrust her away.

'Farewell, Madame Mermaid.'

Without a backwards look he swung up, let the mare quicken and stretch into a full gallop across the parkland, out of her line of sight.

Zan concentrated on putting as much distance between himself and Lydyard's Pride in the shortest possible time. As if he could erase the memory of the woman who still stood on the steps and looked after him. He knew exactly who his mermaid was.

Marie-Claude de la Roche—he'd forgotten her name, if he ever knew it. He supposed he'd never heard it mentioned in his hearing. There was no reason why it should have been in the circum-stances. He had become *persona non grata* in the

Hallaston household after that night. He'd heard later of her existence, of course, from George Gadie, who knew all the Hallaston affairs. French, married to Captain Marcus Hallaston and widowed, cast adrift in Spain with a child, taken under the unscrupulous wing of some French rogue—called Jean-Jacques Noir, was it?—who had held her to ransom to bleed Luke Hallaston, the Earl of Venmore, dry in return for her safety. Threatened to use her as a whore in one of the military towns if the tale ran true. And she had been rescued by Venmore and Harriette in that eventful run to the French coast, bringing her back along with the barrels and bales of contraband.

Oh, yes. He recalled that night, right enough. The night that had brought an unmendable rift with his cousin Harriette. The night when he had been accused and found guilty, albeit without trial, of treachery, wrecking and attempted murder.

He knew the widow had been rescued, but had never met her, nor she him. She did not even recognise his name. Obviously no one had ever spoken the name Zan Ellerdine in the Hallaston household from that day to this. He tightened his hands on the reins to bring the mare back into a more controlled canter. Alexander Ellerdine no longer existed in that august circle.

In the circumstances, he could hardly blame the noble Earl and his family, could he?

Well, he had delivered the pretty widow home and that was that. He had not compromised her sensibilities too greatly, nor damaged her spotless reputation. He set the mare to a low hedge, pushing her on into a stylish leap. And then another as he increased the distance between himself and the Pride. But the speed and exhilaration did not take his attention as he might hope. Clear blue eyes with no hint of shyness. Soft lips that parted beneath his. Smooth fingers that touched his cheek. Desire curled in his gut, tightened into urgency in his groin.

Forget about her. Forget how for those few short minutes she turned your blood to fire. Forget how she made you think that life could have been different. Forget how she called you Zan and wound her fingers into your hair as she wound them into your heart...

When Marie-Claude smiled at him in his mind, Zan ruthlessly banished the image. An unfortunate dose of lust, that's all. Easily remedied. He'd been right all along. Love did not exist. Not for men like him. And certainly not with one of the Hallastons, a family who hated him with every breath it took.

Marie-Claude stood on the steps, ignoring the cold striking up through her bare feet, her boots and stockings clutched to her bosom. She stared after Zan Ellerdine in disbelief.

What had happened? What had she done?

Surely she had not imagined that intense *closeness*. And surely he had felt it too. Some of the things she had said to him… She blushed to recall them. And he had kissed her. He had actually kissed her on the lips. Raising one hand so that she dropped the boots—not that she noticed—she pressed her fingers to her mouth, reliving that moment when her pulse had rioted and desire had flooded her veins. He had kissed her and she had kissed him back. She could still feel him there. Taste him there. Even the scent of him, a purely male blend of sun and sweat and salt-water, still filled her head.

And then what had happened? It was as if a curtain of icy rain had cascaded down between them, separating them so there was no connection, no sense of *oneness* between them at all.

What had he said about the Hallastons and Lydyards? *Once I knew them. No longer.* What was that about? Some mystery here. And he knew about Meggie and her association with the family.

He had been so kind, so considerate. He had taken off her shoes, ordered her tea, kissed her hand, a burning brand that had been anything but a formal caress. Had he not told her she was beautiful? He had rolled down her stockings and dried her feet. She swore she could still imagine the gentle impression of his fingers. And then when he had kissed her she had abandoned all modesty and *offered* herself.

And what had happened? The enchantment had been smashed, destroyed.

It was her name. As soon as she had mentioned Lydyard's Pride. The Hallaston connection had caused the rift.

Well, she would not tell Meggie—for some reason she did not want to talk about this meeting with Zan Ellerdine—but she would find out who he was.

'Meggie…' Once servant and confidante to Harriette Lydyard, now Harriette Hallaston, at present with Marie-Claude at the Pride, as stout and buxom and forthright as she had ever been, was the obvious source. Ask her, Zan had advised with no pleasant anticipation. So she would.

'Miss Marie-Claude! Just look at you… What have you been doing?'

Well, she would ask eventually. First she must soothe Meggie's eagle eye.

'Oh… I was caught by the tide. Silly of me. I'll learn.' She cast her bonnet on to the scrubbed wooden table in the kitchen where she had run Meggie to ground, and prepared to deflect the flood of concern.

'It's dangerous. One minute out of my sight and just look at the state of your clothes…'

'The only things to suffer are my shoes and my gown. Both beyond redemption…although my feet are cold and damp.'

It did the trick. Meggie bustled her out of the kitchen, insisting on ordering up the tub and heated water to Marie-Claude's bedchamber. Nor was Marie-Claude sorry. All things considered it had been an exhausting day.

She sank back into the soothing water with a sigh. Here was the chance as Meggie fretted and fussed around her.

'Meggie—who is Alexander Ellerdine?'

A short expectant hiatus. Meggie angled her a glance.

'Who?'

'Alexander Ellerdine.' Marie-Claude fixed her with an innocent expression.

'Now why would you want to know that?'

'I heard his name mentioned in the village, that's all.'

A pause. The glance became even sharper as Meggie folded a pile of linen. 'Did you meet him?'

'No.' Marie-Claude hoped the flush of colour would be put down to the heat of the water.

'He owns Ellerdine Manor.'

'Oh.' This was not getting very far. 'Is there a—a problem about him? Some scandal, perhaps?'

'Yes.' Meggie folded a linen shift with a sharp snap of the cloth.

'Will you tell me?'

'No.'

Marie-Claude could not help the frown. 'Then I shall have to ask elsewhere.'

'No need to do that. And Miss Harriette wouldn't wish it.'

'Well, if that's so, there must be a good reason.'

Meggie pursed her lips as if coming to an un-pleasant but necessary decision. 'Well, if you must know…he's a smuggler—amongst other things.'

'Is that very bad?'

'Isn't that enough, miss? It's not a reputable oc-cupation for a gentleman, is it?'

Marie-Claude read the disapproving expression on Meggie's face and gave up the hunt. 'No. I suppose not. That must be it then.'

'All I'll say is—no woman of taste or discrimina-tion would seek his company, however handsome his face. Handsome is as handsome does… He's a dangerous man.'

'Is he? Why?'

'He just is! Take my word for it.'

It was clear that she wasn't going to get any further with Meggie. She tipped back her head and closed her eyes, letting her impressions form and solidify. The fact that Zan might be a smuggler couldn't be the only reason. As she understood it, almost everyone in Old Wincomlee had a finger in the smuggling pie. As she knew, from personal experience, Harriette herself had been one of the Brotherhood of Free Traders. Captain Harry, sailing her cutter *Lydyard's Ghost*, swaggering in boots and breeches.

So what was the issue with Mr Alexander Ellerdine? One moment he had looked at her as if he saw her as a glittering prize to be owned and savoured. And the next—he had fixed her with a stare cold enough to freeze the air in her lungs and informed her she had been as mistaken as he. She had accused him of being capricious. But that was not it either. Capricious was too mild a word for his apparent disgust with her. He had dared—he had had the *effrontery*—to swat her aside as if she were an autumn wasp!

Was she prepared to leave it like this and pretend they had never met?

No. She was not.

What's more, she *would* not. Within her, bright anger warred with intrigue, and a little *frisson* of excitement such as she barely recalled curled its way into her belly as she ran her tongue over her lips. She would discover the mystery of Mr Ellerdine, for it was her chief desire that he should kiss her again. Then with a little laugh she rubbed at her lips with the scented water. No daughter of the de la Roche family would bow weakly before the whim of fate, but would seize it, shake it.

Alexander Ellerdine had better beware.

Chapter Three

Mr Alexander Ellerdine—Zan, as she had called him—had told her, before his bewildering volte-face and his descent into disgraceful bad manners, that he would come the next day to the Pride to ask after her safe recovery. Marie-Claude waited, finding an excuse from her previous day's exertions to remain within the house and gardens. She was feeling just a little weary, she informed Meggie—quite understandable. She would stroll and sit in the rose garden and read perhaps. So she did with increasing difficulty. She had never felt so full of energy in her whole life. And of course he did not materialise—and she was not in the least surprised, in the circumstances. He had warned her off, well and truly, with no attempt to soften his words. She paced the rose garden with increasing impatience.

And waited two more full days.
Zan Ellerdine did not come.

Marie-Claude decided to seize the initiative. Events played beautifully into her hands. Meggie's ageing mother demanded her daughter's attendance at her side when a flare of the rheumatics kept her to her bed. With no one to notice her comings and goings, and certainly not to question them, on the third morning Marie-Claude ordered up the cob and trap as soon as Wiggins had cleared the breakfast cups and saucers and asked directions from a stable lad. She dressed with care.

She would wager the pearl bracelet that she clasped about her wrist against his being overjoyed, that she was the last visitor he would wish to see uninvited on his doorstep. *Tant pis.* Too bad. He had made her feel alive again, restored to her a vivacity that she had somehow lost over the years since her coming to England. And the connection between them had been so strong, so undeniable, like knots in a skein of embroidery silk. Until, that is, the unfortunate mention of her name. She must discover what it was about the Hallastons and Lydyard's Pride that had turned his tongue from lover to viper. It was quite beyond her understanding, and it was not in her nature to let it lie.

Marie-Claude considered her imminent conversation with Zan Ellerdine. How to conduct it, she had as yet no idea, but must wait to see whether he would smile or snarl at her. Then she allowed her mind to assess her own personal situation as the cob picked its sedentary way towards Ellerdine Manor. It was a line of thought that had occupied her frequently of late.

The Hallastons were not *her* family, of course, the only one of them who had given her that connection being dead now for—unbelievable as it might seem—almost six years. And her future as a Hallaston widow? She could not imagine what it would hold that would bring her true happiness and heal her heart that had recently acquired a hollow emptiness. Perhaps that was the problem, she mused. She no longer had any roots, not in France, the country of her birth that she had fled those five years ago, not here in her adopted country. Her future, cushioned as it was by Hallaston money and consequence, seemed increasingly solitary and just a little lonely.

Until, that was, she had met Zan Ellerdine. It was as if he had opened a window to allow sunshine into a darkened room. Or opened an unread page in a book, promising any number of new possibilities. Only to slam them both shut again! Marie-Claude swiped her whip at a bothersome fly. She did not think she could allow him to do that.

She would never forget Marcus, of course. Marcus Hallaston, the vivid young man who had awoken her to the delights of first love when their paths had crossed in the battle-torn campaign of the Peninsula War. Rescuing her, he had wooed and wed her before she could collect her thoughts, loved her extravagantly, and then died at Salamanca, leaving her destitute in Spain with a new-born child. She would always remember him, always love him. What a whirlwind romance that had been. A regretful little smile curved her lips. But she had known him so little time. And her memories were growing pale with the passage of the years. Sometimes fear gripped her when she could no longer bring Marcus's face to mind, yet it seemed that her heart was frozen in time, when she was still nothing more than a young girl who had fallen in love with the handsome officer in Wellington's army.

Until Zan Ellerdine had pulled her into his arms and kissed her. With a delicious warmth, the ice around her heart had melted. And then what had he done? Thrown all her reawakened emotions back in her face.

It was not that she was unloved of course. Marie-Claude denied any such self-pity. There was Raoul, her five-year-old son, spending a few weeks with

Harriette and Luke, Marcus's brother, at The Venmore. Raoul had been her whole life since Marcus's untimely death. They had not always been safe. She narrowed her eyes at the cob's ears as the horrors of the past pressed close. Abducted by that villainous individual Jean-Jacques Noir as objects of blackmail to wring money from Luke, it had demanded a midnight run to France by Luke, and Harriette in her old guise as Captain Harry the smuggler, to rescue them and bring them home safe. What an adventure that had been when the Preventives had almost caught them on the beach and Harriette had been shot. Marie-Claude's recall of the details was vague—it had been a time of danger and extravagant emotions with the future of Harriette and Luke's marriage on the line—but she had been accepted and welcomed at last, and her son had reclaimed his rightful place in the Hallaston family.

But now Raoul was growing up and showing a streak of Hallaston independence. Of course he would rather spend time with Luke, in the stables, riding round the estate at The Venmore on a new pony, running wild in the woods, than with his mother. Of course he would. It was to be expected. But what would she do with the rest of her life?

Spend it with Zan Ellerdine…

Ridiculous! He did not want her. She should not

be demeaning herself by going to meet this man. But Marie-Claude's newly melted heart began to throb with some strange elation. She would not step back from him and whatever it was between them that had been ignited in that dingy little room. If he did not want her in his home—then he would just have to send her away.

She would not make it easy for him. She shook up the reins and prompted her somnolent cob into a more sprightly gait.

Ellerdine Manor. Not so very far away. First impressions—not good as she steered the cob into the drive. An old mellow stone house, long and low, stood at the end of the drive. Substantial, attractive it must once have been, but now with an air of dilapidation. The drive was choked with weeds and overgrown shrubs that had not seen a gardener for a decade. It was plain to see as she drew closer that the stonework needed attention. The chimneys were crumbling. So this was where her mystery rescuer lived. She wrinkled her nose. It could have been lovely with time and inclination. With money.

This, Marie-Claude thought, was the point of no return, and her courage nearly gave out. Fearing it would if she hesitated longer, she directed the cob at a shambling trot into the stable courtyard to the rear. Stepping down from the little carriage, she headed for the sound of activity in the range of stalls occupying one side of the outbuildings.

It amused her a little. This area looked as if someone had taken it in hand. Someone was more interested in the stables and their occupants than the house itself. She stepped through the open doorway into shadows, bars of sunlight angling across to form strips across the floor. It smelt of dust and hay and horses, in no manner unpleasant. Dust motes danced and glinted gold in the light. Somewhere in the far depths of the building someone whistled tunelessly.

The first stalls were closed. But the third was not.

Marie-Claude approached quietly.

And there he was. Coatless, in shirt and boots and breeches, he was grooming a dark bay stallion. Long smooth strokes of the brush from shoulder to knee. It was no difficulty for her to simply stand and stare, to watch the stretch and bend of his body. The flex of sinew in his powerful thighs. The fluid, agile play of muscle in his back and shoulders under the linen shirt. He reached and stretched with an elegant grace that set off a silent hum of pleasure in her throat. Turned away from her as he was, she could not see his face, but his dark hair shone in the soft light. Once more she experienced the urge to run her fingers through the dishevelled mass.

Here was her future. She was sure of it. Here was the man who could make her body sing again, even without touching her. And when he did—well, she really had no point of comparison. It was as if all the sparkle and bubbles from a glass of French champagne had erupted in her blood. This was the man who could wake her from the trance in which she had lived and slept since Marcus had died. Like Sleeping Beauty roused from a hundred years of enchanted sleep with one kiss from the Prince.

Marie-Claude was transfixed. Until Zan Ellerdine stood to his full height, half-turned and shook back his hair from his face as he reached up to a curry comb on a shelf above his head. As the light gleamed on the sweat at throat and chest she felt a need to touch her tongue to her dry lips. He was magnificent. And how intriguing. He applied himself again to the animal's quarters, his expression distinctly moody, the lines between nose and mouth heavily drawn, his eyes dark and brooding, snapping with temper. There was no softness in that beautiful face, only a cold ruthlessness, a driving force that would be indifferent to all but the ultimate goal.

But, oh, he was beautiful.

Cold logic immediately took hold. She should run for her life. This was not a man any well-bred woman should seek out. Zan Ellerdine was a man who had no thought of her, of any woman, but only of his own needs, who would take her and use her to his own ends.

A faint noise. She must have moved, scraped her foot against the cobbled floor. Marie-Claude held her breath.

Zan straightened to run his fingers through the stallion's mane. 'How's the mare, Tom?' He raised his voice to the far whistler. 'Just a sprain, I thought…'

He glanced back over his shoulder. And stilled, every muscle controlled, the words drying on his lips.

There, just as she had known. Those dark eyes, dark as indigo, looked into her, knew every secret of her heart, she was sure of it. For a brief moment his features softened as he saw her. The lines that had bracketed his mouth smoothed out. The fierce emotion in his eyes faded. She thought he would smile at her. Hoped he would.

His mouth firming into a hard line, Zan Ellerdine tossed the brush he was holding on to the bed of straw and faced her, hands fisted on hips.

'Go away. There's no place for you here. You shouldn't be here.'

It was like a blade to her heart, a tearing pain. Marie-Claude took a moment to wonder why it should matter so much, if a man she barely knew felt no desire to spend even a moment in her company. And after all, wasn't this what she had feared would happen? If she'd had any sense, any sense at all, even one ounce of dignity and pride, she would never have set foot on Ellerdine property in the first place. Instead she had laid herself open to this.

And she would open herself to more. She simply did not believe that his insolent denial of her reflected that initial response in his face. She summoned all her sang-froid, straightened her spine and raised her chin.

'I have come to pay a morning call, Zan.' There! She had called him by his name. 'Did you not expect me?'

'No.'

'You promised you would come to ask after my health. You didn't.'

'No. I didn't.' Still he stood, uncivil and unwelcoming.

'Did you even care?'

'You had wet feet and a ruined gown, nothing more. A gown that Venmore could afford to replace out of the loose change in his pocket. I doubt you would succumb to some life-threatening ailment.'

So callous. So unreasonably impolite. But Marie-Claude kept the eye contact, even when it became uncomfortable. 'As you see, I am perfectly well, but I was raised to honour my obligations,' she stated, her demure words at odds with her galloping heart. 'So since I am indebted to you, I have come to pay a morning call to offer my thanks in a formal manner.'

His lip curled. 'I was clearly not raised to honour my obligations, my upbringing being lacking in such finesse,' he retaliated, giving no quarter.

'Frankly, sir, I don't believe you.'

That shook him. She saw the glint in his eye, but his response was just as unprepossessing. 'What you believe or disbelieve is immaterial to me. I thought I made it clear our—our association was at an end. I am not available for such niceties as morning calls. As you see, madam, I'm working and you are disturbing me.'

She would *not* be put off. 'Then I will say what I wish to say here, Zan. It will not take but a minute of your *so* very valuable time.'

'Say what you have to say, madam, and then you can leave.'

He would be difficult. He was deliberately pushing her away. Well, she would not be pushed away in that manner. 'My name is Marie-Claude,' she informed him with a decided edge.

'I know your name.'

'You called me Marie-Claude before.'

'So I did. I should have treated you with more *respect*.' His tone was not pleasant.

'But as you have just informed me, your upbringing was lacking in social niceties. So why should you cavil at using my name? I did not think Englishmen were so stiff-necked as to be so rigid over etiquette. Frenchmen, perhaps.' She paused, then delivered her nicely judged *coup de grâce*. 'Since you kissed me, more than once, and I think did not dislike it, I would suggest you know me quite well enough.'

He breathed out slowly, unfisted his hands, but only to slouch in an unmannerly fashion. 'What do you want from me?' Still bleak and unbending.

'I'm not sure quite what it is I wish to say,' she admitted. How hard this was, how intransigent he was being. 'You saved me from drowning, or at least a severe drenching. I think I didn't thank you enough.'

'As I said—it's no great matter. I happened to be there—and I would have saved anyone in your predicament.'

'I think it does matter. Would you deny that some emotion flows between us? Even now it does. It makes my heart tremble.' She stretched out her hand to him, but let it fall to her side as the stony expression remained formidably in place. Indeed her heart faltered, but she drove on. She would not leave here until she had said what was in her mind. 'I think I should tell you that I don't usually allow strange gentlemen to kiss me—or any gentlemen at all, come to that. Just as I don't believe you kiss women in inn parlours—unless it's Sally who showed willing. Then you would.'

'I might,' Zan admitted.

'I envy her.' She raised her chin higher. 'What I don't understand is why you went into fast retreat when you learned my name, as if an overwhelming force had appeared on the horizon.'

His eyes released her at last. Turning from her, Zan picked up a wizened apple from the shelf and offered it to the stallion, who crunched it with relish. 'What did Meggie say?' he asked, stroking his hand down the satin neck.

'That you are a smuggler and I shouldn't associate with you. But that's not it. Everyone seems to have some connection with smuggling here. Harriette was a smuggler. George Gadie is a smuggler and Meggie doesn't disapprove of him. Or not much.'

His eyes snapped from the stallion back to her, fierce as a hawk. 'You don't want to know me.'

'*I* choose whom I wish to know. I am not a child.'

'Your family would disapprove.'

'But why?'

A pause. Would he tell her? 'I'll not tell you that.'

'Then you must allow me to make my own judgements. Do I go, Zan? Or do I stay?'

It was a deliberate challenge. If he wanted her to go, he must tell her so. She would not move one inch otherwise. She could read nothing in his face, anticipate nothing of his thoughts. And so was surprised when she heard him issue the invitation.

'Since you're here, I suppose I must take you into the house and provide you with the tea that never materialised at the Boat.'

Something had changed his mind. She inclined her head graciously. 'It would be polite.'

He retrieved his coat from the stall partition and remarked drily, 'I know the form after all. My mother was a stickler for good manners. I was at least *raised* as a gentleman.'

'I never doubted it. And I would like to see your house.' She fell into step beside him.

'You'll be disappointed.'

He took her hand, drew it through his arm, to lead her out of the stable courtyard towards the main entrance.

Until she hesitated. Looked up at him, head tilted.

'What's wrong? Have you changed your mind after all? Not willing to risk stepping into a smuggler's den of iniquity?'

'Not at all. I simply wondered why you led me to

think that you were raised as an unmannered lout. Not that you will tell me, of course.'

He laughed at her prim reply. 'You'll prise no secrets from me, Madame Mermaid!'

Abruptly he opened the door into the entrance hall and stood back so that she could enter.

Marie-Claude stepped into his home. 'Do you live here alone?' she asked.

'Yes. Are you changing your mind again?'

'No. Are you? Do you not want me here?'

'I invited you. I have a housekeeper. Mrs Shaw.'

'I did not think I would need a chaperon, Zan,' she chided gently. She stood in the centre of the entrance hall and turned slowly round, taking in her surroundings. 'Will you show me around?'

'If you wish. It won't take long.'

He opened the doors that led off the entrance hall, into the library, two small parlours, a withdrawing room, a little room with an escritoire that still held traces of his mother who had used it for her endless letter-writing. He watched Marie-Claude with some amusement as she inspected each room without comment. Without expression. Finally, calling along a corridor to an invisible Mrs Shaw for tea, he led her back into the library, where she sat on the dusty cushions of the sofa, hands neatly folded in her lap.

'Well? What do you think?'

'Disreputable,' she remarked immediately. 'What are you thinking to allow this?'

He gave a crack of laughter at the directness of her censure. Then Zan sobered, frowned. 'No money to spend on it.'

'I was thinking soap and water, rather than money. What is your housekeeper doing? And is smuggling not a lucrative trade? I was under the impression there were fortunes to be made if a smuggler was not too nice in his choice of companions. We hear talk of the vicious rogues in the smuggling gangs even in London. I know all about rogues...' She shivered as if a draught had touched her arms.

'It can be lucrative, as you say, with the right contacts,' he offered.

'Are you a member of a smuggling gang?'

'No. I am not.'

'Forgive me. I did not mean to pry.'

'I'm sure you did mean it! But I forgive you and I assure you I'm not a vicious rogue. When I organise a run, I use my own operation from the bay, and my own cutter.' The door opened to admit the spare form of the housekeeper, bearing a tray. 'And here's Mrs Shaw with refreshment.'

Whilst Zan leaned his weight back against the edge of the desk, arms folded, Marie-Claude removed her gloves and took charge, murmuring her thanks despite the housekeeper's chill disapproval of an unchaperoned female visitor, then proceeded to dispense tea with skilled assurance, measuring the amount from the inlaid box, pouring the pale liquid into fragile china cups. Zan took the cup offered to him.

'I can at least guarantee the quality of this,' he remarked drily.

'I'm sure you can.' She sipped. 'And doubtless your brandy too. Has it paid any duty?'

'Not that I know of!'

'Tell me what you do when you are not smuggling.'

Zan cast himself into one of the chairs and proceeded, against all his good intentions, to tell her the trivial nothings of life on the run-down Ellerdine estate whilst Marie-Claude sat and listened, asking a question when it seemed appropriate. How strange it was. How surreal. There they sat and exchanged polite conversation as if they were in a London withdrawing room, certainly not as if an intense undercurrent throbbed on the air between them. Later Marie-Claude had no clear idea of either her questions or his answers. Only that he had not taken his eyes from her.

Mon Dieu. How confusing this all was. Marie-Claude felt like a butterfly on a pin. His replies were brusque, his dark beauty and stern demeanour never exactly encouraging, yet she felt astonishingly at ease in his company. Eventually she put down her cup. Replaced her gloves. Rose gracefully to her feet and held out her hand to him.

'I must go. Morning calls should only last half an hour, should they not?'

'So I understand. I'm sure you're well versed in such *social niceties*.' He bent his head in a formal salute to her knuckles, a glint of humour lighting his dark eyes at last. His lips brushed softly against her skin.

'You have been most hospitable.' She managed a smile as her heart jolted with desire. 'Will you come to Lydyard's Pride one afternoon? For tea?'

'No. I will not.'

The humour vanished. The whole pleasant house of cards they had just constructed collapsed around them.

'Why not?'

'I would not be made welcome there.'

'But why would you not? What on earth have you done to cause this *impasse*? Meggie will not say, and neither will you. How can I accept what I do not understand?' She frowned at him, her dark brows meeting in frustration. 'You don't like the Hallastons, do you?'

'No.'

'There! Again! That's no answer, Zan.' Her

fingers gripped hard when he would have released them. 'Why won't you tell me the truth?'

'Because I choose not to. Goodbye.' He kissed her fingers once more with an elegant little bow. 'You have made your morning call and repri-manded me for my lack of duty in fulfilling my own obligations to you. You have seen and disparaged the way I live. Let that be an end to it. Whatever is between us—it can be explained away as a mo-mentary foolishness. We should acknowledge it and bury it. It's good advice, Madame Mermaid. I advise you to take it.'

'No. I won't.' The frown became almost a scowl. How effective he was at dismissing her, at putting her at a distance. 'Three days ago you called me Marie-Claude. Your told me I was beautiful and that you had known me all your life. And now you tell me to put it aside as if it had no meaning? Three days ago you *kissed* me.'

'So I did and I should not have done so. Forget what happened.'

'I will not.' A determination stormed through Marie-Claude, to hold tight to what she believed might be if he would only allow it. 'If you will not come to me at the Pride, then I must come to you. But you have to agree. I'll not force myself on you or be a trouble to you.'

'You don't know what you're stepping into. You don't know me.'

'I know what I see,' she persisted. 'A man who is brave, who risked his own safety to rescue an unknown woman.'

'And kissed her in an inn parlour. Hardly a reputable act.'

'Yes, you did. And then you took me home to save my reputation, from some ridiculous sense of honour!'

His lips twisted. 'Don't think too well of me.'

'I'll think what I like, what I know here.' And Marie-Claude placed her palm flat against her heart.

For a long moment he looked at her as if he were reading her thoughts, considering an answer. Even searching for a decision. For the length of that moment Marie-Claude thought that he would dismiss her again.

'What are you thinking?' she asked.

'I am thinking that, almost, you persuade me, Madame Mermaid.'

And Zan Ellerdine, for better or worse, made a decision.

Drawing her close, he released her hands to slide his arms around her waist so that she fit perfectly against him, then lowered his head and laid his mouth against hers. Warm and firm, as was hers in reply. He deliberately kept the pressure gentle, seductive, tender even, sinking into her scent, her soft curves. Even when desire flooded through him, prompting him to pounce and ravage, he maintained the control to keep his demand light. His senses swam and he was suddenly iron-hard, but he lifted his head and smoothed the pad of his thumb over her cheek.

'Very well,' he said. 'I'll not come to the Pride. Come here if you wish. I'll not turn you away. But you must take care—if you tell them at the Pride, they'll try to turn you away from me.'

'So will you meet with me, Zan?' she asked.

'Yes. Come to the cliffs. Tomorrow afternoon.'

'Will you call me by my name?'

'I will call you by your name.' His lips, soft as a breath, devastating as a spear of lightning, a seductive promise on hers. Or was it a warning? Marie-Claude was not sure.

'*Adieu*, Marie-Claude. Until tomorrow. If you dare…'

Chapter Four

She dared! Marie-Claude kept the assignation. Nothing other than the Crack of Doom would have kept her away. And now she found herself seated in the stern of the *Black Spectre*, fighting to catch her breath, racing with the waves and the wind towards the far headland, the sails taut and full.

'Come with me, Marie-Claude,' he had demanded. 'We'll launch the *Spectre*. Come and sail with me across the bay.' There he had stood on the cliff top as if he would bar her way. He was impossibly, outrageously persuasive. And so splendid to look at, his even teeth glinting in a smile that challenged her mettle, his black hair shining, lifted by the relentless breeze. 'I'll make a sailor of you yet.'

Her heart had leapt, with fear, excitement, desire. 'No, I can't.'

'Why not?'

'I think I'm afraid…'

'Afraid?' He seized her hand, tugged, as his careless smile tugged at her heart. 'You have the courage to do anything, Madame Mermaid. I swear water's your element. All you have to do is say yes.'

She doubted, after her recent ordeal, any affinity with water deeper than two inches, but could not refuse. Nor did she need to. He had swept her up into his arms before she could say either yes or no, carried her through the shallows and deposited her, hands firm about her waist, on to the planking of the *Black Spectre*. Zan Ellerdine had a distinct tendency towards the domineering.

Now here she was, denying her basic fear of open sea to be with him, and it was everything she had imagined it could be if she could overcome her trepidation. Windblown she might be, clinging to the side with rigid fingers, but exhilaration sang through her blood. Nor was it the speed and uncontrolled movement of the little cutter that forced her to catch her breath, even though it leapt over the water with the power of a runaway horse. Given the opportunity to study Zan whilst he was occupied, she felt free to watch the flex and play of his shoulders and back beneath the fine linen of his shirt, the strain of his muscled thighs as he braced against the kick of the waves. If she had enjoyed watching him groom his horse, how much more aware of him was she now as he leapt to secure a rope? Of his potent masculinity, the understated power of his body, the smooth control of interlocked muscle and flesh and sinew.

Suddenly he was standing before her, his body blocking out the light.

'Why are you clinging to the side?'

'The waves seem very close,' she admitted as the spray rose and fell between them in a sparkling arc.

'I'll not let you fall overboard. Don't you trust me?'

'I'm not sure.' She squinted up at him through the drops. 'I think the sea has a mind of its own.'

Placing a booted foot on the seat next to her, he leaned to peel her fingers away from their grip. 'There—you're quite safe.' Then he pressed his lips to the very centre of each palm—first one, then the other—before placing her hands firmly in her lap. 'I promise to bring you safe home. Just sit there and enjoy it.'

And then he was gone to trim a flapping sail. Marie-Claude closed her fingers over that invisible imprint, still conscious of his closeness. The heat and power of his body as he had leaned against her. What would it be like to lie in those arms, to feel the weight of his thighs?

She turned her face away and shivered, considering whether she should feel some element of guilt.

It was impossible to deny that she was acting against some unspoken disapproval, but since no one was prepared to spell out the truth for her she could hardly blame herself. She would snatch at the happiness that was offered. Never had she felt so full of joy, so awake to every sensation. So there was no guilt, no remorse, only a close-knitting into a seamless whole of all that she was with him.

Even when he was too busy to give her any attention it felt as if his mind caressed her. Soft, smooth as the silk he admitted to smuggling, she luxuriated in his presence and dreamed. Until she realised that the old fisherman, Zan's efficient crew, was frowning at her.

She raised her brows and he came over.

'What is it, Mr Gadie?'

As weather-beaten as the fishing smacks in the bay, George Gadie propped himself against the thwart at her side. 'The family won't like it.'

Marie-Claude sighed. Here it was again. 'Why would they not?'

'Not my place to say, mistress.'

'Then I make my own decisions. No one has given me a good reason why I should not have Mr Ellerdine as my friend. Why should a sail in the *Spectre* be a subject for any man's disapproval?'

'It'll cause trouble. I'm not saying as I agree with

what's said against him—but don't say I didn't warn
you, mistress.'

'I won't. I see no cause for trouble.' A trip of
anger surprised her. 'And do I not have you or
Meggie as permanent mentor and chaperon?
There's nothing inappropriate in what I do. I am a
respectable widow.'

She knew bright colour surged in her cheeks,
nothing to do with the effect of the brisk wind.
Nothing inappropriate? There was everything inappropriate in the line of her thoughts as her attention
moved to Zan when he loped across the little vessel
to secure a rope with those clever, long-fingered
hands. Marie-Claude's belly became mellow and
liquid with longing. The glamour of his loose-limbed
grace and handsome face struck home once more.

'I will have him as my friend if I choose to,' she
said. 'I'll hear no more from you.'

The old fisherman's lips shut with a hearty smack.
'Aye, aye, mistress.' He saluted. 'You'll do as you
wish, I expect.'

Yes, she would.

But George's words would not go away, spoiling
the moment, forcing Marie-Claude to grasp at
honesty. What was she doing?

Flying in the face of her upbringing, certainly. Of
all she had been taught, all the principles instilled

in her. A daughter of the de la Roche did not engage in casual affairs. Did not throw aside all ideas and tenets of morality and good breeding. A well-mannered husband, marriage, family—that was as her upbringing dictated, that should have been her expectation in life.

'But it is not enough!' she informed a passing gull.

Nor was the life she was leading. Comfort, indeed luxury, a choice of houses in which to live, a thriving son, a loving family. An assured future. She must be the most selfish creature alive to cast all this aside in her mind as *unsatisfactory*. But it was. It was all enveloping, endlessly suffocating. Restricting every thought, every movement to fit with what the London *ton* considered respectable.

'Respectable!' She issued the word as a challenge as the gull circled and dived into the waves.

She lived, breathed, dressed in the most fashionable of garments, enjoying the pretty clothes that her jointure allowed her. When in London she danced, rode in Hyde Park, laughed.

But was smothered by it all. Stifled by respectability.

She was grateful to Harriette and Luke. Horribly grateful. And always would be. But she was only half-alive. Was this it for her, for ever? To exist, only half-awake?

'I have a half-life. And I want to live!'

Marie-Claude gripped hard on the glossy wood of the *Spectre*'s gunwale. After Marcus's death, she had escaped death, dishonour, appalling fear for herself and her baby son. Of course she would never wish to return to those days, but she recalled how her blood had run hot in her determination to break free from Jean-Jacques Noir and his evil plans. In the intervening years her blood seemed to settle into a dull sluggishness that horrified her. Was she now to sink into tedious oblivion, a widow, a doting and ageing aunt to Luke and Harriette's children?

'No! I won't!'

Although the wind snatched her words away, they still lingered to echo in her mind as her eyes again sought the man who stood by the mast in utmost mastery of the vessel, shirt billowing at sleeve and neck. This man had come into her life, had awoken her. Had stirred her senses into flame. Until that moment in the inn parlour she had not fully understood how desolate her heart had become.

At that moment he turned his head, shouted an order to George Gadie to reef the sail as they would tack into the wind. What did he offer her? Ah, that was the problem. He offered her nothing. Nor ever would, she suspected. He was an enigma. A man with dark shadows. He had saved her and surely would not hurt her, but had shown a coldly calculating streak as he had tried to put her at a distance. He would have succeeded if she had not been so determined to have her own way. He could be ruthless too, she thought, given the right circumstances. And there was a guarded secrecy that trapped him, some mystery that he would not talk of. Certainly he had a reputation. He had not denied being a rake or a libertine, had he?

The mere thought of his mouth on hers took her breath away entirely. Marie-Claude closed her eyes and lifted her face to the sun.

You don't want to know me.

Well, she did, despite her confusion. But what did she want from him? Friendship? Zan Ellerdine was not a friend. What he was she did not rightly know, but it was not friendship that placed him at the centre of her thoughts and her dreams. He was a difficult and dangerous man to associate with.

Would she risk his threat to her reputation?

'I am afraid that I might!'

This time there was an answer. 'Are you talking to yourself or the gulls? What do they say? Beware, Madame Mermaid, or they'll *gull* you into believing that happiness is possible in this life!'

Opening her eyes, Marie-Claude laughed. For there he was beside her again, lounging on the wooden seat, head thrown back to the kiss of sun. At once she knew the answer. Yes, she would risk all, whatever the future would hold, to grasp this one chance. Happiness? Who could know? But she would snatch this moment with this man, and all the rest he offered her. And if he was willing, she would have him as her lover. Breathless at the enormity of her decision, Marie-Claude's fingers itched to touch his face, but she was suddenly shy.

'And is happiness not possible?'

'I'd say not. But I'm not the man to ask!'

'I'm happy today.'

'Then that's enough. Well, Galatea? Does it please you, to sail the *Spectre*?' His eyes gleamed, travelled over her face. Gone was the shadow of their previous meetings, the bitter self-regard, even the cynicism of a few moments ago. Today he was filled with a wild euphoria, his spirits soaring. And it was infectious.

'Yes. It pleases me. I feel full of light—as if the glittering spray has become trapped in my veins.' She tilted her chin. 'Galatea?'

'A beautiful woman,' he replied with utmost solemnity, 'who threw herself into the waves when her lover was murdered and so became a sea nymph.'

'What a weak-willed female!' A provocative arch of brows. 'I'm no Galatea!'

'No?'

'Are you flirting with me, Zan?'

'Most definitely, Marie-Claude!'

His gaze grew intense, capturing hers. The intoxication of the glittering sea faded in comparison with the dark glow of his eyes. Marie-Claude held her breath as he leaned close.

'If we were alone, I'd kiss you. As it is…' he whispered in her ear, his breath warm on her cheek. 'As it is, you'll have to imagine my lips on yours until I have the chance to show you.'

'How scandalous you are, Mr Ellerdine!'

'How enchanting you are, Madame Mermaid.' Suddenly his hand caught her chin. 'I regret—but I can neither resist nor wait until we reach land.'

Sliding his hand until it curled round the nape of her neck, he leaned to place his lips on her, a firm pressure that tasted of sun and salt, a riot of feelings. Marie-Claude closed her eyes against the brightness, to fix her senses on the kiss that lingered, enticed.

'Have we shocked the gulls?' she murmured at last, blinded by the light, swamped with pleasure, as he raised his head.

'I fear we have. And George Gadie who's pretending not to notice. Do you care?'

Her eyes snapped to his. They were audaciously challenging.

'Do you care, Marie-Claude?' he murmured, a mere breath from her lips.

'No, I don't.' Scandalous, indeed, Marie-Claude admitted. 'I don't care at all. Kiss me again, Zan.'

They returned to the beach, tacking against the push of the wind. Zan leapt down into the shallows, turning to lift Marie-Claude, lifting her high to set her down on the dry shingle.

'Go on. I'll help George to pull the *Spectre* up. Then I'll come to you.' Zan pushed her gently in the direction of the harbour wall. 'I'll join you. You were a magnificent sailor.'

He watched her plod determinedly up the shingle.

He turned back to his cutter, only to find George looking askance at him—and cursed himself silently for allowing his inexplicable feelings to be quite so transparent.

'Well?'

'Hope you know what you're doing, y'r honour.'

Zan tensed at the implied criticism, but refused to be drawn. 'By God, I hope I do. When did I ever not? I'm no victim of blind chance, as you well know, George.'

'As you'd like to have some of us believe, sir.'

'What am I supposed to understand from that masterly statement?' Zan asked, not entirely pleased.

'Nothin', y'r honour. Just that you might think as you can pull the wool over the eyes of them as knows you best, and has an affection for you. But you can't. Some of us is too old to be fooled. Some of us would say you don't deserve the reputation you've chosen to carry on your shoulders—'

'No! Enough!' Zan snapped, suddenly aware of the direction the old fisherman's accusation was heading.

But George Gadie was in full flow and fierce scowl. 'Some of us'd say you should come clean and put the blame where it lies. No one who knows you could possibly think you've sold your soul to the devil, no matter what you told Miss Harriette and her Earl. And some of us—'

Zan's hand flashed to grip George's wrist. 'And some of us should keep their mouths shut,' he snarled. 'D'you understand me?'

'Aye. I understand right enough. But it's not right…'

'I don't care, George. You'll say nothing at this moment. I don't want to hear even a hint of what you're thinking. If I do—you'll have me to deal with.'

'As you say, Mr Ellerdine.' George was in no way put out by the threat. 'But Mistress Marie-Claude… I just think she deserves—'

'I know what you think. Don't say it.'

George sniffed. 'Not my place, sir. It'll all end badly if you keep it secret. Mark my words.'

'I will. But I've set out my path and I'll tread it to the bitter end.'

'And pray God we all comes out of it in one piece, sir!'

They beached the *Spectre* in sullen silence. Zan felt the weight of George's warning, but he would not think of it. He would hold to the false promise of the future for just a little while. And at least pretend that Marie-Claude had a place in it.

The cutter firmly beached at last, Zan made his way over the shingle to where Marie-Claude sat on the seawall. Seeing her smile as he approached, he thrust all doubts aside. Although he bowed formally, a deliberately elegant and courteous little gesture entirely out of place between two wind-swept figures on a seawall, his eyes spoke his feelings. His mouth on her proffered fingers sent a thrill through her veins.

'George Gadie has just warned me off,' he announced.

'Mr Gadie disapproves of me spending time with you,' she agreed.

'I can imagine.' Zan pushed himself up on to the wall beside her.

'Will you tell me why?'

'No.'

'Why not?'

'You might run away from me. How would I live, how would I breathe and my heart continue to beat when I have only just found you?' Keeping a charade of light flirtation, he set himself to preserve the pleasure of the afternoon.

'I think you would live very well. I dare say you have a score of pretty women laying their hearts at your feet.'

'Only a score? I think you underestimate my attractions.'

'No. I do not. Do I not see them before me?'

His eyes lifted to hers, their focus suddenly sharp.

'There's only one heart I'm interested in owning,' he replied slowly.

'I think you might already have it.' With a quick intake of breath she covered her mouth with her fingers, in shock that she should have spoken such a sentiment.

Zan simply caught her hand and pressed his mouth to her fingertips.

'If you've lost your heart to me, I willingly give you mine in recompense.'

Marie-Claude blinked, startled. 'I shouldn't be saying this, listening to this, should I?'

'Why not? Is it the truth, Marie-Claude, that you have given your heart to me?'

She did not even hesitate. 'Yes. Oh, yes.' Her fingers curled around his.

A man rode up along the quay on a raw-boned horse, pulling it to a standstill beside them. His shadow fell across them. Zan raised his head as he became aware of a shiver running across Marie-Claude's skin.

He looked round.

'Ellerdine. A word…'

'Rackham.' Zan squinted up into the dazzle of the sun, lifting his hand so that he was able to make out the man's narrow features and emotionless stare. Damnation! This confrontation was not what he wanted, not here in this company. But needs must when the devil drives—and Rackham definitely represented the devil. Zan turned back to Marie-Claude, assembling an easy smile despite the tightened clasp on her hands. He deliberately released them and pushed himself from the wall. 'Forgive me, madam. If you would allow me a minute?'

'Haven't got all day, Ellerdine,' Rackham sneered as he dismounted, letting his eye slide over Marie-Claude in a manner crude and obvious enough to instantly heat Zan's blood.

'Nor will you need it, Rackham,' Zan snapped back. 'Wait here for me, madam.'

Marie-Claude watched as Zan leapt down to the

shingle, deliberately leading the man some distance away. The conversation was short, without warmth or humour. Hardly more than the basic good manners expected between men with business dealings. Try as she might, she could catch no more than the odd word, but she thought they had no liking for each other. Then with no more than a raised hand Rackham strode off, remounted and rode away, leaving Zan to return to her side.

His good mood, she decided, had been decidedly compromised, his features settled into an austere severity.

'I should see you to the cliff path,' he remarked coolly.

So he had no intention of telling her what that had been about.

'Who was that?' she asked.

'Rackham? An acquaintance.'

'From the village? I don't know him.'

'No. From Rottingdean.' He helped her down from the wall, brushing the sand from her skirts, his voice clipped.

'What did he want? You didn't seem pleased to see him.'

'Did I not? Merely a matter of business.' His eyes were flat with rejection.

'Smuggling?'

'Yes.' A sharp glance as if he wished she had not asked. 'Does it bother you?'

'No. Not really. I know that my sister-in-law, Harriette, was part of a smuggling gang before she married. It sounded exciting.'

'It is not. It's a foul trade.'

'I thought you were involved in it.'

'I am.'

He said no more as he escorted her to the start of the cliff path, leaving Marie-Claude bewildered. Whatever the man Rackham had said had stirred some strong emotion within him. She didn't like the look of the smuggler from Rottingdean. She would not trust a man with so hard a face or such cold eyes. Nor had she liked the manner in which he had looked at her. She would not like to be alone with Rackham.

It was as if Zan sensed her disquiet. 'Mr Rackham need not concern you, Marie-Claude.' With a wry smile, he tucked a flighty curl behind the ribbon of her bonnet. 'Don't allow him to spoil a remarkable day. It was too good to allow such a man to mar your memory of it.'

'No. I will not. I doubt I'll ever see him again.'

'I doubt you will.' The lightest touch of his fingers on the back of her hand had the power to make her heart flutter. 'Farewell, Madame Mermaid.'

She chuckled at the foolishness of the name he had given her. But there was nothing foolish in the glint in his eye. It was quite predatory, she thought. He was hunting in earnest. She must have a care. Yet still she asked, 'Will I see you again?'

'Yes.' His lips on her brow soft as a blessing. 'Yes, Marie-Claude, you will.'

But as she climbed the steep path her anxiety did not quite go away. She could not quite forget the man Rackham's cold eyes. Nor Zan's equivocal response.

Marie-Claude curled on the window seat of her bedchamber and stared unseeingly at the magnificence of moonlight on silvered waves. Sleep had evaded her, so what point lying in bed reading the cracks in the ceiling? She would not look towards Ellerdine Manor. How fortunate that her room faced towards the sea.

A welter of emotions swamped her. What manner of man was he to stir such feelings within her? When he kissed her, she was lost. What use in promising to keep him at a distance? Easier to attempt to keep the waves at bay like King Canute. He had singularly failed too.

She wanted him. Just the thought of his mouth trailing along her throat curled fingers of desire between her thighs. Every inch of skin was suddenly sensitive to the air. Marie-Claude opened the window to let in the still-warm night air to dissipate the heat of the room. Alexander Ellerdine was probably engaged in doing something entirely reprehensible to do with smuggling. Something to do with Rackham. Leaning on her arms, she wished he was here with her now. But he would not come. He would not come to the Pride. She would not invite him again.

She must dream alone.

At Ellerdine Manor, Zan strode through the library, across the hallway, not even staying to find a coat or a hat. Suddenly every minute seemed precious to him. He would go to the Pride, but not sully its floors with his booted feet. If he would seduce her, it would be on neutral territory...

Seduce? It almost brought him to a halt as he flung back the main door. Was that what he intended? She had asked if he were a libertine in all seriousness.

But he wanted to see her again. He must see her.

In the stables he put a bridle on his mare, hoisted himself up with an effortless flex of muscle in thigh and arm and rode the cliffs without a saddle, holding firm with his thighs. It was many a day since he had done that, riding bareback in his wild youth. He pressed the willing mare on into a gallop, intoxicated, relying on the sure footing of his mount in the moonlight.

And there was the Pride, gleaming white, the home of some enchantress who had put a spell on him. By God, he was bewitched. And so be it. He would accept the spell and walk with her in the moonlight. His lips curved. He would entice her out, to touch her hand, to know the slide of her skin against his. To take her mouth with his, to experience the perfume of her hair wrapped around him. It was no longer enough to know how she felt in his arms. He wanted more.

First to lure her out. Not beyond the wit of a clever man and he knew exactly how to appeal to her. He rode his mare across the lawns. If he knew her, she would have chosen a room with that wild aspect over the sea rather then the gentle order of flowerbeds and ornamental trees. And there was a window open. Was fate once more guiding his steps? He pulled the mare to a standstill and whistled softly. Waited.

Nothing.

Not deterred, Zan dismounted. Picked up a handful of gravel and tossed it lightly at the open window. A soft shriek made him smile. Stepping back, looking up, there she was. Leaning out in indignation, light kissing her shoulders, silvering her fair hair.

'What are you doing?' she whispered.

'Trying to attract your attention,' he replied, bowing low, a courtly gesture.

'You've succeeded. What do you want? It's after midnight.'

'And you are awake. Come down, Madame Mermaid.'

'Now? I'm in my night robes.'

'What better garments for strolling in the moonlight.'

'You must be mad!'

'Perhaps I must. Mad with desire, forsooth!' He struck a pose worthy of Edmund Kean treading the boards at Covent Garden. 'Come down, lady.'

'Are you drunk?'

'Never that. How cruel you are.'

'Go home.'

'Never. I shall stay here and pine until you come down.' He sank dramatically to one knee, hands flattened over his heart. 'Or until you let your hair down, sweet Rapunzel, and allow me to climb up. Now there's an idea. That might be the best course of action…' He sprang to his feet and made to grasp the rampant creeper. If she was half the woman he thought her, that should do the trick.

Another soft shriek. Zan stepped back, hiding a triumphant smile.

'Have you decided, Marie-Claude? Do I come up or do you come down?'

'*Mon Dieu*, Zan! What are you asking of me?'

'To come and walk at my side so that I can tell you how beautiful you are.' He hesitated, but only for a second. This was a night demanding honesty. 'So that I can tell you how much I love you.'

Silence.

'Have you taken leave of your senses?' she whispered, once again leaning out.

'No, fair lady. But I shall if you don't take pity on me and put me out of my misery of loneliness. On second thought, perhaps I'll come up after all.'

'No, you don't. Wait there!'

Don't. Don't leave the safety of your room. He's uncontrolled, unbridled like a mettlesome stallion. Dangerous. You don't know him. You'll spend the rest of your life in regret if you go to him now.

Still Marie-Claude hesitated.

No! Never regret. I know that, even from a distance, he calls to me, touches me, demands that I respond. This was meant to be.

The thrill of anticipation danced through her blood. She thrust the sly inner voice of warning from her mind and answered the insistent demands of her heart as she tugged on a chamber robe over her night attire and flew down the stairs. She had accused him of madness, yet the same frenzy had entered her brain. Did the poets not say that the moon drove men and women to wild, irrational longings? This was irrational. To leave her bed to walk with a man alone in the moonlight after midnight was outrageous. But, oh, she wanted to be with him. She wanted to be in his arms, to feel his strength, his life-force, more than she had ever wanted anything in her life.

Without stopping to think, she drew the bolts on the main door and ran, her soft slippers making no sound on the flags of the terrace. And there he was, waiting for her. Leaning against the balustrade as if it were the most common occurrence in the world. He was laughing, his hair ruffled by the breeze to curl against his throat, his shirt glowing white in the strange luminescence.

For the length of a breath she stopped, still hesitating, still uncertain. How dominant he was, how confident as if he were only to lift his hand to command her obedience. As if he knew that she was his. Surely he would hear her heart thudding so hard against her ribs she was breathless from it.

Go back. This is your last chance. If you go to him now, you are lost. His wildness will infect you and you will be bound to him for ever. This is not how Marie-Claude de la Roche should conduct herself!

You are no tavern slut to leap into the embrace of a man as easily as she serves him a tankard of ale. What will he think of you?

She smoothed her damp palms down the sides of her lace robe.

But desire, hot and sweet, curled like a fist in her belly when the moon glimmered on the flat planes of his face and silvered the swell of muscle in thigh and shoulder as he pushed himself upright and walked softly towards her. His face was solemn now, watchful, his dark gaze possessive, holding hers. She held her breath.

'Marie-Claude.'

His voice was gentle. Yet she recognised in it a command. He lifted his hand, palm upwards. Supplication or demand? She knew exactly which and shivered at his power.

'Yes.'

'You have come to me.'

'Yes.' She walked towards him, close enough that she could see herself reflected in his eyes. And saw them shine with triumph.

'Your courage shines as bright as the moon.'

'I think I should not. I think I must be mad.'

'Then so am I. Let us be mad and foolish together. How could we resist this magnificence granted to us by the gods?' He flung out one arm to encompass the soft grass, the fall of the cliff, the soft hush of the waves on the shingle far below.

'No, we could not.' Marie-Claude placed her hand in his. It closed strongly round her fingers and drew her close. And when he opened his arms, Marie-Claude simply stepped into them.

Zan could feel the tremor of nerves ripple through her body as his arms closed around her. He would be gentle, would not frighten her, so he drew her softly against him and bent his mouth to hers. Whisper soft, as light as a breath. Beautiful she was, ethereal in the moon's beams. No time for second thinking, but he controlled the urging of his loins. He would take her hand in his and walk with her in this magical light, nothing more. Yet her body fit against his, soft curves against hard muscle. Her lips were meant to be kissed, savoured, caressed.

Ravished!

The heat built before he was aware with the kick of a rogue wave. His arms tightened, his mouth took and took until he groaned with pleasure as her lips parted beneath his. Too much, too fast. Breathless, he raised his head, prepared to step back, only to see the blur of blind desire in her face.

'Marie...' He pressed his lips on her brow.

When she raised a hand to touch his cheek, when

her lips curved in shy delight, he was undone. He swooped to crush his mouth to hers.

How wild he was. Uncontrolled raw passion raced through him, lighting an answering flame in her own blood. The power of him, his hands, his lean body, made her want. Need. His desire for her was clear in the hard thrust of his thighs against hers. This was no light flirtation. He was hunting and she was the quarry. And Marie-Claude gloried in it. To be wanted. To be wanted by this man who made her feel cherished and loved and desired.

Her breathing became shallow as his mouth roamed to slide along her jaw in open-mouthed kisses. Then her throat, with the caress of tongue and the nip of teeth.

'I think you have bewitched me,' she murmured, dropping her head back as he pursued a path to the dip of her collarbone. Her pulse leapt and quivered.

'You have bound me in silver chains this night.'

Then he lifted his head, grasped her waist and lifted her to spin her around.

'Will you come with me, Marie-Claude?'

She tilted her chin. 'My conscience says no.'

'To hell with conscience. Damnation, Marie!' A little spurt of temper that both surprised and excited her. 'Can you not feel it? My heart beats for you. It has since the moment I set eyes on you. You have trapped me.'

'As you have trapped me.' She kissed the temper away. 'You are not the only one to suffer from this. Where will you take me?'

'Somewhere—not far—out of the wind and away from prying eyes. I should warn you. I want you—and I'll take you. I've no right to ask it of you. Certainly I've no right to demand it. But you should know—'

She put her fingers against his lips. 'You have every right if I agree, if I allow it.'

'And do you?'

'I do.'

His ravenous gaze raked her. 'Tell me to stop now—if that's your wish.'

'And you will. I know it.' She had no fear of him, however compromised his control might appear.

'I'll leave you here—if you wish it.'

'No. Make love to me, Zan.'

Walking backwards, luring her on, he drew her down into a shallow dip in the cliffs where the grass was nibbled short by the sheep, firm and springy beneath their feet. Thinking that she might be spurred into flight if she allowed stern thought to replace the dazzle of moonbeams in her brain, he kept his hold firm, but she followed his leading readily enough. The expanse of sky above their heads, the bright vista of stars enfolded them as the light wind caressed, warm as a breath. All that mattered was that she was here, she had come to him. And now she stepped forwards into his arms, eyes alight, lips smiling. He could not resist her. Moving close to obliterate any space between them, his lips cruised over her face, lingering on her eyelids, the impossibly alluring hollow at her temple, drawn irresistibly to her lips that opened beneath his and welcomed him. When his tongue savoured the sweetness of hers, she sighed against him. Then he continued, holding her close, applying open-mouthed kisses along the fine length of her throat to the fragile bones of her shoulders, to where the pulse beat hard against him.

His own pulse leapt in fast response. Desire raged through him, hot and urgent, taking him off guard, so that his hands clenched hard on her arms, too hard. He raised his head, forcing himself to relax his grip. Without doubt she challenged his control, but her eyes were wide and trusting on his.

'Zan…' she murmured, raising a hand to touch his lips.

'Do you really want this?' he asked, catching her restless fingers and biting gently.

'Can you ask?'

All the invitation he needed; he released her to loosen the ribbons of her robe, waited for her to deny him the intimacy—which she didn't—then parted the delicate material to slide it down to catch at her elbows.

If he had lost his breath before, this moment was shattering. It was as if she were meant to stand like this, moon-kissed, desirable. A sea goddess, a nymph, or the mermaid he called her, bathed in light that made her skin glow and demand that he touch her. Zan simply stood and looked, making no apology for it. She was so beautiful. The light from sky and sea illuminated her skin, gleaming along the curves, casting enticing shadows beneath her breasts. He stroked his fingers down over the tantalising swell, the hardness of her nipple, until she gasped.

Zan dropped his hand, conscious that her cheeks were now flushed, her expression just a little anxious.

'Forgive me…'

'No.' She stepped closer and when she raised her hands he allowed her to unfasten the ties of his shirt and push it aside. He allowed her to touch and discover as she wished. His blood heated. His body tightened, his erection hardened in demand. She wanted him as much as he wanted her.

'Will you give yourself to me?'

'Yes.'

'Are you afraid?'

'Yes…' A reluctant confession.

'There's no need to be.'

Casting his shirt on the grass, Zan took her hands
and lowered her and proceeded to kneel beside her,
sliding his fingers beneath the fine silk of her night
attire, opening it as if to display a miraculous gift.
For him and him alone. Then he set himself to woo
and pleasure them both, the pressure of his lips a
prelude to the stroke of his fingers, touching, discovering, driving her and himself to an urgency of
need. His command over his senses was iron-hard.
Always gentle, always slow, an insistent awakening,
determined to let her become familiar with this
intimacy before allowing his own needs to surface.
A difficult promise to keep, as her nipples hardened
against this palms, as her breath shortened. His
control, he discovered, was not infinite.

Marie-Claude found herself blinded by the desire
that swept through her so fast she could not contain
it. Her knowledge of these intimacies was so
limited, so distant, but she felt no uncertainties in
Zan's embrace. He would treat her with care. How
could she know that, when she had known him for
so little a time? But she did. She spread her palms,
her fingers, against his chest, marvelling at the firm
smoothness of muscle underlying skin. Like rocks,

smooth and hard and dangerous, beneath fast-flowing water. She sighed in impossible pleasure, her horizon filled to the brim with his glamour as his dark hair trailed across her breast. She gasped as his teeth closed over a nipple.

He bit gently, then soothed with his tongue. All thought vanished, her mind submerged in a sea of longing. This was enchantment and she gave herself up to the enticement of his clever hands.

Zan continued, unhurried, waiting for her response, skimming his fingers over her belly, the sensuous curve of her hip. Tantalisingly, torment-ing, over the satin skin of her inner thigh to the throbbing heart of her.

Her breath caught in her throat on a little gasp.

And his heart lunged from its heavy beat into a gallop. He could wait no longer. It took only a heart-beat to disrobe her entirely. Longer to divest himself of boots and breeches. Sitting with his back turned to her as he hauled off the leather, he felt the brush of her fingers along the length of her spine, and shuddered. In a state of blatant arousal that he could not hide, he rolled and pinned her, yet holding his weight from her on his forearms, he wound his hands into her hair so that she must look at him. And she did, with no reticence. It drove hard like an arrow through his gut.

'You were meant for a night of loving such as this. You were meant to be for me.' He kissed her mouth, filling himself with her sweetness. 'I'll not hurt you.'

'I know.'

Her arms tangled round him to draw him down as she offered her lips to the relentless passion in his. Real and solid, he took her over, her will, her mind, her body. Cool, smooth, he was all male. He was all she wanted. Marie-Claude opened her thighs to receive him.

'Marie-Claude… You have the skill of a siren.'

Helpless to resist, Zan sank into her, deep and full, enclosed in hot silk. With a steady pace in mind, he thrust and withdrew. Thrust slowly again. But she arched her body against him, taking him deeper, and he was lost. A slow loving was no longer a choice he could make. Hunger roared in him and he plunged until she enclosed him entirely. Allowing that same hunger to rule, he swooped and plundered, driving them both to a frenzy of wanting, sweat-streaked, struggling to catch their breath at the onslaught of desire.

Zan filled her. Marie-Claude gloried in his body, in her own, in the way they fit so perfectly and moved together, strained against each other in thoughtless delight. This was right. He was hers. Sighing as he took her, powerful thrust after powerful thrust, owning her. When he moved within her, setting fire to her, giving her no peace, she mirrored his rhythm, trembling beneath him as his flesh moved against hers, stroking every nerve until she could not bear it.

How could pleasure approach so close to exquisite agony?

Quivering, her whole body alight, Marie-Claude felt herself dragged to some inexplicable destination. She was overwhelmed by it and for a moment fought against it, but he was with her. Zan would keep her safe. Her whole world was centred there, in him, and her heart pounded in unison with his. His mouth captured hers, his tongue forceful to part her lips and savour the soft flesh. The power of his thighs became more insistent, irresistible, shattering her senses. All Marie-Claude could do was to hold on, to hold tight, her fingers digging into his shoulders, her nails scoring his flesh.

Lured by her heat and softness, Zan felt the need build to drive home. He held back as long as he could, until he must respond to the tensing of her muscles around him. Until body overcame mind, like the rush of the tide to sweep all before it. With a groan of despair, of inexpressible pleasure, he clung to the edge as the water sucked and clawed.

Then fell in, drawn below the surface of dark-edged satisfaction.

She drowned too in a glittering explosion of sensations.

Slowly Marie-Claude opened her eyes to find Zan looking at her. Their eyes locked, held, as if neither wished to be released from what had just been between them.

'I can't believe it,' she whispered, finally breaking the spell, stretching luxuriously.

Zan kissed her lips, her hair, in a chaste little salute. 'What can you not believe?'

'That you have given me such happiness. I feel as diamond-bright as those stars shining down on us. I feel as if they have got into my blood, to sparkle there.'

'Very poetic, Madame Mermaid. Then if you feel at one with the stars, I am well repaid for my efforts.'

Was that a touch of cynicism? Momentarily unsettled, Marie-Claude reached up her hand as if to smooth his hair from his forehead.

Abruptly Zan drew back, released her. Sat up and pushed himself to his feet in one strong movement. Surprised by his sudden change of mood, Marie-Claude could do nothing but allow him to lift her, to help her don her robe with brisk attention, before putting his own clothes to rights.

'You are very skilled, I see,' she remarked with a

soft laugh, clinging to their previous intimacy against the little distance he had built between them, as he tied her silk ribbons into more than passable bows.

'I have to admit to having some knowledge of feminine attire. Does it bother you?'

'No.'

'It needn't.'

'I have never dreamed of anything like that!' She closed her fingers around his wrists in the softest of bracelets. 'You made me feel beautiful and desired and alive as a woman. What more could any woman ask but to be loved in the moonlight on a night such as this…' *And by a man she finds irresistible*, she added in her mind.

'You have cast an enchantment, Marie.' His voice had gentled again, and Zan pressed his lips to her brow. 'But now it's beyond late and I must take you home.'

Linking his fingers in hers, he drew her with him. Silently they retraced their steps to the edge of the lawns, where he turned her against his arm so that he could see her face.

'Goodnight, my glorious girl.'

He could not resist. A kiss that began exactly as he intended, a gentle, reflective farewell. A light touch of lips against lips. And it took him by surprise. The flood of desire. The blow to his gut like a punch from an iron fist. He wanted her all over again as if he had not just buried himself in her, satiating his needs. Those same needs rose like to shining fish to the surface of the sea, to rack him again.

Marie-Claude clung to him, poured all she had into the kiss, and found her emotions whirled into disarray once more.

'Go in.' His voice was low and rough, again surprising her. Startling her when he thrust her away. 'Go in before I take you again…'

She did not quite understand, but reached to touch his mouth with her fingers. 'Goodnight, Zan.'

'Sleep well, Marie.'

'I will.'

'No bad dreams. No regrets.' The twist of his lips against her hand was wry.

'I will dream of you.'

As she turned from him she thought she saw a hint of bitterness trace its path across his face, or perhaps it was a mere shadow as a cloud drifted across the face of the moon. She could not bear that he might already be regretting what he had done.

Marie-Claude closed the door and leaned back against it, astonished at her boldness, her lack of discretion. How could she have acted as she did?

Chapter Five

Marie-Claude's memory was crystal clear when she awoke. Far too clear, she thought. Had she really done those things, said those things that brought a blush to her skin? Allowed him, invited him, to do those things to her? Marie-Claude's awakening in her own bed, the moonlight replaced by the cool, clear light of an overcast morning, sank her spirits. Humid, heavy, the heat of the previous days threatened to break in a sudden summer storm. The air was as heavy as her heart. A flush of shame washed over her, even deeper. She had lain in Alexander Ellerdine's arms, inviting his caresses. Demanding them. Not only the intimate discovery of his clever hands, but also tongue and teeth and lips. All consuming. And then when he had buried himself deep within her she had urged him on. Given herself completely…

She leapt from her bed to fling open the window to cool her cheeks, despite the threat of drizzle. What would he think of her this morning? It filled her with dread that he should despise her for her lack of discretion. No better than one of the whores who plied their trade, with no more than an enquiring smile, a turn of a shoulder and a show of an ankle, along the quay at Hastings.

She had been no better than they.

She had been much worse! Marie-Claude closed her eyes on the image of Zan stripping her lace gown from her shoulders whilst her blood ran hot and sure for him.

As the rain dampened her skin, her first thought was to pack her clothes and make a run for London. She deserved every degree of shame. But she could not flee. When Zan had coaxed and lured, had he not said that she was brave, courageous?

But if that were so, fleeing in ignominy was not a choice she could make. There was only one thing she could do. Since he would not come to her, not in broad daylight, she must go to Ellerdine Manor, as she had once before, to see if…well, to see if he rejected her with a contemptuous curl of his lip. She flinched in horror as she recalled the intimacies those lips had taken.

And then at the end—something had occurred

between them. Without doubt when he had stepped away from her, dressed her, there had been an unexpected coolness in his actions, in his manner.

Without further thought, Marie-Claude had a horse saddled and set off to face icy condemnation at best, outright rejection at worst. She would face him because she must.

And because she wanted to see him.

He was not at home. His taciturn housekeeper thought he might not be home until evening. Heavy with disappointment, Marie-Claude turned away. She might as well go home before the heavens opened and she was drenched to the skin.

Zan bent his head against the gusting wind and pushed his mare on into a smart trot, in no manner dissatisfied with his morning's work. A vital business meeting, to consolidate his agreement with Rackham and Captain D'Acre, gang master of the Fly-By-Nights. He had had no choice. It would have been too dangerous at this juncture to send an excuse and cry off. But all had gone according to plan.

Except that he now appeared in imminent danger of being caught in a storm.

Of her own volition, the mare broke into a canter as her stable beckoned and Zan did not steady her. Not until, approaching from the opposite direction, he saw Marie-Claude. A swirl of wind brought a rattle of raindrops against his back. In a second he was beside her, gripping her reins.

'Come with me.'

'I can't.' Eyes dark with distress, she tugged on the leather against his damp hands. 'I shouldn't have come.'

'Yes, you should.'

'I thought…I wasn't sure that you would want to see me again.'

'Marie-Claude…' A hand to her chin made her look at him. 'I want to see you. I want nothing more.' A quickly snatched kiss as the drops grew heavier. 'You'll catch your death out here in this.'

'I should go home.'

'No.' His grip tightened. 'I'll not allow it, so don't bother to argue.'

They ran before the approaching storm, the exhilaration of it soaking into their blood. When her gelding stumbled, Zan threw out a hand to grasp her arm, and felt the same surge of energy in her that stirred him.

'I'm safe,' she gasped, the wind snatching at her words.

'And I'll keep you so.' His eyes were wild, his expression unrestrained.

Swinging down from his mare, Zan plucked her

off her horse and pushed her in the direction of the house, then slapped the rumps of the two animals to send them to the stables. No time to lose.

They were in the entrance hall, the door slammed shut against the elements.

Marie-Claude turned to him, a fever in her blood. 'Last night. I should never—'

He closed her mouth with his. 'You should.'

'I thought you might despise me,' she gasped when she could. 'And I was ashamed.'

'Never! Let me show you how much I hold you in esteem.'

Up the stairs to his bedchamber. When Marie-Claude tripped, Zan supported her, an arm around her waist. He locked the door to enclose them and shut out the world.

'Well, Marie. What now?'

'I don't know,' she whispered, catching her breath, but her eyes never left his.

Tension hummed between them, spinning out in lively waves. Then as they faced each other, it exploded into outrageous need, with so much energy that the air almost sparkled with it. Jolted by it, Zan simply pounced, gathering her into his arms, her whole body flattened against his in a need to touch every inch of her, to be aware of every curve and angle even through the layers of silk gown and petticoats. Covering her face, her throat with kisses, he could bring no thought into his mind but that she had braved the storm for him, come to him, that she was here, in his bedchamber, by God, and her mouth was soft under his. Desire rushed through him as fast and overwhelming as a summer flood.

Stripped of all thought, Marie-Claude allowed herself to be swept along with the elemental thrill. This was what she wanted, to be here, with this wild, untamed man who touched her heart and her soul. Marie-Claude did not even try to argue that she should not be here. In his bedchamber in the middle of the day with his hands hard on her back and his mouth hot on hers. It was glorious. She wound her arms round Zan's neck and curled her fingers into his hair, heart beating furiously as the slide of his teeth along her throat tossed her responses into a mad spin. A whirlpool, the water soft and fluid but utterly relentless, whirling her faster and faster into its vortex. The only thought to surface—that he did not despise her. When he groaned, his tongue sliding along the swell of her breast above the lace edging of her gown, she knew the bond between them was unconditional, without limit.

Zan was out of control, dominated by one driving force. To take, to possess, to own. To ravish and devour. Raising her head, he dragged in a breath. He must be careful of her—but the need to hold, to arouse, had the sharpness of a knife-edge. Every movement she made in his arms, every brush of her body, every slide of breast and thigh, saturated him with need. The taste of her, her perfume, the texture of her skin, all melded together to create a feast for his senses. And he was ravenous. As if he had not eaten for days. For years.

'Marie…'

Driven by the hunger, his mouth swallowed her gasp of pleasure as he tumbled her to the bed, pushing aside, snatching at clothing as she fed his arousal.

Marie-Claude found herself pinned under him on the bed. 'Wait!' she gasped.

'Too late for that!'

Her breath sobbed. The tendons in his neck were taut as ropes beneath her lips. She felt a need to brace herself, as if she had been cast adrift in a relentless sea and must weather the force of a storm. His hands, such clever skilful hands, skimmed and roamed, a ferocious onslaught of discovery, searching out new responses. Seducing her. One moment softly reassuring, the next swooping, plundering, so that her skin heated and quivered.

She could not get her breath. Her body strained against his.

Zan was stunned. The ultimate combination of

sleek muscles overlaid by the most satin-soft of skin. He couldn't get enough, but wanted to absorb her, every perfumed inch. It was not enough to re-learn with his fingertips the lovely body he had seen in moonlight. He needed to consume and savour. To trace with his lips the sweet under-swell of her breasts, her hard-tipped nipples. The sinuous dip to her waist, the fluid sweep to her hips. The dark secrets of her thighs. Until the taste and texture of her was in his blood.

Marie-Claude shivered when Zan captured her wrists to stretch them above her head. A lovely long sinuous offering for him. He could not wait. Here was everything he wanted, a banquet of taste and sensation. He was entranced by every shiver. Lost when she arched her hips in mute invitation. When she writhed, he plunged. Buried himself within her with one long thrust of dark and desperate pleasure.

'Yes…' she breathed against his throat, enclosing him. 'Take me.'

He thought, in some distant moment of recognition, that he could not have responded if she had said no, if she had denied him. Too late. Too much sensation crowding in. But she wanted him as much as he needed her. His name trembled on her lips, and in passing gratitude he thanked God for it.

'Zan!' she cried out.

It lit a fire in his flesh and blood. In his very bones. Breath ragged, muscles straining as he pushed himself over her, relieving her of his weight, he lowered his head to brush her lips in the most tender of caresses.

'Hold on.' Raw with emotion he might be, but he would love her well and with kindness.

'I can't. Take me now, Zan.'

It stoked the flames into an inferno that cauterised every doubt that he might have had. All softness was obliterated. Zan thrust hard, sure, piercing her, a relentless demand that gave neither of them respite as passion built and built until nerve endings could withstand it no longer. He felt her shiver, felt it begin deep within her, her muscles clenching around him.

He held on, keeping up the assault, breathing hot and uneven, body rising and plunging, rising again, until her whole body convulsed. Only then, with a hoarse cry, did he allow his own ending.

Chest heaving, sweat slick on his body, Zan looked down at her flushed face, smoothing the hair back from her forehead. She had taken him by surprise. In spite of all his skill, his experience, his knowledge of women, he had not expected this. And when she touched her tongue to her well-kissed lips, he felt a renewed arousal stir his muscles.

'You could be the death of me, my lovely Marie-Claude,' he remarked as calmly as he could.

'I think I have just come alive again,' she replied, the blue of her eyes still blurred with astonishment.

'Then let us be alive together.' He kissed her gently, so tenderly. 'I think I used you with less than finesse, lady.' He stretched to take her wrist in his palm, and frowned at the faint marks he had left there. 'I have less control than I'd like when you touch me. I don't like it.' He touched his mouth to the shadow of the bruises.

But Marie-Claude brought his hand to her own lips. 'You did not hurt me. I think I have never known such pleasure. Don't frown at me.'

'I'll never frown at you.' The disquiet smoothed away from his features. 'And since you appreciated my poor attempts despite my lack of skill—then let us repeat the exercise. Perhaps a little more slowly.'

'Again?'

He touched his tongue to her nipple. 'Again…'

And Marie-Claude shivered at the promise.

Another day of shared pleasure. Marie-Claude could not grasp the joy of it, the burning anticipation of the next minute, the next hour, even the next second that they could snatch to be together. Climbing the cliff path from the beach to the Pride,

Zan helping her to scramble over a rock fall, his hands splayed firmly around her waist, his lips stealing a kiss, the evening sunlight blinded her to reality. Mouth firm, tasting of salt from the sea wind, he was everything to her. Nothing could ever change that. She looked back over her shoulder to where he followed her in shirt sleeves, carrying his coat slung over his shoulder with careless grace. Her heart leapt in her chest. He caught her gaze and responded with a smile that melted all her reservations that they were being anything but discreet. What did it matter? Who would care how she spent her time? She could do nothing but return the smile. Her lover! How shocking! Long past any shyness with him, she stretched her hand back to touch his, gratified when he laced his fingers through hers. If there had been any hesitation, it had been momentary. He wanted to be with her as much as she wanted to be with him. She knew it.

Had he not given her proof, that very morning? If a man gave a lady something so foolish as a parasol—and went to such much trouble to get it— then he must be in love.

'To replace the one you lost,' he had said, handing over the slender, carefully wrapped package.

She had unwrapped it. 'Oh! It's French…'

'It is. I can vouch for it.'

'Come with the contraband?' she'd gently teased.

He had simply smiled. It was beautiful, elegantly sophisticated. Cream silk, stretching over the frame to a delicate scalloped edging, a carved ivory handle with a cream silk-tasselled decoration. Entirely inappropriate for a stroll on the beach, but she had unfurled it anyway, angling it with neat precision.

A man had to be in love to give so particular a present.

'It's lovely.'

And he had kissed her. 'Not nearly as lovely as you.'

She carried it now.

'Come.' Zan pulled her on when she would have lingered. 'It's growing late and you should be home.' He led her on until they reached the cliff top and the spread of the gardens of the Pride beyond, and there he allowed her hand to fall.

'This is where I must leave you.' A shadow wove its way between them, the first of the day. Nor was it dispelled when Zan touched her cheek, then let his fingers smooth the wind-whipped curls at her temple. His smile owned not a little regret.

On an impulse Marie-Claude caught his wrist. 'I wish you would not.'

'It's better so.'

'Stay with me.' Oh, she wanted him to stay. 'For a little while.'

'You know I would not be made welcome here.' The sardonic lines appeared, deepened. 'I have enough integrity not to take advantage of Venmore's absence. I'll not be with you within the walls of the Pride.'

Marie-Claude tilted her head. 'I know you won't explain, so I won't ask again. But I can't believe the rift's so serious that you won't set foot beyond the door.'

'Believe me, it is.'

'Then I must accept it. But there's no one here, Zan.' Soft, velvety, persuasive, her voice, her words eroded his will-power. 'No one will be here to disapprove if that's your concern. Meggie's not here. You need not stay long. A glass of brandy, if nothing else. Please come, Zan. Stay with me.'

She placed a hand on his arm. Her eyes were shining with love, beguiling with unspoken hope. Answering her clasp on his arm, he gave the reply he knew she wanted.

'How can I resist such a charming invitation, Madame Mermaid!'

His mouth was warm on hers, the flames of desire leapt into a conflagration, and shook him to the core as his mouth took and ravished. The flames leapt from him to her, scorching.

He lifted his head, looking down at her with an expression that sent a ripple of concern through her.

It was quite speculative, perhaps not very pleasant. The lines beside his mouth were deeply etched.

'What are you thinking?' Marie-Claude asked, suddenly anxious. For a moment she had sensed a darkness, a sadness in him despite the fire, the heat of his embrace.

But then he smiled and the darkness was gone. 'I'm thinking that I have no desire to leave you. Very well. I'll see you to the door. And drink a glass of brandy.' His smile acquired a touch of malice. 'I'll do it if only to challenge the absent Hallastons.'

Chapter Six

Leaving Zan to collect his mare from the stables, Marie-Claude ran up the steps and flung open the door into the entrance hall, which was empty. Untying the ribbons of her bonnet, she considered her victory. Zan had at last agreed to set foot inside the Pride. It would be quicker for her to fetch the brandy herself rather than run Wiggins to ground in the kitchens. She would take it into the library where—

She stopped in her tracks as she heard the footsteps above her on the first floor. She looked up to where a figure appeared at the top of the staircase and leaned over the banister to smile down at her. The curl of rich brown hair, the shine of silver-grey eyes.

'Harriette!' Pure pleasure was her first reaction. 'How lovely to see you. I didn't expect… Did you send a letter I've not received?' And then the brush of uncertainty. Of doubt. Of fear. 'I thought you were settled at The Venmore. Is something wrong?' Her heart tripped. 'Is it Raoul?' But surely not. Harriette was smiling.

Harriette ran down the stairs. 'No, no. Raoul is too full of the new pony to have time and thought for anything but what it eats, when it sleeps and when he can ride it again. You know how it is!' She clasped Marie-Claude's hands to search her face. Nodded as if satisfied. 'Marie! How well you look!' They stepped into each other's arms. Five years of affection and sisterly closeness. 'Sea air suits you. You're glowing again.'

'Yes. It does. The weather's been a blessing. I have spent so much time outdoors.' She saw the shadow in Harriette's eyes behind the smile. The fine lines of tension. Felt the grip of Harriette's fingers around her own. 'Is Luke with you?'

'Yes.' Harriette turned her head to glance up the stairs, waiting.

There was something here between them... And suddenly Marie-Claude knew why they had come. It was as if she could scent the suspicion, carried in on the wind. She *knew* why Harriette had come. But she would still make Harriette say it.

'Why have you come?' she demanded more sharply than she had intended.

'We just thought—I thought—it would be good to spend a few days here with you. I thought you might be too much alone.' A tumbled rush of words. But it was not in Harriette's nature to dissemble. 'That's not it! I received a letter,' she remarked bluntly.

'A letter.' Marie-Claude felt a cold hand close around her heart. 'And the purpose of this letter?'

'Well, it seems that…'

And Marie-Claude felt anger pulse in her veins. She knew very well, did she not? Some local busybody who would see fit to inform the Earl and Countess of Venmore that their sister-in-law, obviously French and flighty, was spending her time with a self-confessed smuggler. Far too much time and unchaperoned, even if she were a widow! He might be a gentleman by birth, but she wagered there would be any number of local matrons who would view his dissolute lifestyle as scandalous and her acquaintance with him questionable.

Well, she would not have it. She would not be questioned and criticised as if she were a child. She would spend her time with Zan if she chose.

'And who might have sent you this communication?' she asked, deceptively sweetly, before Harriette could find a reply to her previous demand.

'It was unsigned.'

'But it brought you here hot-foot?'

'Yes—Marie, it said that—' Harriette turned her head, relief obvious. 'Ah! Luke…'

Luke Hallaston, Earl of Venmore, descended the stairs more circumspectly than his wife, smoothly elegant as always, and leaned to kiss Marie-Claude's cheek. Marie-Claude saw the deep affection for her, the look of concern in his eye. And a glint of some deeper emotion in the sharp green. There was a strong will behind the Earl of Venmore's handsome face that it was never wise to discount. It had been strong enough to fight for Harriette's love in the early days of a marriage beset by scandal and danger, strong enough to risk his life to bring Marie-Claude to safety in England, even when her veracity as his brother's widow was in doubt. On this occasion her deep love and gratitude to him was marred by irritation.

'Harriette was about to tell me why you felt the need to come all this way on a whim and ask after my good health,' she observed tartly.

'It's not that, Marie. We were just concerned—'

'Concerned for me? I can think of no reason why you should be. As you see, I am in perfect health. Perhaps you will explain.'

'Yes. We need to talk.' His hand was gentle on her arm, soothing her obvious annoyance. 'We'll go into the library—'

A voice interrupted from the doorway. Low and smooth and full of humour. Dangerously unaware. 'Marie-Claude, I've just—'

There was Zan, coming to an abrupt halt.

'Ah!' A soft exhalation. 'I see you have unexpected visitors. Now, this should prove to be entertaining.'

He stood, back lit by the evening sun, face cast in shadow, but the tautness in Zan's stance could be felt. The edge to his voice could be tasted, sharp as young ale. No one moved as if all were turned to stone by the Gorgon's stare. Marie-Claude felt the weight of it press down on her shoulders, on her heart with a terrible forewarning.

She knew that she must intervene before... before what?

'Zan...' Shaking off Luke's hand, she stepped towards him, which did nothing to break the tension. The only sound was Harriette's low murmur of rejection.

The atmosphere tightened unbearably. Marie-Claude found herself isolated, Zan rigidly motionless in the doorway, her family, Luke and Harriette, at the foot of the stairs. All her earlier certainties drained away. What was here in this room that she did not understand?

'Zan!' Harriette whispered with what could only be an expression of anguish on her face.

Whilst Luke walked slowly to Marie-Claude's side, placing a proprietorial hand on her arm, but his eyes were on Zan.

'Ellerdine.' How dismissive he was. Luke's voice was more hostile than Marie-Claude could have believed possible in a man who had given her all the physical comfort of her present life, all the emotional ties of family that she had lost with Marcus's death. His hand on her arm was heavily controlled.

'Venmore.' If Luke was hostile, Zan's reply was viciously cold. 'I didn't expect to see you here.'

'No. I'm quite sure you didn't. I expect you thought you had a free hand to wreak all the havoc you could. Where you failed once to destroy what was most valuable in my life, you would succeed the second time.' Luke laughed harshly. 'And break my innocent sister's heart into the bargain if I read the circumstances right.'

'Luke!' Marie-Claude could only gasp at the crude accusation. It felt as if she were held fast by invisible hands and unable to escape, some winged creature set in amber. How was it possible to grasp the waves of intense emotion that swam in the room, beating at the walls? Here was more than a casual dispute between neighbours. Here was more than a distant acquaintance that had gone sour. Here was pain and grief and betrayal. She looked to Harriette for enlightenment, but Harriette was staring at Zan, eyes wide in horror, face pale as the lace at her throat.

Marie-Claude turned to Zan, lifting her hands in bewilderment. 'What is this?'

But it was Luke who replied, 'I wager he's not told you the truth, has he?'

'About what? I know Zan's a smuggler, if that's what you mean. Is that so heinous a crime?' She glanced at Harriette, expecting support from that quarter at least. Captain Harry would hardly damn a fellow smuggler out of hand.

But silently Harriette shook her head.

'There are worse crimes,' Luke admitted. 'Did he tell you the rest?'

No. No, he hadn't. He had refused to give any account of the reason for the enmity between the families. As had Meggie. In her innocence, Marie-Claude had denied it, arguing that it could not be so very bad. From the antagonism in Luke's face, Marie-Claude began at last to fear that it could.

'He said you would not approve of our…of our friendship,' she said.

'Not approve?' Luke showed his teeth. 'By God, I would damn him to hell for daring to lay his hands on you!'

Marie-Claude drew her arm from Luke's hold and

walked across the space to stand before the man who was being accused of unmentionable crimes.

'Zan? Will you explain to me?'

'My dear Madame Mermaid! So trusting!' She thought it was a sneer and her heart quailed. 'Let my cousin and her virtuous husband explain.' Zan's eyes were dark, were almost black, flat and bleak, his expression set and unyielding. There was nothing of the passion that had existed between them.

And then his words made some connection in her brain.

'Your *cousin*?'

'Oh, Zan,' Harriette murmured. 'So you did not even tell Marie that!'

Marie-Claude brought her eyes back to Zan's, willing him to say something, anything, to put it all to rights. For a long moment he returned her gaze and she saw emotion storm in the depths. The lines that bracketed his mouth became deeply indented.

'Marie-Claude…'

Then his mouth tightened against whatever he might have said, and turned away from her towards Harriette.

'No, cousin, I did not tell her.' He inclined his head in a little bow. 'I'll not court difficulties before they arrive at my door. You look in excellent health. Marriage obviously suits you.' It was definitely a sneer. He cut his eyes to Luke. 'Tell her then,

Venmore. Tell Captain Marcus's pretty widow the disgraceful whole and put the blame where it lies. I'm sure you'll do justice to the telling.'

'Yes, tell me, Luke,' Marie-Claude managed to say. She'd had enough of secrecy.

So Luke did. Sparse, undetailed, but enough to fill her with dismay.

'It doesn't make for comfortable listening, Marie, but you deserve the truth and you'll not get it from *his* mouth. You never met Ellerdine, did you? He organised the smuggling runs with Harriette in the old days. But you'll recall the night of your arrival when we rescued you and Raoul from France. The run that went wrong—when Harriette was wounded and the Preventives almost caught us all on the beach because they'd been alerted to the run. I don't think you ever knew who was to blame for that. Adam had taken you to London before it was all finished. There was no need for you to know.'

'Yes. I remember.' Luke's brother Adam had wrapped her and the baby up and transported them from the Pride. She had never known the outcome.

'Who was it?' she demanded. 'Who informed on us?'

Luke lifted a cynical brow at Zan as if expecting him to reply. When he did not, Luke wielded the dagger.

'Ellerdine, of course.'

How impossible it suddenly was to read Zan's expression. Marie-Claude studied the hooded eyes, the unsmiling mouth. His face was engraved in stone.

'Zan? Is it true?'

'As Venmore says. Guilty as charged.'

'You informed on us to the Preventives? But why? Why something so despicable, to put us all in danger?'

'Oh, that's simple enough,' Zan replied calmly, as if it were merely a matter of conversation. 'I tipped off Rodmell, the Preventive Officer, that there was a run. All part of an intricate little plan to preserve my well-planned organisation for smuggling.'

'I don't see—'

And Harriette, low-voiced, explained, 'It was to keep *me* here in Old Wincomlee and to keep Lydyard's Pride, my home, as a centre of operations for signalling and storing contraband. I gave up smuggling when I married Luke and forbade the use of the Pride with the Smugglers' Lamp in the Tower. It threatened Zan's ambitions. So my cousin tried to put a rift between myself and Luke and destroy my marriage so that I'd stay here and stay in the venture.'

Memory swept in from that night five years before.

'I remember. You were wounded that night. You were hit by a bullet.'

'Yes. The bullet was intended for Luke, not me, but still—'

'*Murder?*' She swung back to Zan. 'You would have shot Luke? Surely that was not…'

She stopped, lifting a hand to her mouth. If Marie-Claude had thought the truth would bring her distress, she had not known the half of it, whilst Zan simply stood there, listening, accepting. Horribly, cynically silent.

'Is there nothing you can say to this?' she finally asked.

She saw him take a deep breath, but there was not one flicker of emotion in his face. It was as if he did not care.

'Why should I?' Zan drawled. 'It's true enough. I put the run in jeopardy. I fired the shot that wounded Harriette. What use is there in making excuses?' He lifted his shoulders as if to shrug off the guilt. 'Now you've heard the worst. Now you can despise and condemn me as much as the rest of my family do.'

'Not quite the worst,' Luke interjected. 'I don't suppose during your *flirtations* you told her of your involvement with the *Lion d'Or*.'

'No, I didn't.' Zan's smile was viciously sardonic. 'So why not tell her of that too, Venmore, so that you have damned me entirely?'

'I'll do it. It affects me most.' Harriette stepped to stand beside Marie-Claude with an arm around her waist, but her eyes were on Zan. So, Marie-Claude thought. This was to be even worse, whatever it was. 'It was a ship out of Dieppe full of silk, wrecked here on the coast. Brought aground by the Smugglers' Lamp lit in this tower to signal a safe haven in a storm when there was no safe haven, only death and destruction. And you, Zan, blamed it on me. So that Luke would hate me and cast me off.'

'Yes, I did. Not one of my most honourable moves, I admit.' He lifted his head as if, Marie-Claude thought, to brace himself. 'Go on then, Harriette. Don't stop there. Tell her the rest—or are you going to let her work it out for herself? Perhaps I'll do the honours. I was to blame for the wrecking. Who else could have ordered the lighting of the lamp, here at the Pride, but me?'

'No!' Marie-Claude whispered.

'Why not? Because if it was not Harriette, who else is there to blame? It's what the whole neighbourhood thinks, whether it's true or not. So not only am I a smuggler, but I'm a wrecker too.'

'Exactly!' Luke stated.

'But is it *true*?' demanded Marie-Claude.

'It doesn't matter any more, foolish girl.' For a moment Zan's voice softened, then light flashed in his eyes with a return to the old defiance. 'You see before you the rogue you've spent the past weeks associating with.' Zan's sudden grin was wild and white. 'Not an edifying thought, is it? I'm sure you understand, Madame Mermaid, why I did not broadcast my sins on our first meeting.'

'Enough!' Luke cast one glance at Marie-Claude's white face.

'Oh, I quite agree.' Zan bowed curtly in a curiously graceful gesture. 'I told you you did not want to know me. And I was right, wasn't I? You should have believed me from the start.'

All Marie-Claude could do was look at him in horrified disbelief. 'I know what you told me but— I had no idea. Could I have guessed this depth of depravity?' And then grief began to replace the horror. 'Why did you do it, Zan? Why did you seek me out, spend time with me…?'

Luke stepped forwards, between her and Zan, as if to protect her, face alight with anger. It was as if her words had lit a fuse to one of his Majesty's cannons.

'So it was revenge, was it, Ellerdine? You couldn't harm me directly, so you set your sights on those I love. That's despicable beyond words. And to use an innocent woman to further your own illicit ends. I told you five years ago that you were not welcome here in this house!' Luke's verbal attack was savage. 'How dare you come here again? How dare you foist yourself on my sister?'

Zan cocked his head, challenging, stirring the flames. 'Do you think I forced her? I'll not take that layer of guilt, Venmore. I'd say she was willing enough—with a little encouragement.'

'So you seduced her to get your revenge on me!'

'No!' Marie-Claude cried out.

'Believe what you will!' Zan smirked insolently.

And Luke sprang, one fist making contact with Zan's jaw, taking him by surprise so he fell to the floor. For a moment he lay there. Then as Marie-Claude covered her mouth with trembling fingers, he propped himself on his elbow, tossing his hair out of his eyes.

'This is getting to be a habit, Venmore.'

'And you deserved it on both occasions—when you put Harriette in danger and now when you have deceived Marie-Claude. Get up!' Luke snarled. 'Get out of my house!'

Zan pushed to his feet, brushing the dust from his shirt and breeches. Reclaiming his coat, he wiped the blood from his mouth with his sleeve. For a moment his eyes were on Marie-Claude, hot and wilful. Wild. Reckless, as if he would speak and act as impulse dictated. Then the emotion drained to leave his face as white as hers and icy cold. It was as if a flame had been quenched.

With ridiculous dignity, inestimable grace, he

bowed, a full court flourish, to the company. 'Cousin. Venmore. Your servant, as ever.' Then turned at last to Marie-Claude. 'Madame Mermaid. Our acquaintance was very sweet. I regret its ending. Perhaps you should thank the noble Earl for saving you from my clutches. Obviously a fate worse than death.'

'Zan!' She stretched out her hands, torn hopelessly between disgust for this man who had bewitched her for the worst reasons, and an irreparable sense of loss.

Zan ignored her. He spun on his heel and walkcd out.

Before she disgraced herself by dissolving into tears, Marie-Claude evaded Harriette's compassion-ate arms and ran to the refuge of her room.

With Marie-Claude fled and Alexander Ellerdine shown the door, Harriette and Luke were left to face each other in the deserted entrance hall with the rags of emotion clinging to the walls.

'Oh, Luke!' Harriette flattened her palms against her heart. 'What a terrible mess this is.'

'I know.' When he took her wrist in a light clasp, she looked up to see the anger beginning to die in his eyes. 'Come with me, love. We've aired our dirty linen in the entrance hall for all to hear. Let's try for some privacy now.'

He drew her into the library, hunted up a half-decanter of brandy, poured and gave a glass to his wife. 'Drink this…' He threw back his own measure without enjoyment. 'It won't help, but it might steady your nerves.'

She did not drink. 'What have we done?'

'It was not of our doing, Harry.' He moved to sit beside her. 'None of it.'

'No. But she didn't *know*. We dealt with it and pushed it aside—for five whole years—as if it had never happened. We never talked about it—I don't think we ever mentioned Zan's name—so she did not know. That's at our door. A sin of omission, if you wish. She didn't even know he was my cousin!'

Luke nudged her hand until she took a sip. 'I agree. But it was Ellerdine who saw the chance and spun his web to entrap her. It didn't take him long, did it? I think she'd barely arrived here when he cast the lure.'

'Do you think he was truly so—so cold-blooded?' Harriette's eyes were wide with distress, grief shimmering beneath the pale silver. 'That he hunted her, to use her in that way?'

Luke eased his shoulders in an uncomfortable movement. 'You still believe the best of him.' A wry twist to his lips.

'No… I don't know. Zan was always wild, with nothing to anchor him to good behaviour, no love or affection at home. So he took to smuggling to prove a point, I think. But he was never vicious.'

'I don't recall any affection in *your* upbringing, Captain Harry. It pleased me to rescue you from your brother's less-than-tender care!' A kiss. A soft touch. 'It's no excuse for your cousin's bad habits.'

'He was kind to me when I was growing up and not very happy.'

'He put a bullet in you!' Luke protested.

'Unintentionally.'

'Yes. It was his intention to put it in me! As I recall, he had murder in mind. I can't forgive him, Harry. You can't expect it of me.'

Harriette sighed. 'I know. I don't mean to defend him. It's just that…' She lifted her hands in despair.

'I'm sorry. How can I think well of him? He would have destroyed our marriage simply to keep control of the Pride. His plans were foiled, but only at the eleventh hour. I nearly let you go. I nearly let him persuade me that you were a blood-soaked killer. When I think of that I could plant my fist on his jaw all over again!'

In understanding, Harriette touched his cheek with her fingertips. 'I can't defend him, can I? If we had parted, I would have lived with pain and grief for the rest of my life.'

'Thank God we stopped him. But because we did—why would your cousin not want his revenge on us?'

'By seducing Marie-Claude?'

'Of course. A perfect weapon. He can't hurt us in any other way.'

'No.' She leaned into his arms, letting them soothe her as they closed round her, full of love.

'Look up,' Luke murmured at last. 'I despise him for what he did to you. I'll not let him hurt you again. Nor Marie-Claude.'

'No, I suppose not. So much evidence of his guilt. He admitted to it all. Even the wrecking.' Harriette wiped the dampness from her eyes as she recalled the outcome of the scene in the hall. 'Oh, Luke! I hope he has not broken her heart.'

'Marie-Claude has more sense than that.'

Which just showed how little men sometimes understood, Harriette thought. 'She's lonely, Luke. It's six years since Marcus was killed. She'll never love him any less, and Raoul is the centre of her life. But I know she's lonely, although she'll never admit to it. I know what love is. You gave me that. Would we want to deny Marie the chance? I would not have Marie live without it for the rest of her life.'

'No. Nor I. But not with the likes of Ellerdine.'

'No. But she's not happy.'

'She'd be even less happy with Ellerdine!' he exclaimed.

Harriette kept her own counsel. What had she seen between Zan and Marie-Claude? The vibrations between the pair of them, even in the welter of anger and betrayal—well, they had been nothing less than astounding.

It was nothing that she could mention to Luke.

In the terrible aftermath of the storm, Marie-Claude sat in the middle of her bed, her arms around her knees. Her face was dry of tears, her heart set in stone. She *would* not weep, but it was difficult to breathe, she noticed inconsequentially. Difficult to think. Difficult to *be*. It was as if her mind had been belaboured by a heavy club until it could absorb no more. So many accusations. So much knowledge. So much evidence!

And Zan standing there, accepting it. Making no attempt to defend himself. Admitting to every accusation thrown at him.

It was impossible to take it all in and put it into some form of order, but she had enough recall of Zan's sins to freeze her blood. Why had she had no sense of all this? Smuggling, yes, but not all the rest. Attempted murder, no less. Deliberate sabotage of a run that might have brought both Harriette and Luke before the Justice of the Peace. And then there was the wrecking. Bloody deeds that could never be excused. There was so much he had not told her. If he loved her, if he were innocent, would he not have told her?

They won't want you to know me.

Well, he had been right about that!

But he had not given her the choice to make up her own mind. Could she ever forgive him that? But in truth it wasn't *that* that tore at her heart. What if Luke's accusations were true? That Zan had never loved her, but seen her only as an instrument for revenge? And she had willingly thrown herself into his company, into his deceitful embrace, believing that his emotions were as engaged as her own. She had seized this unexpected chance at life, at love. She had *trusted* him. And what had he done? Only cracked her heart in two.

All lies. All a cruel charade. Misery washed through her and, head bent, she hid her face against her knees. Well, she had learned a valuable lesson, and should be thankful for it, she supposed. She did not think she would ever trust a man again.

A knock on the door roused her.

'Come in.' She lifted her chin. She would not be an object of pity. 'Harriette…'

Of course, Harriette would come to find her.

'Marie… What do I say to you?' She sank on the bed beside her.

'You never warned me.' That was all she could think. 'I did not even know Alexander Ellerdine was your cousin.'

Harriette sighed her guilt, taking Marie-Claude's hands. 'I'm so sorry. I didn't think I had to—that it was at all necessary. It wasn't a connection I was very proud of after all that had happened.' She grimaced a little. 'And I suppose I never thought this would happen. But, yes, Zan's my cousin. His mother, my aunt Dorcas, was a Lydyard. James Ellerdine, Zan's father, was pleasant enough, but too weak-willed to control his wayward son. So Zan got into smuggling—above his head.'

'I don't recall you ever talking about him, not even mentioning his name. I would have remembered…'

'No. You can understand why.'

'I suppose so.' She rested her chin again on her knees. 'Is it all true? All the accusations? I suppose it has to be.' A question. A last grasping at hope.

'Yes. He never denied it,' Harriette said gently.

They sat together for a little time, hands clasped.

'I'm sorry he took advantage of you.' Harriette finally broke in to her thoughts.

'So am I. Do you truly think he was using me out of spite against Luke? Or even to get a foothold in the Pride again? He wanted it five years ago—perhaps he still does.'

'It's possible. Luke thinks so.'

'So all his words were false.' Tears burned, but she would not let them fall.

'There's no blame on you.'

'But I was taken in. I pursued him. Even when at first he refused to see me again. I don't think I was so innocent in this.' Her eyes flashed. 'I feel so stupid. He made me believe what was not true. How could I have been so weak?'

'He is very charming. And cunning. I know to my own cost.'

'So he lured me on to make the first move? He appeared reluctant so that I would beg that we should meet again?' She all but cringed at the thought.

'Marie—don't dwell on it.'

'How foolish and gullible I must have seemed to him. How needy.' Bleak acceptance caused unshed tears to gather. 'He kissed me, you know, and held me in his arms, on our very first meeting. He rescued me from the sea—that was genuine enough. After that I was bewitched.'

'Oh, Marie!' A pause. 'Did he…did he take further advantage of you?'

'If you mean did he seduce me… No.' Which was true. By then she had given herself of her own free will. Oh, how naïve and over-trusting she had been. But she could not talk about it, not even with

Harriette. What passed between them on the moonlit cliffs was too precious. Too painful now. How could she possibly talk about that?

'You haven't fallen in love with him, have you?' Harriette asked anxiously.

'No. Certainly not! What a pathetic creature that would make me.'

But she had. Oh, she had. Shame swamped her that she should have been so wilfully taken in.

Her heart wept within her when Harriette had finally, reluctantly, left her.

'I can't believe it of him,' Marie-Claude murmured to herself. 'I simply can't.'

You have to believe it. Do you trust Harriette and Luke to tell you the truth?

Yes, she did.

So if the answer was yes, then she had to believe it.

Did Zan deny any of it?

No, he had not.

Devastating.

And the worst of it all? That his wooing of her had meant nothing. That he had embarked on it, a cold calculating ploy, simply to avenge his treatment at Venmore's hands. Or even to get access to the Tower and the Smugglers' Lamp to send the signal for the incoming contraband. Once he knew who she was, he had made a plan to use his knowledge. How despicable was that, to use her in that way, wooing her, seducing her, overwhelming her, only to use her as a weapon or to gain material advantage, whilst she had rejoiced, believing that she had met the one man who could turn her limbs to water and her blood to fire. And whilst her heart had been full of love, he had been cultivating her with hatred and cold planning in his mind. It had all been part of a scheme to further his own ends. She had become part of the scheme.

What's more, she knew the exact moment when he had seen the possibilities. When she had first gone to Ellerdine Manor. To start with, he had been determined to send her away. And then he had changed his mind, invited her into his home. Had made an assignation to meet her on the cliffs. That was it. And she had been so stupidly intoxicated that she had leapt willingly into his arms, had opened herself to his cruel manipulations. From that moment he had set himself to seduce her with such skill she had not stood a chance.

'Oh, Zan!' she whispered. 'Did you feel nothing for me but lust and revenge? What a lowering thought. You have humiliated me. Your punishment has been as bad as you could ever have envisaged.'

Marie-Claude rubbed her hands over her face. She must accept what she knew. He had felt nothing for her. It had all been false. After all, he had never said that he loved her.

Even the gift of the parasol had been a means to entrap her.

Her heart was broken.

But still, Marie-Claude decided as she lay sleepless on her bed, until she learned it from his own lips that he had never loved her, never felt even the most mild affection for her, she could not fully accept that her world, so new and bright, lay in ruins round her feet.

Chapter Seven

For a whole week Marie-Claude endured the company of Harriette and Luke. Endured their surveillance, their constant presence. They were very kind. They were endlessly compassionate. They surrounded her with love and sympathy, as if she might sink into some life-threatening melancholy if left alone for more than five minutes! Existing in a bleak grey world, immured from the ever-changing beauty of sunlight glinting on the waters of the bay, Marie-Claude was conscious that Harriette watched her like a mother hawk anxious for the health of its solitary chick. In the end she could not bear to be watched with such solicitude any longer so she pinned on a bright smile and set herself to get on with her life. It was difficult—no, it was well-nigh impossible to pretend that her heart was not in pieces—but she would do her best. Since time—

was it only a week since the man who had become the centre of the world had so cruelly betrayed her?—was not healing her pain, she must learn to live with it.

She had her family, her son, all the luxuries that money could buy. She was young and strong. Her heart would heal as well as any other wound, with hardly a scar to show for her pain.

But then Harriette suggested she return with them to The Venmore.

'I think you should come with us,' she persuaded. 'So does Luke.'

'Yes, I will—but not yet.' Marie-Claude was adamant.

'You'll enjoy the company. So will I.' Harriette was not of a mind to give up easily. 'Raoul misses you…'

A low blow that her sister-in-law had used without compunction! Marie-Claude had to swallow hard against that, with the suspicion that Raoul was perfectly content with the dogs and horses and freedom of his present life at The Venmore. She steeled her heart and made her decision. She had, after all, unfinished business in Old Wincomlee.

'I wish to stay here for a few more weeks. Don't you trust me to remain at the Pride and steer clear of your cousin?' Marie-Claude asked, uncomfortably forthright.

'Of course I do.' But Marie-Claude saw the quick blush in Harriette's cheeks.

'I'm not likely to go anywhere near him, am I?' she stated firmly. 'Not after the humiliation he inflicted on me. Besides, I'm not the best of company at the moment. I think the sea air would prove rejuvenating.'

'I suppose…' Harriette murmured, doubtful but weakening. They could hardly drag her off against her will, could they? 'Are you sure you won't come?'

'I will. I promise. After a week or two.' Marie-Claude managed a smile and squeezed Harriette's hands. 'I need my own company for a little while and Raoul's safe with you, I know. Go back to The Venmore, Harriette. I know you're missing your own children.'

'Yes, I am. If you're sure…'

So it was settled. But not before Luke, to Marie-Claude's mind in an entirely unscrupulous manner, introduced his own man to the Pride, Mr Samuel Temple, young and energetic, ostensibly to act as steward under Wiggins's overall authority. Marie-Claude was not fooled for one moment.

'He's an able man. He'll see to your comfort, far more efficiently than Wiggins,' Luke said.

'I'm sure you're right.' She kissed Luke's cheek.

But Mr Temple, urbane and obliging though he might be, was a Hallaston spy.

'You'll send for us if you need us, won't you, Marie?' Harriette asked finally as their coach was made ready.

'Yes—' a touch waspishly '—I most certainly will, especially if the Pride is invaded by a horde of Wincomlee smugglers led by your obnoxious cousin! And if *I* don't send for you, I'm sure Mr Temple will.'

'I was thinking more along the lines of the Fly-By-Nights led by that monster D'Acre and his cold-blooded lieutenant Rackham!' Harriette replied sharply—but had the grace to blush.

Then they were gone and Marie-Claude was free to take steps to close the door on this most painful part of her life. Was Zan guilty? He had stood there and accepted every accusation hurled at him by Luke. Well, perhaps he was. But there was the answer to one question she needed to hear, from Zan himself, if she was to put it all behind her.

I can't shut him out, as if I had never known him! He's with me every waking and sleeping moment! I can't escape. Her heart wept.

You must. You've no choice. He lied to you. Or at least he did not tell you the truth—which comes down to the same thing. Her head had no compunction in outlining its condemnation.

Marie-Claude could find no argument against such a harsh judgement.

Hardly had the Hallaston coach vanished round the bend in the drive then Marie-Claude avoided both Meggie, now reinstated at the Pride, and the supremely efficient Mr Temple, claiming a need to pay a purely social call on Sir Wallace and Lady Augusta Lydyard, Harriette's brother and sister-in-law. Dull but perfectly innocuous. Ordering up the cob and trap, conveniently tacked up by George Gadie, who added to his fishing and smuggling activities with occasional work in the Pride's stables, she sought some information.

'One thing, Mr Gadie. Something Harriette said—' She managed a nice touch of false insouciance. 'Tell me what you know of Captain D'Acre. And a man called Rackham?' Now there was a name—and a face—she recalled.

'Captain D'Acre's a bad man, mistress.' George spat in the dust. 'Leads the Fly-By-Nights—out of Rottingdean. You don't want nothing to do with the likes of him.'

Rottingdean. She remembered that too. 'Is he another smuggler?' Was *everyone* involved in the Trade?

'Amongst other things. He's vicious to get his own ends. Murder, torture, rape... Beggin' your pardon, mistress. He runs the gang—has done for a score of years now—with as tight a hold as ever he had. No one can touch him.'

'And Rackham?'

'D'Acre's second-in-command. They runs a tight ship together and don't care who gets hurt. Bad doings...' George shook his head. 'Smugglers beaten to death for passing information to the Excise—not that they had, you understand. Another with his hand chopped off because he dipped his fingers in a package of lace from one of D'Acre's runs.' George spat again. 'Pardon, mistress.'

'Can the Preventives not put a stop to his cruelties?' she enquired curiously.

George Gadie shrugged. 'Preventives've tried to find evidence, mistress. No one'll speak against him. Too afraid, y'know. D'Acre's a long arm and Rackham's the heavy fist at the end of it.'

Marie-Claude thought she did know. Knew too much as another hurt bloomed in her heart. If her suspicions were correct, Captain D'Acre and Rackham would provide the final, fatal wound in her love for Zan Ellerdine.

A week could last a lifetime, Zan discovered, in which to consider the list of his crimes as displayed by the Earl of Venmore.

A callous scheme to ruin Harriette's new marriage. A smuggling run condemned to failure with the threat of imprisonment or death for all concerned, because he had laid the information into the hands of the Preventives. A bullet intended for Venmore that had found Harriette instead. She had not been seriously injured, true, but that hardly drew the poison from the act. She might have died. As for the wrecking of the *Lion D'Or*—did not the evidence against him speak for itself? As he'd said in self-accusation, who else could be guilty of lighting the Smugglers' Lamp to lure that ill-fated ship on to the rocks?

He could make excuses, of course. There had been reasons. He had made the choice all those years ago, young and arrogant and ambitious for power as he had been, and in the same circumstances, he would make the same choice again. He was as guilty as hell and must live with it.

Zan showed his teeth in what was not a smile and got on with his life. He rode into Lewes on legal estate matters, he sailed the *Black Spectre* to test a new rigging. He rode the Ellerdine land, shutting his mind to the ravages caused by lack of investment of time or money. He organised a run for the following week. He was summoned and met with Captain D'Acre, pursuing his goal to its inglorious end.

And when the shadows of his past did not loom and encroach, in the evenings when he sat alone in his library with wine or ale to hand, there was Marie-Claude to despise and censure him, hating him to the depths of her soul.

He sensed her approach the moment she stepped on to his land, lifting his head as if her perfume, the soft but spicy tones of lavender, reached out to his senses. He heard the outer door pushed open, her footsteps on the paving in the hall. Of course she would come. He had never thought she would run away from her problems to The Venmore. She would remain in Old Wincomlee, out of pride if nothing else. He had known her so little time, but his instincts told him that she would not let it lie as they had parted.

He considered her, as he had left her in the entrance hall at the Pride, as dispassionately as he was able. Beautiful, and somehow fragile under the weight of truth that she had been forced to accept. Bewildered and confused as she had every right to be. She had looked at him with disbelief, and with such sadness, such hurt.

All his own doing.

Zan snarled, and lifted his tankard in a mocking toast to himself.

'Your affectionate father was right after all. You're a worthless unprincipled rake at heart.'

He shook his head as if to dislodge a series of unpalatable thoughts, not least of his long-dead sire, from his mind. Now was not the time for such regrets and recriminations. Now he had to face Marie-Claude whether he liked it or not.

There she stood in his library as she had once before. She had come with a purpose. As pretty as ever in her favourite deep blue spotted muslin, as composed and confident as if engaged on a formal social call. Her straw bonnet had a high frame and sweep of feathers that curled to draw his eye to her lovely face, her magnificent eyes. Today she carried her parasol. His gift to her. He thought she carried it today of all days as a challenge, a deliberate slap in the face. How inconsequential that he should notice it. And that her fingers were hard-clenched around its ivory handle. She was not as composed as he had thought.

Zan steeled himself to conduct this meeting on his own terms.

He did not move a muscle as the library door was thrust open.

Marie-Claude came to a halt in the open doorway.

'Come in, Madame Mermaid. I thought you'd be here before too long, once you managed to escape your watchdogs.' Disdainful, sneeringly ill mannered, Zan remained where he was in his habitual slouch, his booted feet on the desk, a tankard of ale in his hand. Insolent. Wilfully discourteous. 'Come to heap your own particular condemnations on my head, have you?'

It had taken all her courage to come here after all. It nearly failed her as Zan's boorish welcome hit home. But she would not be daunted. 'Yes, I have come. There's something I need you to tell me.' She kept her tone cool, direct. She breathed deeply against a sudden spasm in her belly.

'Go away,' Zan growled, not stirring one inch. 'We've nothing to say to each other.'

Marie-Claude simply looked at him. A long, level stare. 'Is that all you have to say?'

'What more is there? I think enough has been said. In God's name, what can possibly be achieved by raking over the ashes of my past sins again and again? It's not going to change the facts, is it?'

'So you lied to me.'

'No. I never lied. I just did not tell you the truth.'

So there it was. Impossible to believe—so brutal, so unfeeling—but stated so unequivocally.

'I loved you, Zan. I think I still do,' Marie-Claude stated with amazing calm, the product of many hours of thought. 'My sentiments are not so shallow that they can be destroyed simply by accusations when you have made no attempt to defend yourself. I have come to hear your defence.'

An unmannerly, mocking little tilt of his head was his only reply as he raised the tankard to his lips.

'Why will you not answer me?'

'Because you don't need to hear my *defence*, Marie-Claude. You say you love me, but you don't.' He put down the tankard, locked his fingers behind his head and tilted back his chair. Was it possible for him to be any more ungallant? 'Face facts, my dear. It was a harmless flirtation to while away the summer months. Now you believe the worst of me. And why shouldn't you? You've heard all the unpleasant evidence from Harriette. I'm sure she described to you every sin and crime in lurid detail. Overwhelming, isn't it? Face it—I'm not the man for you.'

She gripped the handle of the parasol even tighter, fingers bone-white within her gloves, struggling to find a reply. 'I find it hard to reconcile what I hear with what I know.'

'This is what *I* know!' His lips twisted. 'You're guilty of romanticising smugglers and smuggling, my dear girl. It's not romantic—rather hard and brutal with no room for principles and higher emotions.'

'Then are you hard and brutal too?'

'So it seems.'

'I don't believe you.'

'Then you're more foolish than I thought.'

She faced him, did not retreat one step. 'Is it true? Everything that Luke said?' she demanded.

'You heard it all. The damning evidence against me on Venmore's lips. Was it not strong enough to convince you?'

'I want to hear it from *you*. Did you truly do all those terrible things?' In her despair, in her inability to claw through her confusion, Marie-Claude's accent became more pronounced.

'Yes. I'm guilty as charged.'

'All of it?'

'Yes. All of it.'

A tremor touched her, but she remained staunchly determined. Her fingers clenched strongly enough that the fragile ivory was in danger of snapping.

'I don't believe you,' she repeated.

'You have known me a bare few weeks. How would you know what I'm capable of?'

She placed one palm against her breast, as she had once before. 'Because you are here. In my heart. You wouldn't lie to me. I know it.'

'You have no choice but to accept it, Madame Mermaid. Would Harriette lie to you?'

The question took Marie-Claude aback. For a moment she had to think. 'No. I don't think she would.'

'I'm her cousin. Would she blacken my soul if there was any chance of my innocence?'

What terrible stark demands his logic made on her. 'No. No, she would not.'

'You know how the landing went awry. You were there.'

'Yes. I was.'

'You know that Harriette was shot.'

'Yes.'

'Well, then. The pistol was assuredly mine.' He raised his tankard in a silent toast. 'Guilty as charged,' he said again, deliberately.

She flinched. It was as if he had struck her a physical blow.

'Did you *intend* to kill Luke?'

'Why not? He threatened my whole operation.'

'You would kill a man to keep your pockets lined with gold?'

Zan shrugged.

Marie-Claude, all her hopes, that somewhere in this morass she would find an answer, draining away through the soles of her feet, gathered all her resources to withstand this breaking down of her convictions. *I must breathe. I must remember to breathe.* Was this the man she had given up her heart to? Was this her lover who was destroying her love with such callous efficiency? Such cruel words.

There was a recklessness about him today. A cold-blooded, wanton carelessness. Even his clothes were dishevelled, his cravat hanging creased and unfastened round his neck. His slovenly attitude was an insult to her. She suspected this was not the first tankard of ale he'd consumed. He looked louche and dissolute, a dark unshaven shadow on chin and cheeks. Surely this was not Zan.

'I don't understand,' she stated abruptly.

'What's so difficult, Madame Mermaid?' Even the manner in which he addressed her—the name he had once used in such tenderness—was an insult. 'Your own experience should tell you that men can not be trusted when there's the prospect of gold to line their pockets.'

Again she flinched inwardly at his callous reference to Jean-Jacques Noir who had taken her prisoner, who had controlled her and threatened to use her as a whore in a French military town, offering her as bait in a plot to blackmail Luke. Yes, she knew how despicable men could be. But Zan was nothing like Noir. Marie-Claude struggled to order her thoughts into some recognisable pattern. It felt as if she were back in the bay, wading through incoming tides that threatened to sweep her away.

Still, she must discover… She would beg if she had to.

'You say you are less than honourable,' she admitted. 'But I need to know one thing from you. Tell me the truth. If you will do nothing else, I beg this of you.'

'Of course. I've nothing to lose.'

So she would ask it. It was the one question that had kept her from sleep.

'I need to know if you used me. Did it mean nothing to you? Did you not love me at all? Were they all empty words, meaningless kisses? Was I a convenient means of you getting your foot in the door of the Pride for your smuggling ventures?' She took a breath. 'Did you do it to get possession of Lydyard's Pride?'

'That's easy to answer, dear Mermaid. I could have got it without your involvement. Wiggins was hardly going to stop me, repelling me at the door with a shotgun! If I presented him with a bottle of port, he'd invite me across the threshold. If you recall, I did not visit the Pride, even at your most kind invitation—until that final afternoon. I didn't need you to get the Pride.'

He hadn't needed her. Such brutal truth. But she had demanded it and must withstand its wounding power. 'So was it revenge?' she asked. 'Was it just to get back at Venmore for snatching Harriette and the use of the Pride from you?'

He tilted his head mockingly, sneered. 'That's harder to answer. What do *you* think?'

'I think I can't accuse you of seduction. I was willing enough, wasn't I?' She too could show disdain.

'You fell into my hands as softly as a ripe plum. I simply wanted you. And took you. A weapon against Venmore? That was just an added dessert.' His smile was bitingly cruel. 'But I have to admit it did add to the piquancy of the occasion.'

'So you did it to punish me for my connection with Luke and Harriette.' She felt as if he had taken her trust and shredded it into tiny pieces. 'I trusted you. I gave you my heart and you trampled on it.' It was as if she had held the glory of the moon and stars, only to have them filter through her fingers, lost for ever in the fine shingle of Old Wincomlee bay. 'I loved you.' Marie-Claude took one step towards him.

'No, you didn't. You enjoyed the novelty, the excitement. The secrecy of our meetings. You'll get over it.'

Harsh, wounding words searing the air between them.

Zan put down the tankard and pushed to his feet to walk towards her.

'Goodbye, Madame Mermaid.' Before Marie-Claude could move, he swooped, gripping her shoulders with his hands and pulling her hard against him. His mouth took hers. A demand, a possession, carefully controlled, yet punishing in its intensity. At first she struggled, pushing ineffectually against his chest. But then his arms slid round her to hold her, and when he changed the angle of the kiss, against all her intentions her body betrayed her and her lips parted beneath his.

Furious with herself, she could do nothing but be overwhelmed by the bittersweet power of his embrace.

Until Zan lifted his head, pushed her away.

'Yes, you're pretty enough,' he observed dispassionately. 'Did I love you? Lust, rather. What man wouldn't want you? And you were so willing...'

It restored her to reality, cutting into her flesh like ice on a winter pond. Released to stand alone, Marie-Claude felt as fragile as glass but she held herself together. She could feel him on her lips, taste him there. In spite of everything he still had the touch to stir molten desire in her. But not any more. His words were cynically cruel, reminding her of her wanton behaviour. She would not be so ingenuously trusting again.

'You must excuse my lack of modesty, if the fault was then mine!' she managed, aware of nothing but the heat in her cheeks.

'Go home, Marie-Claude,' he advised harshly.

'Forget these past weeks, unless it's as a lesson in not giving your trust too indiscriminately. Marry a good man with honour, who can give you more children to fill your heart and your days. A man your family can respect and welcome. Who will bring you happiness.'

At the comfortable domestic picture painted so viciously, Marie-Claude felt temper surge to replace hopelessness. She was grateful for it. Anything was better than the vast emptiness that had opened up where her heart should have been. And finally her temper snapped. She allowed it to escape because suddenly she wanted to hurt as she had been hurt.

'How dare you tell me what to do? Who are you to give me good advice as to what might or might not bring me happiness?'

His face became still, his eyes flat. 'There, you understand perfectly. I knew you would. Who am I, indeed?' He stretched out a hand to draw the back of his fingers softly down her cheek—until she flinched back out of his range. 'No one but a smuggler and wrecker, an unprincipled rogue with no reputation and no honour.'

'And how misguided I was to be taken in by a handsome face and soft words. Without reputation and honour? That's not the half of it. Now that I can see clearly, I think you are still in league with the worst scum of *gentlemen*! What an unfortunate term. You told me that you belonged to no smuggling gang. I know that *that* was a lie too. I was there, if you recall. When the man Rackham came to find you, the man I now know to be Captain D'Acre's lieutenant. I suppose you're in business with them—the Fly-By-Nights, isn't it? You're no better than D'Acre is—and his tally of crimes is worse than appalling. George Gadie told me so.'

She saw his eyes widen, then the sardonic lines around his mouth deepened into a smile that held no amusement. 'That's true. Of course it is. Captain D'Acre and I are hand in glove—always have been.'

'I *despise* you,' she spat.

'Then why are you still here? Unless it's to gloat over the failure of my schemes to pay Venmore back. You've been mercifully saved from my wicked clutches.'

'So I have. I never want to see you again. How fortunate I am to discover your disgrace so soon.'

She turned on her heel and strode to the door, halting to look back over her shoulder.

'Do you know what my greatest relief is?' She did not wait for his answer. 'That Raoul, my son, was not here with me at the Pride. I had let him go with Harriette and Luke to The Venmore. Sometimes I regretted it. I thought how much he would enjoy sailing in the *Spectre*.' The pain in her heart was almost unbearable now. 'How fortunate that he was not here. I would not have wished my son to be anywhere near you. Not even in the same room as you. I would not have him influenced by a man with so little integrity, so little honour.'

Zan inclined his head, a mocking little salute. 'Then you must be thankful, Madame Mermaid. There are always some blessings in life.'

It was too much for her. 'God damn you, Alexander Ellerdine!'

With her hand she swept the glass lamp that stood on the table by the door on to the floor, where it shattered and spread in glittering diamonds across the boards.

The fall of her footsteps echoed in the hall. The outer door slammed.

The foolish parasol lay abandoned on the floor amidst the debris of broken glass.

Chapter Eight

It was one thing to be determined to remain in Old Wincomlee to show that she was no coward, but quite another to actually do it and keep her nerve. How much more sensible to take herself off to The Venmore, be reunited with Raoul, and forget. Forget everything. Forget him. But Marie-Claude had a point to prove. That Alexander Ellerdine—she would never again think of him as *Zan*, except when she forgot!—meant nothing to her, that her love for him was dead—in fact, had probably never existed except in her own imagination. She had meant every word of it when she had told him she despised him and all he stood for. She would prove that she could live in the same universe as so despicable a man without every beat of her heart being a painful memory when she had believed it had beat only for him. That she could exist without turning her head, expecting to see him outlined before her in sun or shadow. He was a wrecker with blood on his hands by his own admission, for goodness' sake. A liar, a cheat.

So she would do it.

Marie-Claude set herself to steer clear of his haunts. It was easy enough to do if she kept her wits about her, and there was no fear that he would ever seek her out. Meggie and Mr Temple need have no fears that the smugglers would gain access to Lydyard's Pride through her innocent co-operation, or that Alexander Ellerdine would ever again lay siege to her heart and her virtue. When the *Spectre* sailed in the bay, its dark sails shimmering in the gusts of wind or catching the light from the sea, she remained at the Pride, turning her face inland. No one need know that her heart fluttered uncomfortably and her face flushed. When moonlight flooded her bedchamber, who was to know that in her mind she walked the cliffs with him? Who was to know that she remembered how she had lain in his arms, taken him into her body, shivered beneath his weight? Who was to know—and it would never happen again. As he had said, she must be more discriminating in whom she put her trust. Never again would she act on that strange force that had seemed to catch and bind them together in the parlour of the Silver Boat, turning the miserable little room into a place of heart-stopping brilliance.

Never again.

It was easy to pass the heavy July days, despite the necessity of pretending contentment. She drove the gig. The Gadies, father and son, took Marie-Claude across the bay in *Venmore's Prize* so that she returned windswept and flushed from the sun. A gusty morning tempted her for a brisk walk along the cliffs where the wind would blow the cobwebs away. It was a risk, being so close to Elleredine Manor, but its owner would be unlikely to be at home. Busy elsewhere, doing something illicit and nasty with Captain D'Acre, without doubt.

Weary and sun-warmed, she turned for home, and Marie-Claude's simple pleasure in the day made her careless. Climbing out of one of the steep ravines, she looked up and back, towards where Ellerdine Manor nestled in a stand of wind-blasted trees, only to see his distant figure, sitting on his mare, looking out to sea.

Zan! It was the first time she had seen him since their bitter confrontation. Her heart leapt to her throat as if to choke her. There he was, no figment of her imagination, but flesh and blood. Immediately she turned and retraced her steps back into the ravine, hurrying along before he could see her. Then hesitated, looked back, senses alert at the quiet beat of hooves on the thick sward as a second rider approached. It was obviously a pre-arranged meeting. They both dismounted.

So who was the newcomer? Not Rackham. Was it D'Acre?

Narrowing her eyes against the bright light, Marie-Claude recognised some familiarity about the figure. Another smuggler of D'Acre's band, come to agree details of a run with Zan? But if so, how would she recognise such a man? As he turned in profile, she thought it might be the Preventive Riding Officer, Captain Rodmell, an easily recognisable figure with a tall stooping posture. In an impromptu charade, she had wept tears on his chest the night Luke and Harriette had brought her here, Raoul still a babe in arms. Yes, even at this distance, she was sure it was the Captain.

So what was Zan doing with the Preventive Officer?

Passing false information to protect one of his precious runs, most likely. There was no love lost between smugglers and excise-men. Zan was hedging his bets and sending the Captain on a wild-goose chase whilst the contraband was safely unloaded.

The two men remounted, business done.

No, he had not seen her.

Marie-Claude turned her back, conscious of a lingering regret.

Zan had seen her. He knew she was there from the moment she arrived. Knew when she looked across at him. The strand of connection, strong as new rope, still tied him to her. With a lift of his shoulders he turned his back on her and gave all his attention to a most detailed exchange of information with Captain Rodmell.

The business complete, he turned back, but she had gone. Marie-Claude had not seen him. The bond between them had been severed at last. Finally she was forgetting him.

His mouth tightened as he turned his mare in the direction of Ellerdine Manor. He did not look back again.

A week of storms, high winds from the south-west together with torrential rain, was hard to tolerate, keeping her indoors. When Marie-Claude saw a clear morning with relief, her spirits lifted. She must get out—but unfortunately not in *Venmore's Prize*. The severity of wind and waves had kept the fisherman of Old Wincomlee landlocked. Too dangerous to put to sea for the duration of a week or more and the results were obvious. No work, no catch, no money. They would be feeling the pinch in the village. Food would be sparse. Today the menfolk would all be putting out to sea—would already be there—so there would be no one with the time to spend on her leisure pursuits.

She would take the gig along the coast towards Hastings.

Early, before breakfast, she took herself to the stables to find anyone who might not be fishing to tack up the cob.

'George? George?'

No reply. Not entirely unexpected but surely there was some stable-lad left to do the job. There must be someone here.

First she heard a soft whicker of greeting. Then she saw.

There was a horse, saddled and bridled and warm from an energetic ride, tied in the courtyard. A chestnut mare with a flighty eye who raised her head in interest when Marie-Claude approached to run her hand down its neck. It didn't take much of an inspection for Marie-Claude to recognise the pretty animal.

Disconcerted by the little throb in the region of her heart, she ran her fingers through the silky mane. It was no better, no matter how often she might try to convince herself that it was. Time did nothing to assuage the pain. A sense of loss overwhelmed her, to the extent that she was horrified by the sudden threat of tears. It was no better. It was no better at all.

She patted her cheeks with her sleeve. She would not weep.

'Your master is a villain,' she whispered to the mare. 'He's unprincipled and manipulative. I will not love him.'

Retreat or challenge?

Definitely not retreat.

With a final caress of the mare, she walked into the open stabling where she could now hear the rumble of voices. Two culprits together, she decided, both knee-deep in contraband and methods to circumvent the law. She should be disgusted with the pair of them. Alexander Ellerdine and George Gadie. The throb in her heart became a bound that took her breath as her eyes travelled over the tall, leanly muscled figure, the familiar fall of dark hair.

She was in time to see Zan hand over a flat package that George tucked into his jacket with a nod of thanks and a brisk salute.

'Much obliged, y'r honour.'

'You'll know where it's best needed.'

'Aye, sir. There's a number of families where it'll be welcome. What about D'Acre?'

The name of the notorious smuggler slammed into Marie-Claude's mind.

'Nothing yet. I'll let you know.'

'Dangerous work, sir.'

'But necessary. Keep an eye on things here, will you? Don't put yourself in unnecessary danger. Just let me know if—'

So they were in league with D'Acre over some nefarious act of law-breaking. Marie-Claude waited to hear no more.

'What are you doing here, Mr Ellerdine?'

Both heads snapped round. George Gadie acquired a look of extreme innocence. Zan became still, brows raised.

'You are not welcome on this property.' This was not what she wanted to say at all. How harsh it sounded even to her own ears, but her throat was dry and she was horrified at her reaction to simply the sight of him within touching distance.

High colour slashed along his cheekbones. The muscles in his jaw tensed, his chin lifted, his mouth set in a firm line. For the briefest of moments she thought that Zan, caught out in this dubious transaction, would simply leave without a word. Instead he obviously decided to brazen it out. He made a supremely ironic bow.

'Madame Mermaid,' he drawled. His teeth glinted in a careless grin. 'An unexpected pleasure.'

'Hardly unexpected. This is my home.'

'So it is. Allow me to make my apologies for sullying Hallaston land with my disreputable feet.'

The drawl became more pronounced, insolent in its smoothness. Marie-Claude drew in a breath as she caught a breath of emotion behind the apparent contempt. She did not know what to say in the face of such bitter irony. Then realised that he had no need of any compassion from her when, entirely composed, Zan turned from her to look back over his shoulder to George.

'My business is done here, Gadie. There's a packet of tea for your wife in my mare's saddlebag if you would collect it.'

'Aye, y'r honour. She'll be grateful.' George moved between them, giving a strong impression that he would be glad to escape. 'Excuse me, mistress. Beg pardon... D'you need me for something?'

'Harness the cob to the gig, if you please, George,' she replied coldly. 'I'll drive along the cliff.'

'Aye, mistress.'

He stomped off, leaving Marie-Claude alone with Zan.

She found that he was watching her, a smile on his face that was bleak and unforgiving, but whether directed at her or at himself she could not say. His eyes were dark and impossible to read. As he sauntered towards her she felt suddenly breathless. Intimidated.

'You are not welcome here,' she heard herself snap.

'And as I said, my business is done. I'll be off.'

He took one more stride to walk past her, then stopped, too close for comfort, eyes narrowing on her face. A hesitation. 'You are too pale. It looks like you have not slept. Are you well? I don't like to see shadows…' He raised a hand as if to touch her cheek, the faint shadowing there.

Marie-Claude flinched. 'I shall be better when you have left.' Then tensed against his instant response. He looked strained, savage almost. Definitely menacing. Perhaps it would have been better not to provoke him. She held her breath.

Zan flung back his head as if she had struck him, letting his hand fall away. Abruptly he moved to push past her, as if he could not bear to be in the same space as she, to breathe the same air. As pain tightened around her heart, Marie-Claude turned her face away so that he might not read her grief, and stepped awkwardly back against the stall door. Immediately he reacted. He was so close. She felt him halt, stiffen. Then Zan seized her wrist so that her eyes snapped to his.

His words—that were seemingly wrung from him—startled her.

'Listen to me, Marie-Claude. Forget your hatred of me for a moment. If anything happens to worry you… If you feel threatened in any way—however trivial it might seem—send me word.'

'How should I be threatened here at the Pride? The only threat comes from *you*.'

'Anything that troubles you,' he persisted, ignoring her accusation, 'send Gadie to me. Promise it.'

'No! I need no help from you.'

'Promise, Marie-Claude.'

'I will not. Why would you care?' she said bitterly.

'I care because…' He shook his head as if to dislodge an unwanted thought and tightened his hold on her wrist that suddenly seemed fragile in his larger hand, against his obvious power. 'That's not important. Promise me!' he demanded with a heavy frown.

'Very well. I'll say the words,' she retaliated in a cold little voice even though her blood hummed at his closeness. The heat of his body, the sheer maleness of him, turned her knees to water. She hid it perfectly, callously. 'I promise to send George if I feel threatened. Will that do? Why not perjure myself? Since promises are cheap and mean so little to you, I don't have to keep it. And I'd thank you to let go of my wrist!'

'Ha!' He lifted her hand and pressed his lips to the centre of her palm. 'As soft and pretty as ever, my Sea Serpent!' He laughed when her hand promptly clenched into a serviceable fist. 'And just as forceful. But I doubt you'll use it against me.'

'It would be below my dignity!' But still her fingers were tight-clenched.

'I've no intention of allowing you the liberty!' he retorted. He took possession of her fist, holding tight when she would have snatched it away, smoothing out her fingers against her will. Once again he pressed his mouth against her palm, watching the emotion chase across her face as he did so. It did not seem to please him. His own emotions were instantly masked by a shuttered coldness, an icy bleakness enough to turn a knife in her heart. Then he gave her hand a little tug, taking her by surprise, so that she must step forwards against him. His arm slid around her waist. His hand caught her chin.

'Madame Mermaid,' he purred, 'I recall your kisses with delight. Perhaps we should repeat the experience. It makes me remember the soft gleam of moonlight on the cliffs, on the curve of your shoulders…'

'How dare you! Let me go!' she gasped.

'Oh, I dare. You have no idea what I would or would not dare.'

Before she could sense his purpose, his mouth took hers. A thorough owning, exploring the softness of her lips with his tongue. Growing firmer, more forceful, so that her lips must part beneath his. He held her hard against him when she struggled to be released, driving his fingers through her hair to hold her still beneath his possession. Instinctively, to protect her tumbling emotions, Marie-Claude forced herself to become rigid, refusing to give him the satisfaction of acknowledging her dislike of his touch. Or the wicked delight that insisted on creeping through her veins, betraying her rejection with its sweetness. She stood in his embrace, straight and unbending, as he took his pleasure. Horrified when her lips softened, warmed, entirely against her will, and lured him on. When he gentled his kiss, sweeping his tongue over her bottom lip, then sliding his mouth along her jaw to the tempting hollow below her ear, she was lost. The scent of his hair, his skin, swam in her brain… She gasped as his manhood surged against her in physical demand and he pressed her hard against him so that she would know his need.

Abruptly he released her, to press a final salute between her brows, against her temple. Then he pushed her away.

'Exactly as sweet as I recall. A shame the Earl and Countess broke up our liaison.' He gave a harsh laugh.

'You are the most despicable man I have ever met!' she cried.

'No matter! There are plenty of sweet lips and willing arms in Lewes. Other arms more accommodating than yours.'

'Then make yourself free of them. I care not!'

'No, I know you don't. Goodbye, madam. Remember your promise. I expect you to keep it, no matter your opinion of me.'

He raised his hand as if he would have touched her cheek again, but did not. Instead he strode to where his mare waited impatiently. With a brusque summons to his spaniel, and a flamboyant wave to Marie-Claude, completely at odds with the sudden harshness of his handsome features, he mounted and rode out of the courtyard.

Marie-Claude watched him go.

Furious with herself. With her reaction to him. With her own foolishness in putting herself within his reach. If she hadn't the sense to stay away from him, she deserved to be punished by his mocking behaviour.

Oh, Lord! She could still feel his lips on hers. Every inch of her skin was sensitive to the warm air as if she could still feel the slide of his fingers. Her blood ran hot and urgent in memory of what had been between them. Heat warmed her cheeks and… How humiliating this all was. That her heart should still hold such need for a man whose cruel indifference to her feelings was entirely heartless. Damn Zan Ellerdine and all he stood for! And how could she allow herself to be so weak willed, to be drawn into a response?

Marie-Claude marched over to the stall where

George was tacking up the solid cob. Beside him in the straw was the promised packet of tea. And hidden in the pocket of his coat, as she knew very well, was some entirely different commodity.

'What did Mr Ellerdine want?' she demanded brusquely.

'Just to bring a packet of tea, mistress.' George's glance in her direction, she decided, was infinitely untrustworthy. He turned away to continue to fasten the buckles with his gnarled fingers.

'I think that was not all,' she remarked, stepping to the cob's head so that the old smuggler had no choice but to give her his attention.

'No, mistress. That was all—and news of the run planned for next week. Nothing to trouble your head over.'

She pursed her lips in thought. So he would treat her like a child with a pat on the head. He had no intention of telling her any more than that.

'Nothing to do with Captain D'Acre? With smuggling business here at the Pride?' she persisted.

'No smuggling here, mistress. The Earl don't approve and Captain Harry's given up.' George gave a gusty sigh. 'Those were the days when we used the Tower room and the cellars when the Preventives came down on us. Wonderful cellars, they be. But now—'

Marie-Claude broke in before George could become well set in his reminiscences. 'Are you so certain you can vouch for Mr Ellerdine's intentions?' she asked. 'Has he some dangerous scheme afoot?'

George Gadie was suddenly serious. 'Mr Ellerdine'll do nothing to harm you, mistress.'

'I know he's in communication with D'Acre and Rackham. Can you deny it?'

'A difficult one, that.' He rubbed his nose thoughtfully, but with a sharp glance. 'I'll not say. But as for Mr Ellerdine—perhaps you'd do well to trust him, mistress.'

'How can you say that? Even you warned me off.'

'So I did.'

'He lacks all sense of honour, with no thought for the truth. He breaks his promises.' How could she love a man like that? She stoked her fury, pouncing on the one trivial moment to creep into her mind. 'Even that first time—when he rescued me from the tide—he promised to come and see me the following day. To ask after me. He even broke that promise. I should have known better than to trust him from the very beginning. He did not care.'

'He did care.' George's voice was gruff with emotion. 'Mr Ellerdine thought he should not come himself. And I can't say as I blame him. But he sent

Tom, his groom, to find out what he could. Early the next morning. And I told him.'

'Oh!' Marie-Claude blinked, furious that she had misread him. 'But it's not the same!'

'No, mistress, perhaps not. But he asked if you were well—had suffered no hurt.' Unexpectedly George stretched out his hand to touch her arm, his calloused skin rough but warm. 'All I'll say is— don't take everything as you sees it, mistress.'

'How can I do otherwise?' she asked despairingly.

Chapter Nine

To Marie-Claude's mind the atmosphere in Old Wincomlee underwent a subtle change, bringing an air of unease, of waiting. A threatening heaviness in the atmosphere that owed nothing to the sultry heat of the July days.

'You shouldn't be going out into the village alone, miss.' Meggie was at her bossiest. 'And certainly not along the cliffs.' She scowled as Marie-Claude selected a day gown of cream-striped muslin, suitable for striding along the cliff top. A charmingly elegant picture.

'Why not?' Marie-Claude, who valued her freedom of action in the vicinity of the Pride, looked up sharply. She'd had enough of social strictures on young women who walked unchaperoned in London; she would not give up her independence here without a fight.

'Miss Harriette would never forgive me if you were caught up in the goings-on hereabouts. A God-fearing place we were,' Meggie pronounced with dark inference. 'Our smugglers were a threat to no one, and a more peaceable place as Old Wincomlee I've not known. And now a body never knows what she'll meet…'

'What's happened?' To Marie-Claude this smacked too much like Zan's strange warning of impending but invisible danger.

'Nothing as yet. But the warning signals are out. The Fly-By-Nights.' Meggie sniffed her derision. 'Out and about round here, God rot them. Up to no good, I'll be bound. All I'll say is—take one of the servants when you go out, mistress. Or one of the grooms. George Gadie if you can get him to stir himself from the stables or his fishing boat. I'll have a word with him.'

Marie-Claude stifled a sigh. 'I will if I must.'

'And don't you go talking to Mr Ellerdine,' Meggie warned with an arch of her eyebrow.

'I've no intention of talking with that—that reprobate!' she responded, on her dignity.

True enough. But neither had Marie-Claude any intention of rousting out one of the grooms, or George Gadie, every time she wished to take a walk, but she agreed to be more circumspect. It did not trouble her overmuch. When she sailed in *Venmore's Prize*, as was her intention later that day, either George or Gabriel was always with her. How could she come to harm in Old Wincomlee where she knew every face, where the fishermen and their wives greeted her?

She was perfectly safe.

So she lingered to exchange the time of day with Mistress Gadie outside her cottage near the little quay, leaving George and Gabriel to pull the cutter up on to the beach. It was pleasant to stand and talk of her day and her plans for the next. Eventually she waved farewell and threaded through the cottages, deciding which route to take towards the Pride, opting for the village street with its interesting nooks and crannies to investigate. She strolled leisurely, whilst in her mind she registered that it was noisy at the Silver Boat, which was unusual for this time of the day. Horses were tied up outside. And an empty wagon as if a delivery had been made.

The raucous bellow of laughter took her attention. Marie-Claude slowed her steps as half-a-dozen men, men of the fishing community by their clothing, pushed through the open door to fill the seats and benches in front of the inn. Their voices were raised, fuelled by drink as became clear when tankards and jugs of ale were carried out by Sal and passed around. Not Old Wincomlee men, she decided, recognising no one. Perhaps, on closer inspection, there was more than a touch of affluence in their garments, rarely seen in the village fishermen. A fine cloth coat. A pair of new boots. And an air of sharply confident arrogance that repelled her.

A foreboding blew across the nape of her neck, lifting the fine hair. It dug deep along her spine when two men emerged from the inn to mingle, obviously part of the crowd. Marie-Claude felt the shiver of anxiety expand to grip her belly with fear. There in the midst of the fishermen was the man she recognised from her previous meeting, Rackham, and the stout red-haired, bearded figure with a stamp of authority in his face and gestures next to him must be the notorious Captain D'Acre.

Then she stopped in the middle of the street. Striding from the dark interior of the Boat to take his place amongst them, hip propped against the wooden table, was Zan. Perfectly comfortable in his company, now in the act of raising a tankard snatched up from Sal's tray. Much as she despised herself, from that moment she had eyes for no one but him.

He fit well into the Fly-By-Nights, she thought. Coatless, hatless, an embroidered brocade waistcoat worn open over his linen shirt, dark breeches tucked into highly polished topboots, he had the air of a successful but ruthless smuggler. Even down to the pistol tucked in his belt. He tossed back his dark hair so that she could see his vividly handsome features, the gleam in his eyes.

'To our enterprise,' he announced.

'To our successful venture,' replied D'Acre with a broad grin, casting his flamboyantly feathered hat on to the table, before he too drank deep. 'And failure to all Preventives.'

'Failure to our noble J.P., Sir Wallace Lydyard, and all men of like ilk!' Zan added with a sweep of his arm.

'Damnation to the government!' D'Acre said for good measure.

'Amen to that.' Zan lifted his hand to Sal. 'Another round, my girl. And then you can stay and keep us company.' His smile glinted wickedly, his voice fell into a disreputably seductive purr that Marie-Claude recognised. 'We've a celebration in mind. It's not every day the Fly-By-Nights agree to pass some of their wealth and success in the direction of Old Wincomlee!'

'Let's drink to our association with the village,' Rackham added. 'Long may it last.'

The smugglers drank, breaking out into loud laughter and ribald comment as Sal laughed and swayed her hips.

Marie-Claude stood transfixed, unable to look

away. Zan's air of dissolute rakishness horrified her. If she had needed any further proof that he was hand in glove with D'Acre's gang, this was it. He was entirely at ease with them, laughing at some aside from the grizzled leader. Instinct warned her not to pass the inn with its volatile customers even as her spirit urged her not to show such despicable weakness. Why should she not be able to walk unharmed along her own village street? But perhaps on this occasion discretion would be a sensible choice, as she had promised. She made to turn down between two cottages, back towards the beach, and take the longer path up on to the cliff.

'Now there's a pretty picture!'

The voice, louder than the rest and definitely raised in her direction, made her quicken her steps. She recognised it. That was Rackham, the man whose eyes had frozen her blood. She would not flout fate. She needed to be out of there, and fast. Marie-Claude hastened even more.

'Now why would you think she'd want to escape from our attentions? Such a pretty little thing as she is. And we such gentlemen.' Plain enough to hear on the still air.

'Why don't you persuade her to stay, Rack?'

A surge of laughter followed. Marie-Claude hated the sly, almost ugly, amusement at her expense.

Footsteps sounded, following her. A little spurt of panic urged her onwards. She almost broke into a run.

'Not so fast, lady.' Her arm was caught in a heavy grip that tightened when she tried to wrench away.

'Let me go!' Her eyes flashed as she was pulled to face the looming smuggler.

'We'll let you go.' Rackham's grin was lascivious, leering, enjoying her fright and his fingers were iron-hard, digging into her arm. 'But not yet. Our Captain would like a friendly word and the pleasure of your company. Don't be frightened. He'll not hurt you— unless you're reluctant to take our invitation. Captain D'Acre's used to getting his own way.'

All the time Rackham's arm was sliding around her ribs. Marie-Claude found herself dragged back towards the inn clamped against the side of the man who was far too strong for her to resist. Full-blown fear rioted through her body so that even breathing seemed difficult. There was no one to save her here, no one to come to her aid. No point in looking to Zan. He was one of them. How would she come out of this with her honour intact? She fought against the paralysing terror even as she felt her courage ebbing away with every reluctant, stumbling step.

'Stop that!' Rackham snarled a laugh as she raised a fist to pound on his arm. He grabbed her wrist, at the same time continuing to drag her ruthlessly towards the Silver Boat where Captain D'Acre waited, sprawled in a chair. Marie-Claude fought and struggled every inch of the way. If only George or Gabriel was there. Zan would not help her. Seeing her plight, he hadn't come to her rescue, had he? So much for his promises. When she was released to stand hot and dishevelled in front of the grinning, hooting crowd, she turned her furious stare on him.

Alexander Ellerdine. The man to whom she had given her heart and had loved enough to lie naked in his arms. The man who had loved her with his body. And she had believed him.

There was no love in his face now. It was closed, expression immaculately bland. He gave no recognition of her, no sign to the men around him that he even knew her name. She made her stare a challenge. She would not make this easy for him. He would have to reject her openly, without any pretence of still caring for her. Had he not promised his help if she were in need? She would make him stand by that facile promise—or break it in the full light of day so that both of them would see his treachery.

If you feel threatened—send me word.

Well, that was an empty gesture! She had never felt more threatened in her life. Her heart quailed at the lack of warmth in his gaze as it touched on her. Icy cold, without concern, without compassion. She held his gaze with her own, daring him to allow this public humiliation.

And felt her heart sink as he continued to sit, spine rigid, the only movement the gentle swinging of one booted foot against the table leg. Every muscle in his face was tight, controlled. He had no intention of protecting her from this scum. If she hadn't already done so, she would doubtless discover the worst of him today.

'Well, pretty girl. And I thought you were about to run away from us.' The Captain's rasping voice held terrible insinuations.

'I am not your pretty girl!' she retaliated with a renewed flood of fear.

Thrust forwards by Rackham, stumbling again, she found herself directly in front of Captain D'Acre, who leaned forwards and grasped her wrist to pull her even closer so that her muslin skirts brushed against his body.

'Perhaps not yet. But I think you'll be mine very soon. Softly, my dove.' Raising his hand, ignoring when she automatically flinched away, he pressed it against her breast, sliding it down. His eyes were beadily intent. 'All you need is a little soothing. Me and my men'll be pleased to accommodate you…' He angled an invitation of a glance to his right. 'Unless you prefer Mr Ellerdine here. I see that you know him. And I'd wager he knows you. I'd say he's made himself free of your charms already.'

'Yes, I know him,' she answered contemptuously. 'And I wish I didn't.'

'So he didn't please you?' D'Acre's face crinkled with sly humour.

'He did not!'

'Well, then!' D'Acre leaned back. 'What do you think, Ellerdine? Is she worth my cultivating her affections? How well do you know the lady?' His sneer grew. 'Pretty well, I'd say.' He leaned towards Marie-Claude again, his breath foul. 'What do you think of our pretty gentleman, my girl? D'you prefer him to me?'

Unable to think of a word to say in reply to that appalling suggestion, Marie-Claude simply pressed her lips together and vowed to resist.

For the length of a heartbeat, indecision gripped Zan with a hard hand. What malign fate had brought Marie-Claude through the village today of all days? What had possessed her to stare at him in so blatant a challenge, demanding even in her silence that he acknowledge her and come to her aid, and finally to make it clear to anyone of any wit that she knew him and he knew her.

Well, of course she had. Hell and damnation! If a

man made a thoughtless promise to come to the aid of a lady, a knight errant to the rescue, simply because he could not tolerate the thought of her living in fear, she should expect no less of him. And he had promised her just that. He saw the shattering fear in her beneath the raw courage that kept her facing D'Acre and knew he had no choice. He must act, and fast, before events got out of hand and beyond his control.

But, by God, this had put him in danger too. And here he was sitting as undecided and ineffectual as a gull on a rock in the harbour. He must get her out of this, whatever the cost to him.

'So she knows you, does she, Ellerdine?' D'Acre needled again, a harder note creeping in at Zan's silence.

It would take so little for D'Acre and Rackham to question his new authority in the Fly-By-Nights. He dare not risk it. His brain scrabbling furiously to work a path through this disaster, Zan made the only reply that would be accepted by D'Acre.

'Yes, she does know me. And as you so perceptively observed…' he let boredom lie heavy on his tongue as he achieved an insulting leer '…I know her. I know her very well. I've passed an hour or two, sampling her charms. I've been in more welcoming beds—but she's good enough for a brief dalliance.'

* * *

If Marie-Claude was afraid before, Zan's callous reply filled her with dread. What had his words implied? That she was no better than a whore to entertain the likes of D'Acre and his gang? Not only had he done nothing to extricate her from this, but he had implied that her morals were as loose as his own. The possibility of escape for her vanished, if, indeed, it had ever existed.

She must do what she could as opportunities unfolded. She focused all her attention on D'Acre, hiding her disgust of his breath on her face, the reek of ale, the grossness of his body. She would not flinch. She would not show the disgust for all smugglers—and one in particular—that in that moment flooded her from head to foot in a cold hatred.

'A lady of discerning tastes then, if you've set your eye on Ellerdine here!' With a gleam of amusement, D'Acre's hand stroked over Marie-Claude's shoulder whilst she set her teeth at Zan's betrayal and turned her face away, unable to look at D'Acre's ugly features without shivering in horror.

'What's your name, miss?'

'None of your concern,' she snapped.

'Oh, ho. A high-spirited filly. I warrant you gave Ellerdine a run for his money. Perhaps you'll like me better after all. I can be very—kind—with the right incentive.'

D'Acre yanked her even closer as he rose to his feet. Every muscle in her body tensed as he took her chin in his hand to force her to look into his face. For a little time he studied her and his smile grew. Marie-Claude held her breath, then exhaled slowly at a little reprieve when D'Acre dropped his hand and walked round her, inspecting her as if she were a mare for sale. She forced herself to stand straight and tall.

'Not a village girl, then. Staying hereabouts?'

'Yes.'

'And where would that be, miss?'

'Lydyard's Pride.' She turned her head, looked him in the eye.

'The Pride?' He seemed surprised. 'Now I'd thought that to be empty apart from old Wiggins. One of the Hallastons, are you?'

'Yes, I am.'

'She's the widow of the Earl's brother.' Zan's information curtly delivered, totally dispassionate.

'Staying at the Pride. Interesting. Useful, perhaps.' Again D'Acre made a circuit of her, brushing too close for comfort. It was as if he couldn't keep his hands from her. 'You could certainly be of use to me.' The odious grin again flashed on his face, breath hot on her cheek. 'You could be of use to all of us. Couldn't she, Ellerdine?'

'You'll not get my help in any of your disgusting schemes,' Marie-Claude stated, deliberately misunderstanding the obvious innuendo.

'And French by your accent. Well now, how charming. Why did you think I was referring to one of my *schemes*? I had my mind on something far more—personal.'

His hand was back on her shoulder, over her breast, and down to the dip of her waist. Marie-Claude read lust in his eyes and drew in a sharp breath, determined not to cry out. No possibility of flight—she was surrounded. No one to cry out *to*. She would not look at Zan again. Was he enjoying this? Was he just going to stand there and watch whilst D'Acre continued to humiliate and degrade her? Since she had been manhandled before them like a piece of contraband merchandise, he had only made one move—to push himself from the table's edge to stand balanced on both feet. He looked tense, his face stern and remote, yet every muscle held in check, primed for action. But not on her behalf, she thought bitterly before terror took its hold once more as D'Acre began to drag her towards the open doorway of the inn.

'Don't struggle.' D'Acre spoke softly. 'See how

thoughtful I can be. If you're shy, pretty girl, I'll seek a quieter room for us.'

'No! I will not.' But however much she dug in her heels on the wooden planking, she was pulled inexorably forwards. Despair made her beg. 'Let me go! Please…' she begged.

D'Acre's rough hands were hard and impatient.

'Now why would I do that? You might bring the authorities down on our heads. We wouldn't want that, would we?'

'No. No…' To her horror Marie-Claude felt the dampness of tears on her cheeks.

Then Zan was at her side, one hand curled around her forearm, gently enough.

'Let her go, D'Acre.' His voice was soft, but deadly serious.

D'Acre cocked his head. 'I don't think I will.'

'Let her go, I said.'

'As I recall, *I* am Captain of this League of Gentlemen.' D'Acre's warning was dangerously clear.

Zan did not hesitate. 'She's not yours, D'Acre. She's mine. And I don't give my permission for you or your men to touch her. She's out of bounds, d'you hear me?' Marie-Claude felt his hand tighten, and she froze, waiting. 'She's mine. If she spends time with anyone in a quiet room, it's with me. Now let her go!'

* * *

Zan waited for whatever outburst his challenge precipitated, his body superbly balanced for D'Acre's reply. He'd found himself faced with little choice. No choice at all, in fact. Completely innocent in all this, completely unaware, Marie-Claude had dug a possible grave for him. His gut had roiled as he watched D'Acre touch her with such intimacy, and his hands had clenched into fists. Fury beat in his brain. He couldn't allow D'Acre to use her as some bar-room slut. But unless he could step cleverly, the outcome could be bloody, and if it came to violence, he was outnumbered. They might both end up paying the highest price. He set his mind to dictate the pattern of this nasty little situation, using all the authority of his birth and local standing as an Ellerdine and a Lydyard. D'Acre would not be open to persuasion, of that he was certain. So he must force the issue. Never had it been as necessary for him to fall back on the weight of his name as it was now, if he were to salvage anything from the possible wreck of his plans and the degradation of Marie-Claude.

'Are you standing in my way, boy?' D'Acre asked, smooth as old French brandy.

'Yes, I am. The woman's mine.'

'I could fight you for her.'

'And would you fight fair, D'Acre? If you did it would be the first time in your life.' Zan knew that in the resulting mêlée he would die with a knife between his ribs. He deliberately sneered at his rival. 'Since when were you short of a cosy armful, Captain, to have an interest in another man's woman? Have you lost your touch?'

Still D'Acre kept his grip around Marie-Claude's wrist. Zan was conscious of nothing but her stillness under his hand, her tense watchfulness, poised to run if chance allowed.

She wouldn't get ten feet unless he took a hand.

'The Ellerdine and Lydyard names stand for authority in Old Wincomlee,' he stated, leaning towards D'Acre, an overt threat. 'If you don't accept that, then go back to Rottingdean and take your henchmen with you. If I say I want the woman, then she's mine. My word's law hereabouts.' Would the Captain back down? Marie-Claude shuddered against him. 'And if you want my co-operation in your plans, then you've the sense to see where your best interests lie…'

He left the threat open. Felt the sear of Marie-Claude's disgusted glance.

D'Acre's eyes slid away, the first sign of retreat. 'She's yours, you say,' he observed mildly enough. 'She doesn't look overjoyed to see you.'

'We've had our differences in the past. Nothing that can't be put right with a short…conversation, shall we say.'

'Want me to teach her a lesson first, in respect?'

'I can teach my own lessons,' Zan growled, eyes fierce and predatory on the smuggler Captain. 'Do you deny me that right?'

The outcome still tottered on a knife edge. No better than two fighting cocks, circling, threatening, intimidating. Who would be the first to bow to the vicious spurs of the other? Zan was conscious of the smugglers at his back, intent on the outcome of this show of force.

'No, I'll not deny you.' The Captain suddenly guffawed. 'Let's see you in action, boy.'

'My pleasure,' Zan snarled. 'She was less than amenable when we last met. She deserves a lesson in obedience…'

And Marie-Claude found herself summarily released by D'Acre, thrust into Zan's arms that banded around her to plaster her against him. Despite her shocked cry of disgust, he lowered his head to take her mouth in a kiss, hard and fierce. She instantly stiffened against him, refusing to comply, but his arms were like steel, his mouth ruthlessly possessive. As if she were truly his woman who must be taught a lesson. It was as if a black cloak enveloped her. She could do nothing but ignore the humiliation even as her senses recognised the taste and scent of the man who held her and kissed her so furiously. As at a distance, Marie-Claude heard the appreciative drunken cheer. And D'Acre's voice.

'When you've finished, we can reap the benefits. Break her spirit. A filly always responds better when she knows who's master.' D'Acre threw himself back into his chair, obviously intent on watching her being brought to her knees.

Zan raised his head. 'Oh, I will, never fear.' With her still firmly held against him, he stepped a little apart. 'Give me some space here. I may need to take a riding crop to her sides if she remains recalcitrant.'

'You wouldn't *dare*!' Marie-Claude could not find the words to express what she felt for him.

'Would I not?' Zan grinned. And kissed her again with savage thoroughness. She could feel every taut muscle in his body moulded to hers. Was aware of his arousal even in these dire circumstances. When she struggled to gain some freedom of movement, he simply set those muscles to resist. She could not escape him. Would he drag her off into the inn as D'Acre had threatened? She feared that he would.

Suddenly, without releasing her or relaxing his hold, Zan pulled at the ribbons of her bonnet, snatched the pretty straw and cast it away before burying his face in her hair, turning as if he would savage her throat below the ear as his hand tightened in her curls.

Zan cursed silently and fluently in his mind. Hell and damnation! This was the moment, he decided, the one moment. Now or never. He prayed she would keep her wits about her and obey even when her instinct was to fight him.

Well, he supposed on the ghost of a laugh, this was her one chance to do him some damage.

'Run!' he whispered, his mouth against her skin. Felt her tense against him. 'Kick hard—and run.' He applied his teeth gently to her throat. 'Understand? Run!' A sigh of a breath that he prayed would be inaudible to any but her. He felt with relief the stiffening response in her, then the slightest nod of her head.

'You're not very compliant, mistress,' he said aloud, splaying a hand over her hip to pull her hard against him. 'Perhaps my lesson needs to be—more graphic!' He bent his head as if to take her mouth again, and said, 'Now!'

And Marie-Claude reacted instinctively. She did not altogether know why he would do this, or if she would be successful, but she did as she was ordered, seeing a glimmer of hope. It was not easy because there was no space between them, but she did what she could as she felt the slightest lessening of Zan's hold on her. Raising her foot, she brought the heel of her shoe down on to Zan's instep as hard as she could. And then again, at the same time beating her fist against his chest.

He flinched magnificently, pulled away with an oath. When he stretched out as if to grasp her hair, she swung round, grabbed his wrist and sank her teeth into the soft flesh of the side of his hand.

'Curse you!' He lifted his hand as if to strike her.

Without compunction Marie-Claude raised her knee with all the force of her body to connect with his groin, grateful for the first time in her life for her experiences in the seamy stews she'd inhabited under Jean-Jacques Noir's control, where she'd learned a thing or two about self-preservation from the whores who offered themselves outside the inns and along the quayside.

Zan doubled up in a roar of agony. Genuine or part of the charade she had no idea, but that didn't matter. In that moment she was free and running.

'Vixen! You'll pay for that!' Zan lunged to recapture her, his co-ordination impeded. 'The sly cat! She's too quick for me. And too much ale, by God!'

Marie-Claude did not stop, did not look back, but simply ran. Behind her shouts and cat-calls echoed, cruel mockery at Zan's failure. Crude laughter. Zan's voice, ragged at the edges.

'Farewell, mistress. I'll make sure I see you later. You owe me a bitten hand and a ruined boot!' His voice rose to a raw shout. 'Not to mention a strike against my manhood. I'll make you wish you'd never learnt that trick!'

She fled, not stopping until she was well on the way to the Pride, where lack of breath caused her to slow. Even then she did not allow herself to stop. Only on the cliff top with the Pride well in her sights and no sign of pursuit, she let herself to sink to the short grass and catch her breath, where her thoughts raced in an impossible turmoil of uncertainties and tumbled sensations.

What should she make of the events of the past hour?

Captain D'Acre had some reason for being in Old Wincomlee, and Zan was involved in it. How could he allow himself to be inveigled into joining such a vicious gang as the Fly-By-Nights? But then she knew he was without principle. If the price was right, he would make a pact with the devil himself. It merely consolidated all she had discovered about him to his detriment.

She shuddered in the warm sun as she recalled the overt threats, the slide of D'Acre's obnoxious hands over her. Sudden nausea churned in her belly when she realised what the outcome could have been.

And Zan had sat and watched without raising a voice in her defence.

But then he had saved her from their assault. His methods might be rough and entirely too intimate, but he had secured her release in the only way possible, using his possession of her as a screen to get her out of there. Even she could see that. And at what cost to him? He'd been reluctant to take any initiative. Would there be a price to pay for his losing the object of their torments? As if a cat had allowed a mouse to escape.

What would be the price for Zan at D'Acre's hands?

Nothing more than coarse mockery, she decided. She had no sympathy for him at all.

But her heart still beat fast. From the fright and the run up the cliff path, of course. She'd had no pleasure in his kisses, had she? Marie-Claude surveyed her feelings with brutal honesty. Fear, abject terror had robbed her of clear decisions, but even when she resisted him, still she felt the attraction that refused to die. The thrust of his body against hers and the demands of his mouth had relit the flame so that desire had mingled with the dread.

There had been a tension in him, almost a fear that had required a deep inner control. She had felt it in every muscle of his body, the strain of every tendon when his arms had held her. What did that mean? She had no idea, but what she did know was that Zan was now one of D'Acre's gang, a despicable brother-hood of rogues capable, if George Gadie's tales were true, of severing a hand from one of their number.

Alexander Ellerdine was not worthy of one moment of her time. Not of one thought. Not of one regret. He was everything as bad as she had thought. Yet she fought against a shocking welling of tears.

Could he be so very bad, when he rescued you?

Yes, he could.

She could not fathom his motives, but there was no reason to read honour into them. More likely male possessiveness—that D'Acre should not take what he, Zan, could not have. A quick rub of her sleeve removed the tell-tale moisture as Marie Claude admitted quietly, despairingly, but with calm honesty, for her own ears.

'In spite of everything I know about him, Zan Ellerdine has a place in my heart. I wish he hadn't. It's a place I can never offer him, nor would he ever wish to claim from me. Unfortunately, I love him still.'

The gulls swooped and dipped overhead with raucous cries. The sadness of them found an echo in Marie-Claude.

'I must mourn his loss. I must live without him. Perhaps one day I shall forget he ever existed.'

But she knew she would never forget.

* * *

At the Silver Boat Zan endured his body's reaction to the assault on his groin with as much sang-froid as he could manage. Easier to tolerate was the coarse ribbing, which he did with trenchant good humour that effectively masked any other emotions that might stir him. He would consider those later. For now, he had got away with it against all the odds. Marie-Claude was safe. Perhaps he could even argue that his supreme discomfort had been worth it. If he caught a speculative glance in his direction from D'Acre, it could not be helped.

'Playing a deep game, are you, Ellerdine?' Rackham's jaundiced eye rested on him as he passed him another tankard of ale.

'Nothing deep about me, Rack,' Zan retaliated with a grin and a heavy swallow of the ale. 'Just an eye for a pretty girl. As you have. Sal's casting an eye in your direction…'

And as Rackham let himself be diverted by Sal's attentions, Zan sat down with D'Acre to work out the fine detail of an undercover cargo of contraband, planned to make land in Old Wincomlee.

'Now tell me.' D'Acre fixed Zan with a speculative and acquisitive gleam. 'Tell me again about this double cellar in Lydyard's Pride. And how we can make use of it. How do we get into the property that's locked up right and tight? Tell me how you plan it, Mr Ellerdine, that Lydyard's Pride should fall into the hands of the Fly-By-Nights without a shot being fired.'

Chapter Ten

Zan paced the elegantly balustraded but weed-strewn terrace at Ellerdine Manor and allowed his dilemma to invade his mind. By God, it had sharp teeth! It had kept him awake, and he was no nearer a solution than when he had first realised the problem. He'd been struggling—unsuccessfully—to keep it at bay since the day of the Incident at the Silver Boat, as that terrible afternoon had come to be named in his mind. Now the dilemma loomed imminently and dangerously.

Momentarily his eye was caught by the scuff marks and deep gouge on the instep of his boot that all his polishing could not remedy. Marie-Claude's heel had been applied without pity. His lips curled in appreciation at her thoroughness, then twisted in uncomfortable memory of the more personal agony she had inflicted on him. Now where had she learnt that trick? In the hands of her French captor Noir, kept in a smuggling inn in a port, she had probably learned all the tricks to keep herself from harm. She'd certainly been effective. His lovely girl had not held back. His jaw tightened at the remembered jolt of pain that had almost brought him to his knees.

But he was digressing.

The night of the crucial run was almost upon him and could not be changed. Zan knew he must not even raise the possibility of postponing it for another week or two. If he did it would stir immediate suspicions and he dare not risk it. Nor was he certain that a post-ponement would remove the essential difficulty. No, it had to be next week. It was perfect weather, calm and still, and the night of a waning moon—no bright moonlight to highlight suspicious vessels putting silently into a bay after dark—when the tides were running right to get D'Acre's two cutters to France and back, fast and safely. D'Acre's enthusiasm for the enterprise grew with each day, as did his ambition to make a killing with the large shipments of contra-band, unloaded and snugly hidden from view in the double cellar at Lydyard's Pride. This was the largest, most ambitious operation D'Acre had planned for years. Zan curled his lip. Perhaps he was feeling his age and was set on bowing out with a grand gesture. A superb swansong.

Except that Zan could never see D'Acre handing over the reins to any other man. He enjoyed the power and the fear he engendered in his smuggling compatriots. No, D'Acre might be advancing in years, but he was still a force to be reckoned with. For now.

Zan's part in this run, as he well knew, was crucial and still a subject of intense scrutiny. It was the first time he had joined hands with the Rottingdean smugglers on so major a scale. Oh, he had run with them often enough in recent months, deliberately so, astonished at the financial reward when the business was in the hands of a man such as D'Acre who had blood on his hands. The Captain had no compunction in removing any obstacle in his path, with the result that no one stood against him. The Captain drove a hard bargain and obliterated rivals. So Zan had lent them the use of the *Spectre*. Passed information on the whereabouts of the Excise. Even joined in with a handful of their bread-and-butter operations. Just enough to make a toehold in their brotherhood. Financially it had done him no harm at all—Zan's lips thinned in displeasure as he considered the accumulated wealth—no harm if he had the stomach to spend blood money.

And this imminent operation? Zan felt a shiver of unease down his spine. D'Acre still watched him carefully—he watched everyone—but Zan didn't think the Captain had any doubts about his commitment to this run. Some of the Fly-By-Nights—well, that was another matter. They suspected anyone not native to Rottingdean. Rackham's lively suspicions were often turned in his direction. A new man in an operation was an unknown quantity. Of course he would be an object of interest and speculation. Zan only hoped he had made enough of a reputation to offset any major doubts.

On the other hand he could not afford to be complacent. What if…?

But Zan shrugged. Perhaps he was looking over his own shoulder far too much. He had covered his tracks. His neck was safe enough. The proposition for this run had been his, and much of the planning. The gang had enough trust to go along with him since the resulting gold to line their pockets would be more than they had earned in the past six months. All should go according to plan. No reason for it not to. Within a week it would be over and done with.

Except that…

Zan scowled at the spaniel that kept pace with him.

Except that… And here was the burden that sat on his shoulders, the knife that twisted in his side. The essential difficulty to this neat little scheme to bring D'Acre down. Marie-Claude was still in residence at Lydyard's Pride.

How could he have guessed that she would remain here for so many weeks with no suggestion that she would leave? How could he have believed that she would have put her experience at the Silver Boat aside? Not to mention his own unforgivably heartless treatment of her. True, she was out and about in the village far less than before, never alone, and who could blame her? He had spies enough to tell him of her comings and goings. It must have been a terrifying experience, enough to drive most women into headlong flight. When she did venture out, there was a servant or one of the Gadies with her.

But she was still at the Pride. Marie-Claude was not most women to turn tail and run!

And this could cast the whole operation into jeopardy.

Well, no, he acknowledged, coming to a halt to stare across the fields towards the Pride where the lady would be passing her day with no inkling of the storm cloud that was gathering over her head. The operation would go ahead as planned. Marie-Claude would simply not be allowed to stand in its way. And that was the dilemma that ate at Zan's mind. At his heart. If D'Acre found Marie-Claude threatening his magnificent triumph, and was of a mind for it, he would do whatever was necessary to remove her interference. Lock her in her room. Shoot her dead. Toss her over the cliff…

D'Acre would not give a damn one way or the other.

Zan's mind refused to move on from that appalling picture of Marie-Claude having fallen to her death on the rocks of the bay. He would live without her if he had to—had already made up his mind to that, even though he knew it would be like tearing away one half of his soul. He could live, he supposed, knowing that he had brought her nothing but distress and a broken heart. He thought he might just be able to tolerate the crippling pain that he had brought sadness into her life. But if he helped to put her in physical danger or worse…

How could he live with that?

His thoughts swung back to his meeting with her in the stables at the Pride where he had gone to confirm arrangements with Gadie. She had looked drawn and pale despite her spirited challenge. The faint violet shadows printed below her eyes had made her appear more delicate than he knew her to be. Haunted by her, he had been driven to an ill-considered gesture of gallantry, to make his offer of help when he had intended to say nothing at all and simply get himself out of there because he could not bear to see the sorrow he had created. And then when he had moved to walk past her, she had turned her face away and deliberately flattened herself against the stall door so that even the ruffles of her gown would not come into contact with him.

Rejection was hard to take. The fact that it was all of his own making, and deliberately so, did not make it any easier at all. He had played the rogue superbly.

Her words had bitten deep.

'How should I be threatened here at the Pride? The only threat comes from you.' He remembered the pain of the strike, fast as a snake. *'Why would you care?'*

He had been able to think of no reply that would not destroy the whole edifice he had so carefully created since that grim confrontation when she had come to the Manor to force him to tell her the truth. Already he could read the quizzical expression in her eye as she took note of his offer of help. Definitely an unwise move, to give her cause to think him capable of finer, more honourable motives. It had been necessary to undo the damage, to reinforce his alter ego of unscrupulous libertine. It hadn't been difficult, only at some cost to his own control.

He was not proud of what he had done.

He had kissed her. Not with the tenderness that she deserved, but with hard demand. He had ravished her lips, mastered her struggles, setting himself to ignore the thrust of her hands against him for release. A disgraceful performance on his part, but it had had the desired effect. She now hated him magnificently.

It had been for her own good.

He made a turn at the end of the balustrade, stepping round the spaniel. His frown deepened. He supposed he had been effectively punished for his actions towards her. Her taste, her scent, the soft lure of her mouth had stirred his desire for her all over again. Not that it had ever been quenched, but that one kiss had caused it to leap again to a raging torrent. He loved her beyond reason, but could never have her.

Her words struck home again, as clear as if she was here beside him, flinging her hatred at his feet. *'You are the most despicable man I have ever met.'*

And the emotion he had seen in her lovely eyes. Outrage. Bright fury. A flush of humiliation. But not love, nothing tender. He had destroyed that well enough. And the worst thing she had said to him?

I would not have wished my son to be anywhere near you. I would not have him influenced by a man with so little integrity, so little honour.

The memory attacked his heart with sharp claws. Oh, yes. He had been punished. Why had he not simply told her? Why had he not told her the truth? For one shattering moment he had been tempted to do just that. For that one moment he had felt an overwhelming need to put himself right in her eyes and remove the hurt that swam there beneath the courage that it had taken her to face him. Until sense took hold. What proof did he have? It would be his word against all the formidable layers of evidence. Nor was he entirely innocent. Guilt trickled through his blood and formed a sour knot in his belly. He was no good for her. He shouldn't have sought her out. Shouldn't have touched her. Marie-Claude deserved someone fine and upstanding, a man with a reputation without stain.

So he had ended it.

And the easiest, most deadly way to do that?

He had lied. What was one more sin in the great scheme of things? Best if she thought the worst. She'd recover all the quicker for it. He had played the deceiver with impeccable dishonour and cruel attention to detail. He had lied and broken her heart, but at least it was a clean break that would heal under the onslaught of hatred that she now undeniably felt for him. And his penance? That he would live without her for the rest of his life. Except in his mind. In his heart. She swam in his blood like quicksilver.

Was that enough penance for any man?

But now he must take matters in hand. Marie-Claude must leave. Or be removed before the event. His mind ranged through the possibilities. Kidnapping her and bringing her back to the Manor to lock her up here until it was all over? Or even for ever. Ha! A beguiling picture. He could imagine her fury. And for a moment it brought him to a halt, an appreciative smile to his eyes. The lady would not willingly allow herself to be taken prisoner.

So not an immediately practical idea, and one sure to create a scandal of major proportions, damaging to the lady's reputation. His pacing continued. He would do it if he must, but first he'd attempt to persuade her to leave, even though it would ensure that he would never see her again.

He wouldn't think of that.

His own Madame Mermaid, the delight of his life, wouldn't listen to *his* words of persuasion. Nothing was more certain. So here was an obvious task for George Gadie.

Whistling to Bess, he set off for Old Wincomlee, his mind a little easier that, away from Old Wincomlee, at least Marie-Claude would be in no fear of her life. But his heart was sore.

Later in the afternoon of the same day, a heavy knock disturbed Marie-Claude as she sipped a cup of tea in the parlour.

She was lonely.

She was lonely for one man. And he was not for her.

Deliberately, to prove to herself that Zan meant

nothing to her, she tried to bring Marcus's face into the forefront of her mind, and was horrified when her memories were vague and indistinct, an impression of colouring and shape, but when she tried to bring features to mind, she failed. Instead she saw Zan Ellerdine all too clearly. It was as if he had entered the room and stood before her.

She closed her eyes to block him out.

At least the knock offered a distraction.

George Gadie entered, snatching off his cap. 'Afternoon, mistress.'

'George!' She smiled. A chance for some distraction. 'Can we go to Lewes one day? How long would it take if we left early?'

'Ah, well… That's what I wanted to see you about, mistress.'

Marie-Claude's eyes and ears sharpened. If she were not mistaken, the old sailor was not at ease. But still determined on the path he had set himself, he cleared his throat.

'I think you should leave, mistress.'

'Leave?' Not what she had expected.

'The village. The Pride. It's too dangerous. Too much going on…' The words fell rapidly from his mouth, as if they were lines he had learned by rote.

'Are we speaking of Captain D'Acre?' she asked bluntly.

'Aye, mistress.' He seemed relieved that she had introduced the smuggler's name. 'I heard about the… the unpleasantness the other day at the Boat. I think it's not safe for a young lady here on her own.'

'You think I should leave and go back to London?'

'Aye. Or the Earl's fancy estate, wherever. Safer for you.'

Marie-Claude considered. She could, of course. But not London. Too hot and airless. Venmore's town house would be closed up until the autumn season began. The Venmore? No, she did not want to be a burden on Luke and Harriette at The Venmore until she had to, encroaching on their privacy.

Her eyes rested on George's seamed face. He was watching her anxiously.

'You should have a care for your safety,' he muttered, his gaze falling before hers. 'Wouldn't want you to fall foul of the likes of the Fly-By-Nights.'

He was very anxious for her to go. But indeed, she was in no danger. Had she seen any sign of the Fly-By-Nights over the past week? No. Had she seen anything of Zan? No. Not even a distant view to set her heart beating. That was all over, of course. If she was careful and circumspect in her movements she could see no danger.

Captain D'Acre was hardly likely to take the Pride by storm, was he?

'Thank you for your concern for my welfare, George. But for now I'll stay at the Pride.'

'Aye, mistress.' He shuffled to the door with a sketchy bow. 'Thought you would.'

Zan lounged at his desk that same night, damning all foolish, intransigent, entirely desirable women, and scowled even harder. Bess, sitting expectantly at his crossed ankles, whined to catch his attention.

'Why could she not just do as she was told! I wager Gadie was too circumspect by half and let her ride roughshod over him. For so small and feminine a woman, she has a wickedly opinionated demeanour! And French to boot! I doubt she's ever followed an order in her life. I've a good mind to…' The prospect of kidnapping rose again and sent a spasm of heat, of brutal desire, straight to his loins. It was entirely too pleasing a prospect to have her under lock and key and under his dominion. Except that that was no way forwards for either of them. There *was* no way forwards. 'Perhaps not.'

The spaniel whined again and pawed at his leg.

Zan grinned and stroked her ears. 'It's not you, Bess, who drives a man to distraction. How difficult can a woman be? She worries me like the devil, but

I have to admire her wilfulness. Why was it necessary for me to play the villain in her eyes? And by God I did it well, did I not? I can play a role better than most men. I played that one to the hilt.' The grin died at the memory of some of the things he had said to her. 'So, she won't take advice. What shall we try? An anonymous letter from a well-wisher, with just enough of a threat to frighten her into retreat?'

He raised a glass of fine brandy to his lips, drank. Considered.

'It could work. I doubt it, but it might. At least it's worth a try.'

He opened a drawer, rummaged to find ink, quill and sheets of paper. Then set himself to write two letters.

One, brief and very much to the point, to Captain Rodmell in Lewes. Zan read it through and nodded, satisfied, then quickly sealed it and put it aside to be delivered.

He sat and thought about the second. Much more difficult, to achieve a nice blend of warning, compassion and threat. He set pen to paper.

To Marie-Claude Hallaston
Your presence at Lydyard's Pride has become dangerous to your safety. The Fly-By-Nights have become a force for evil in the village.

That should grab her attention, although he was sure Gadie had told her as much without effect. Zan passed the quill over his lips, imagining her as she read it. The line between her brows, the tightening of her lips. And he remembered the softness of them against his own, her sweet breath…

Damnation!

He wrote again.

Those who wish you well can no longer guarantee your safety. It would be better for you, and for all those connected with the Pride, if you left. And soon. You are already aware of the perils to your reputation and to your person. If you remain at the Pride, you open yourself to further humiliations and possibly physical harm.

The Fly-By-Nights have neither honour nor principle.

This warning is in your own interests. If you choose to ignore it, the price could be higher than you could imagine.

From A Friend

How melodramatic was that! And it contained a hint of cruelty that would worry her. Hopefully she would recall D'Acre's unpalatable overtures. A weight of guilt settled like a rock in his belly, but it couldn't be helped. It would be much worse to leave

her there to face the consequences of her stubborn-
ness. Far from convinced, he sealed the letter,
praying it might do the trick.

'Come!' He snapped his fingers and Bess instantly leapt to follow him as he went in search of
Tom. She would receive it within the hour. With any
luck she could be packed and off to London
tomorrow. And then his life could get back to
normal. Or whatever passed for normal.

He would never see her again.

'A letter, ma'am. Came this morning.'

Marie-Claude took the letter from the tarnished
silver salver offered by Wiggins at the breakfast
table. Opened it.

'Who delivered it?' She looked up sharply.

'No idea, ma'am. It was left on the hall table.'

He shuffled off, leaving her to read the single
sheet. It took a matter of seconds and Marie-
Claude did not appreciate what she read. The
second warning in two days. Someone wanted her
gone from the Pride. Placing it on the table in front
of her, she read it again. A cold hand squeezed her
heart.

A warning, true. But also an overt threat. If she
refused, what next?

Well, why not go? Common sense told her to do

exactly that. Why not just give in, pack her possessions and join Harriette?

'*Mon Dieu!* Why should I?' she demanded of the
lines of black script.

This all had to do with smuggling. She was sure
of it. And if it was, it had to do with D'Acre and his
crew. George Gadie had more or less admitted it—
although this letter was not the old smuggler's work.
She'd be surprised if he could do more than write
his name. Was this letter from Captain D'Acre, to
get her out of the Pride under the pretence of being
a concerned friend? Friend! She was no fool. Nor
was she a weak woman to simply run in the opposite
direction when danger threatened. If her suspicions
were right, D'Acre had his eye on the Pride as the
centre for his operations, just as it had been when
Harriette had sailed her cutter as Captain Harry.

Marie-Claude blinked as the truth struck home.

Of course that was it. Of course he would want it.
Anyone of sense would see where D'Acre's
presence in the village was leading. The Pride was
the perfect place, empty for much of the year apart
from Wiggins, who would stand firm against no
one! A Tower room and a Smugglers' Lamp to
signal smuggling vessels home to safety. Or lure the
helpless storm-tossed wrecks if that was the intent.
Spacious cellars to store the contraband. That's

what it was, and D'Acre would rather not have her in residence when he came to take it for his own.

Well, she would not go.

She sat and sipped her cooling tea thoughtfully. It needed careful thought. The Pride was in danger. It was Harriette's own much-loved inheritance. She had lost her own cutter, *Lydyard's Ghost*, to vengeful retaliation by the Preventives. How heart-breaking it would be if she lost the Pride to a gang of bloodthirsty cutthroat smugglers. Could they take and hold it? She was sure they could.

And how demeaning if she simply ran and left them free to take possession.

Furious at the underhand scheming, Marie-Claude hatched her own little plot.

She would make it known that she was leaving. Have the house shut up as if it were empty. It would not curtail her activities for more than a day or two. She had the strongest feeling that whatever was about to happen was imminent. She would make sure the doors and windows were locked and barred every night, with strict instructions to Mr Temple and Wiggins to open the door to no one.

She would inform Sir Wallace Lydyard of her fears. If he did nothing else, he would make sure that Captain Rodmell kept a close eye on the Pride.

Should she warn Luke and Harriette? No. No

reason to do that. After all, the threat might never materialise if it was only a figment of her overactive imagination. How ridiculous to bring them down to Old Wincomlee on some absurd enterprise.

When D'Acre came to do whatever nasty trick it was he planned, he would find the Pride locked against him and the Preventives armed and ready, lying in wait. She would sleep with a pistol underneath her pillow if she had to. And D'Acre would find himself behind bars in Lewes gaol.

She pushed the note away with a gesture of distaste. It was probably all a lie. How could she not be safe at the Pride? Yet she still decided to ask George Gadie when the next night for a run was planned.

One question remained in her mind for which she had no answer. What role did Zan have in all this? Was he part and parcel of it all? Was that why he had joined forces with the Fly-By-Nights? Even worse, although he had denied it and she had been inclined to believe him, was that the reason why he had sought her out in the first place? To seduce the occupant of the house would be a far easier means of getting control of the Pride than organising an attack. To step in the door, through the invitation of a silly, gullible, love-struck woman.

Marie-Claude thumped her fist on the polished surface of the table. Zan was involved. She would wager her silk stockings on it! He did not care for her, he never had, and she had been such easy prey for his scheming. But she was no longer a love-struck woman. Marie-Claude tore the warning letter into small pieces and cast them into the empty fire-grate. Whatever her weakness then, she was well over it.

She would do all in her power to foil Alexander Ellerdine—and Captain D'Acre.

Mr Temple and Wiggins were given to understand that the French lady would be leaving Lydyard's Pride in two days. It was not unexpected. Surely she had been lonely without a Hallaston family gathering to keep her company. She had enjoyed her respite from the heat and bustle of London, she explained, but was now to join the Earl and Countess at The Venmore. Few preparations would be necessary, merely to pack her clothing and order up the travelling coach. The house could be closed up and put under Holland covers.

Those who had any interest in such news in the village were soon brought up to date with the French lady's intentions. Zan heard as soon as any. *Thank God!*

Within two days she would be gone and he could

stop thinking about her. Could stop expecting to see her whenever he set foot outside Ellerdine Manor. Whatever the outcome of events at the Pride, it would have no bearing on her life. She would be safe and—eventually—content away from Old Wincomlee. Her memories of the summer would fade and die until she would think of it only as some dream, some summer madness that had afflicted her, but from which she had, thankfully, escaped.

It would fade and die for him too. Wouldn't it? Why did it seem that all the brightness in his life had drained away, no matter how sunny the days? Moonlit nights were an agony of loss. The sooner she was gone the better, and he could turn his mind to stop thinking about her.

But he could not. She persisted in his dreams and his waking hours. Until against all the promptings of common sense he knew that he must see her one more time, even if she damned him anew for his vicious treatment of her at the Silver Boat. He would tolerate that if he could have one more moment of her nearness, to carry the memory with him when she was gone.

Fool! he admonished. Far better to remember her when fate smiled and love seemed a possibility. That's what a man of good sense would do, and steer clear of her.

* * *

When Tom had brought the information, courtesy of George Gadie, that the French lady planned on her final morning to ride to make her farewells to Lady Augusta Lydyard at Whitescar Hall, Zan had changed his mind and was lying in wait on his mare on the cliff top to waylay her on her return.

It was like the inundation of the sea at high tide. She filled every part of him, every sense, the minute he saw her cantering along the cliff top towards him, making the most of the short sward, enjoying the exhilaration of the wind and the view of the sea. He knew when she became aware of him, when she lifted her head and looked towards him. Momentarily he saw her make a check on the reins, but he had no fears that she would retreat. He watched, waited, as she applied her heels and continued on her chosen path, only pulling her mount to a standstill when he manoeuvred his mare so that she had no choice but to speak with him.

She raised her chin in defiance. Her eyes were brilliant, rivalling the sunlit waves, and they met his with no embarrassment over their last meeting.

How could he not admire her?

Only the disdain in the curl of her lips wounded his heart as if she wielded George Gadie's ancient cutlass. He steeled himself to weather the storm of her hatred and contempt.

'You are in my way,' she stated with a toss of her head.

'But not for much longer, I understand.'

'News travels fast. I'm sure you'll not be sorry.' The edge to her voice twisted the blade.

'I think it's a sensible decision.' All he could think to say.

He hadn't realised she could ride so well. But then, why should he? Truth to tell, he barely knew her. Had no knowledge of her likes and dislikes, her skills and accomplishments. Even his knowledge of her past was sketchy. How could a woman he had known little more than four weeks have come to mean more to him than anything else? But then he had been lost after that first hour in her company, had he not? And did he not know enough? That she had untold energy. That she was a woman of courage and independence. That she had a predilection for blue gowns and bonnets trimmed with flowers and ribbons. And foolish fripperies such as parasols. That her lips were soft and her arms all-encompassing, her body a delight that he longed to sink into until the day he died. But he knew that she had no tolerance for a man without honour who could betray her and hurt her with lies and deceit.

Today she wore a riding habit in deep green, not an outfit he had seen before. The jacket fit her slight figure snugly, the skirt sweeping to the toes of her polished boots. The jaunty hat anchored to her fair curls was decorated with a feather that curled and teased her cheek with every movement. Colour had been whipped into her cheeks—if he leaned just a little he would be able to touch it with his fingertips.

How much he loved her. More than every breath he took.

'When do you leave?' he asked more brusquely than he had intended.

'That's not your concern, sir. But tomorrow I shall be gone.'

He bowed his head in acknowledgement, no more to say. Since when had he become so tongue-tied, so lacking in social graces? But then, this was no social occasion.

'I suppose I should thank you for rescuing me for a second time,' she said, surprising him.

'Thank me? I deserve no thanks from you, rather that you should damn me for my presumption. My methods were despicable.'

The abrupt reply startled Marie-Claude. How dark and glowering he was. Intense and brooding. Her heart shivered. How difficult it was to keep her composure when her whole body seemed to tremble. But she would do it, she would not show him how much he mattered to her in spite of everything.

'I would rather your despicable methods than

D'Acre's assault,' she replied coldly. 'And as I recall, he threatened to throw me in the way of his men after he'd had his pleasure. You at least spared me that even if I had to suffer your embrace. I suppose I should be grateful—' that same disdain coated her words, dripped like venom '—but I still find your methods hard to forgive.'

'Then you must add it to the rest of my sins.'

She saw his hand tighten white-fingered on the reins, causing the mare to sidestep uneasily. She thought he was going to say more, but his mouth closed in an uncompromising line. Suddenly she remembered how he had kissed her in the stables and refused to let her go. And here he was barring her way again.

'I wish to go on,' she announced. 'If you would let me pass…'

Immediately with a muffled oath he dragged the mare aside and Marie-Claude shook up her reins.

But Zan stopped her, a hand to her wrist, forced into an apology he'd not intended to make.

'Wait, Marie-Claude. I've nothing to say that you'd listen to—but I regret any distress you've suffered.'

'So do I. I made a mistake. I did not know you— that's my only excuse.'

'And now you do know me.' If his hand did not hold her still, his eyes did.

'It was a lesson,' she snapped, forcing herself to look away, 'in not giving my trust where it is not warranted.'

She was so close. It took no effort for him to bend his head and to take a final kiss. Nor did she prevent him, but sat passively as his mouth took. Soft, gentle, tender. Heartbreaking. Encompassing all that he felt for her, telling of passion promised and destroyed. Hopes of love obliterated. This was truly the end, Zan acknowledged, and the beginning of an endless lifetime of sadness and loss for him.

'Farewell, Marie-Claude,' he whispered against her lips.

Stifling a sob, Marie-Claude placed her hand on his chest to push him away, and Zan, with no more words, drew back and bowed his head.

'Goodbye, Zan. You promised me so much. I thought you had turned my life to gold. Instead it was all dross.'

He sat and watched as she cantered along the headland and disappeared behind the distant stand of trees that obscured the Pride itself. It was as if she had taken his heart with her. An empty space opened in his chest, ached. She was gone. But at least she would be safe.

Marie-Claude wept as she allowed her horse to

find its own way home, tears blinding her. Now she must set herself, as George Gadie would have said, to batten down the hatches and repel all boarders.

Chapter Eleven

Zan let himself into the Pride through the kitchen door. It had been easy enough to charm a key from Jenny, one of the village girls who worked at the house. It was nearing midnight, a dark night with a blanket of cloud and no hint of the sliver of moon. The maids were long gone home to the village. Temple was in his rooms—Venmore's installation of the efficient manager had not aided his plan, but there were ways around it. Jenny had been very useful on the predictable habits of Venmore's employee. Wiggins, as expected, sat alone at the kitchen range, dozing over his habitual bottle of port.

'Wiggins!' Zan roused him from his stupor, a hand on his shoulder.

He blinked owlishly. 'Mr Ellerdine…'

'Evening, Wiggins.' He kept his voice low, even

if there was no need. It seemed the right thing to do on the occasion.'

'What did you want, sir?'

'Don't disturb yourself. I need the keys to the rooms in the house.'

Wiggins blinked again, rubbed his eyes, but made no demur, merely lurched to his feet to rummage in the drawer of the kitchen table. 'Are you wanting the keys for the cellars too, sir?'

'Yes.'

'I'm not sure about this…' A puzzled frown worked its way through the fumes of alcohol.

'Don't disturb yourself. Go to bed. Whatever you hear, keep to your room. As in the old days with Captain Harry. Understand?'

Wiggins thought about it for a long time, until Zan's patience threatened to snap. 'Yes, sir,' he muttered eventually and shuffled off with the port and a candle. Zan exhaled slowly and tossed the keys in his hand. So far, so good. If the rest of it ran according to plan… He fastened a black mask over his face and pulled down his hat low on his brow. How melodramatic.He grinned sardonically beneath the black cloth, but better not to be recognised if Venmore's man was on the prowl.

First he opened up the door that led down to the cellar. Time enough later to reveal the well-camouflaged double cellar when the contraband arrived. Then, carrying a branch of candles, he walked from the kitchen into the entrance hall where he unlocked the front door. At some point in the proceedings that might be necessary, either as access or escape.

Back to the kitchen, he collected some necessary items. Time was moving on. He looked at his watch. Not long now. The cutters should be here within the hour—sooner if the operation on the French side had been slick and well managed. Time to signal them home to a welcoming bay, a safe landing and a well-organised dispersal of the contraband. The perfect end to a well-planned venture. D'Acre would already be anticipating the value of the silk and tea in gold coin weighing down his pockets, filling the coffers in his lair in Rottingdean.

He'd actually been talking of moving into the Pride. Of taking personal possession of the house.

By God, he wouldn't! Zan swore. Over his dead body! There'd be no scion of the ignoble D'Acres living in Lydyard's Pride. Zan's mouth twisted in dark humour, diverted, as he climbed the stairs to the Tower room, only to pull his thoughts back. For now he must do everything in his power to ensure a smooth outcome. Nothing must go wrong at this final hour after all the months of planning. The silence of an all-but-empty house wrapped around him. He'd always had a soft spot for it and regretted its passing to Harriette in his mother's will. Not the time to be thinking of that now. It was not his and would never be his. Making a short diversion along one of the landings, he took the precaution of locking the outer door to Temple's rooms. The last thing he needed was Venmore's man coming out to investigate, or not until it was all over.

At least there was no Marie-Claude to worry about.

For a moment outside her door he closed his eyes and breathed deep.

It was better this way.

Zan climbed, rapidly now, to the Tower room. The turn of the stair, the slide of the banister under his hand were intensely familiar. How long since he had done this? Not for five years, since Captain Harry's last run and his own final fall from grace. He grimaced at the memory of it as he unlocked the door. Unused and long shut up, it had the musty smell of mildew and stale air. For all the improvements and refurbishment at the Pride, they had not touched this room. Now if he had his way he would furnish it as a place to sit to watch the sea and the clouds, the ever-changing picture of the coast with the ships, the fishing vessels, the sea-birds.

The use of this room would never be his choice to make.

Zan rolled his shoulders. Time to get busy. He'd come prepared, but there was the old oil lamp still sitting on the floor in the corner. The scarred table still positioned in the widow embrasure. Zan set himself to refill the lamp with oil and remove the shutters from the windows.

This, he thought as he struggled to unfasten and fold back the warped wood, would be the final time he signalled from this room. The last time he signalled to a cutter waiting in the bay. A fitting swansong for him. D'Acre might not be planning this operation as his final flourish, but, by God, Zan was! His smuggling days were over. Under D'Acre's expansive grip, they had suddenly become distasteful.

And then what? He had no very clear idea.

He lifted the lamp on to the table. Checked the wick, trimmed it and lit it from the candles. The light grew until the little room was filled with it, shining out, its beams cutting through the darkness across the sea to welcome the cutters home.

So it was done. Now he must retrace his steps to the kitchen and wait for D'Acre to make contact. He took a pistol from his coat pocket.

If she were one of the Brotherhood of Free Traders, with a run to plan and carry out, Marie-

Claude decided that this would be the night. The tides were right. There was a dark sky, with a fitful moon. What better night?

Marie-Claude sat at her window, seeing only her reflection in the glass. How alone she looked, the light from the single candle highlighting her hair, darkening her eyes with shadows, touching the lace at her neck with a soft glimmer. A creak of settling boards somewhere in the house. The scrabble of a mouse behind the old wainscoting. Marie-Claude stiffened, senses stretched to catch every noise, but she knew all was locked and barred at her express orders. Neither Mr Temple nor Wiggins would let D'Acre and his rabble in. If D'Acre chose to make use of the stables, she could not stop him, but he would not set foot in the house. She was perfectly safe.

Her breathing grew easier again.

Footsteps! She stiffened, breath held. Relaxed with a little laugh. Wiggins, of course, shuffling to his bed. Earlier than usual. She heard a distinct stagger in his step, followed by a muttered curse. It crossed her mind that perhaps she should restrict the bottles of port he managed to consume in one day.

Silence again.

Was she being ridiculous, staying on here? She decided she was. Well, she would give it a few more days and then leave the Pride to its fate.

Marie-Claude considered going to bed.

A footstep. Soft. Not Wiggins. Too sure. Too young. Moving swiftly, silently, Marie-Claude went to stand at her door and listened, head bent. Mr Temple, perhaps? She did not think so. The creak of old timber under booted feet. There was no hesitation. The intruder was not searching for anything. The steps came to a halt outside her door and she held her breath. He must be only three feet away. She closed her eyes. Then to her relief they moved on, fading. More soft creaks and she immediately knew where—on the stairs to the Tower room.

Without hesitation, Marie-Claude kicked off her shoes, snatched up a candlestick and opened her door. She could see the glow of the intruder's candle from the turn in the stair. Heart beating in her throat so that she could barely swallow, she followed. It might be far more sensible to lock herself into her room, but she would not allow this…this *miscreant*—one of D'Acre's men for sure, but how had he got in?—to make use of Hallaston property! He had no right to be here and since she had the advantage of surprise she would put a stop to his plans.

By the time she reached the Tower room, the glow made it obvious that the old oil lamp was lit, signalling to whatever was waiting out in the bay. And there was her intruder, about to come out of the room on to the shadow-wrapped landing. His clothing was dark, hair covered by an old-fashioned tricorne, his face in shadow. Not that she would recognise him—as he half-turned she saw that a black mask covered his features, showing only the glitter of eyes. In one hand he held a candle, in the other a pistol.

Smuggler! Definitely up to no good.

She did not wait or think longer. As he turned to assess the state of his handiwork in the room for a final time, Marie-Claude stepped forwards through the doorway, raised her candlestick in both hands and brought it down on the man's head. With a groan he dropped candle and pistol and fell in a crumpled heap at her feet.

Marie-Claude stared in startled amazement at how effective she had been, shocked at what she had done. No time now for second thoughts—not that she had any. He was an intruder and deserved everything he got at her hands. What to do now? A smuggler possibly dead at her feet, the Smugglers' Lamp still shining to bring D'Acre's contraband into the bay.

She acted quickly. First she relit her own candle. Then, stepping over the inert body, she blew out the lamp. There'd be no illegal signalling from this room tonight. D'Acre would get no help from the Pride. She considered closing the shutters, but that could wait. Instead she grasped the smuggler's shoulders and began to pull him fully over the threshold into the room. It was hard work, but she tugged and pulled enough to get him clear of the door so that she might lock him in and send for the Preventives.

She studied him where he lay face down. One of D'Acre's crew, for sure, but not D'Acre himself. Too tall, too well muscled. Rackham, perhaps? Proud of her initiative in bringing him down, whoever he might be, she crouched and, with a hand to his shoulder, pulled him over on to his back. Stripped away the hat. And her heart stuttered as the familiar fall of dark hair brushed over her fingers. And then with a hand that trembled as her suspicion became irrefutable, she untied and removed the mask.

Marie-Claude sat back on her heels. *'Mon Dieu!'* Well, it should not have surprised her, should it?

Alexander Ellerdine, breaking in, invading her home and lighting the Smugglers' Lamp.

Had she killed him?

Sensations, feelings, raced through her; her thoughts whirled into a spiral of doubts. She placed her palm against his chest, relieved at the solid beat of his heart. Turning his head, touching his hair, she discovered that she had hit him hard enough to break the skin and draw blood. Hardly surprising, then, that his face was so pale. She touched his cheek with her fingertips in momentary remorse. But regret and relief quickly fled as any fleeting hopes that she had misjudged him were snuffed out as effectively as she had doused the light from the lamp.

Kneeling beside him, Marie-Claude forced herself to accept the truth. Zan Ellerdine was up to his neck in this. Using the Pride, the Smugglers' Lamp, using D'Acre's power for his own ends. This part of the plan must have been his—to get access to the house. Only he would have known about the double cellars. Her heart sank even lower as she remembered. He had denied that he had set himself to charm and seduce her to get entry to the house. Obviously that had all been lies too.

But he'd refused to come to the Pride, a faint voice of reason insisted in making itself heard.

True. She stamped down hard on the little voice, but only to lull her into a false sense of security. Whatever route his devious, devil-driven plotting was meant to take, he was here now. When his scheme had foundered, when she had turned her back on him and she had proved to be worthless to him, he had found another even simpler means. Bribing Wiggins to open the door.

Marie-Claude huffed out a little breath of disgust. Zan deserved no sympathy from her. As unyielding and as cold as stone, she turned his face so that she could see it clearly. The face of a rogue for all the unquestionable glamour. She need feel no guilt over her future actions, not even for the blow on the head. She would hand him over to the Preventives with pleasure and hoped he would rot in gaol. He had betrayed her. His whole life was nothing but charade and deceit. It was impossible to deny that she had loved this man, as it was impossible for her not to touch the hand that lay inert, fingers lightly curled on the dusty boards of the floor. He had such beautiful hands. Clever, skilful, wakening her to such pleasure.

Marie-Claude snatched her hand back as if the contact burned. Beautiful and skilful they might be, but they had blood on them for sure. How was it possible that so much depravity and evil existed behind those finely drawn features?

This is no good. Sitting and wishing is not going to change the man he has become.

Marie-Claude pushed herself to her feet and stalked out, having the presence of mind to lock the door behind her.

Some little time later Marie-Claude was back, carrying a large jug. She frowned. He was exactly where she had left him. She must have hit him harder than she had thought—but she would have no compassion. Or not very much. Marie-Claude relocked the door behind her, then poured half the jug of water over Zan's face.

Zan groaned and turned his head. Winced at the obvious pain. 'By God…!'

Marie-Claude emptied the rest of the water in sharp pleasure as he flinched, muttering another oath. He deserved it. He deserved all the pain and indignity she could heap on him.

Zan gasped at the second deluge and opened his eyes. She stood at his feet and watched as consciousness returned, as furious recognition dawned—of her and of his surroundings, his predicament—to be replaced by resignation. And then, she thought, as his mind began to work again, by a wave of sheer horror.

Marie-Claude offered no explanation. Let him make the first move. Let him try to make his excuses as to why he might be innocent. She would not believe a word of it.

Zan struggled up on to his elbows, and frowned at her.

'Madame Mermaid…!' He flinched, eyes closed for a moment, as if even the effort of speech was painful. 'I thought you'd gone from here.'

'I know you did.' She gave him a brilliant smile. 'But I hadn't. And now you're my prisoner.'

* * *

Zan raised himself up on to one elbow, cautiously pressing his fingers against the back of his head where the pain was centred, spreading out in dark waves enough to rob him of any sensible thought. He winced, closing his eyes again. Even the candle-light made his head throb. Then he struggled to focus on his fingers that were smeared with blood. What in God's name…!

Opening his eyes again, he took in the pair of neat shoes and the frilled edging of a blue silk skirt. He lifted his gaze with difficulty to the face of the woman who stood over him.

She was holding his pistol. And it was pointed at the centre of his chest. He found a need to pray that she would keep calm, but he had little hope of it. Her lovely face was alight with fury, her eyes flashed fire. Her fingers around the pistol were white with tension. She looked as if she would like nothing better than to put a bullet through him.

'You hit me!' he said. And how ridiculous that sounded. How obvious. It was the one astonished thought that came into his head. As well as reluctant admiration that she could display such presence of mind when faced with an intruder who had broken into her home and might not wish her well.

'Yes, I did.' Despite the tension in the hand that

held the pistol, her voice was remarkably calm, poised. 'You broke into my house.'

'I did not break in. I used a key.' He took a breath against the pain, wondering at the idiocy of that statement.

'So that makes it any better? Wiggins, I suppose, bribed by a bottle!' Her voice changed, now raw with contempt; she held his gaze in a challenge. 'You frightened me. And you were masked—how was I to know it was you? Besides, you are as much a criminal as the rest of them and deserve no better treatment. I would do it again without a second thought.'

Yes. She would. He had no doubt about it. Carefully he sat up, freezing for a little on an intake of breath as nausea struck. When it ebbed, all he was conscious of was the insistent throb in his head that seemed capable of breaking his skull.

Zan tried to force his mind into action, away from the problem of Marie-Claude looming over him with a lethal weapon. He must pull himself together. Time was passing and here was an unlooked-for complication. He marshalled his wits as much as he was able. Marie-Claude was still here and the con- clusion of the run was imminent. If nothing else he must get her out to safety, away from the Fly-By- Nights. As for his own future at their hands—he would face that as and when. If there was ever a time

for acting out a charade, this was it. He only hoped
his abused wits were up to it…

'Don't move. If you do, I'll shoot you.'

Which forced him to give his wayward attention
back to her, ridiculously struck by her beauty, her
fragility. Except that she was holding a pistol to his
head! There she stood, like an avenging angel in ce-
lestial blue silk, daring him to make a move.

Zan sat up, rubbed his hands over his face as if he
might bring some clarity of thought. And then it
struck him. He lifted his head, turning sharply, then
wishing he hadn't, and saw his worst fears confirmed.

'The lamp…it's not lit.'

'I know. I put it out.'

'By God!' He couldn't think of what the repercus-
sions of that single fact might be. The Smugglers'
Lamp plunged into darkness, leaving D'Acre's contraband to find its own way into the bay, unsure of
its route or its welcome. What would D'Acre think?
What would D'Acre do? If the viciously single-
minded Captain decided on a quick retribution
against anyone within his reach who might have
hindered his plans, there was no way Zan could
prevent it. He would be the first object of D'Acre's
fury, since the responsibility for lighting the lamp
had been his, but he might not be the only target for
D'Acre's notoriously unpredictable ire…

He must get Marie-Claude out of here.

'I'll not have you signalling from this room. Not for D'Acre. Not for anyone,' she informed him conversationally, breaking into his uneasy thoughts.

'You don't know what you've done,' he snapped back.

'Oh, I do. I've stopped your little venture, Mr Ellerdine. If the smugglers try to bring the contraband here, they'll not succeed. I should tell you I've locked and barred the kitchen door. I suppose that's how you got in. And I've relocked the front door—which I found was inexplicably *unlocked*. There'll be no access for D'Acre to make use of the Pride's cellars tonight. And I should tell you—' she raised the pistol threateningly '—I'm quite prepared to shoot the first man who tries to get through the door.'

Worse and worse. Zan cast about for a new direction. The whole intricately constructed plan had been torn to shreds by this woman's determination to thwart D'Acre. Hell and damnation. At last he pushed himself upright to his feet, even though the result was a shaming experience. He almost staggered. Forced to stand, head bent, arms braced on the back of the chair as his surroundings heaved, he could do nothing but allow the waves of darkness to flood through him, until his surroundings settled back on a stable level. Only then did he let himself take a deep breath, snatching at the train of thought that had scattered once more. He dragged it back and forced himself to concentrate.

Marie-Claude was in danger. They were both in danger. For him it could mean death at the hands of D'Acre's bullies. For Marie-Claude... His jaw clenched as he buried the thought deep. If he allowed himself to consider how she might be used by a gang of smugglers, how she might be made to suffer, they would both be lost. Carefully he stood to his full height, relieved when the floor level remained steady beneath his feet even though the beat of pain in his head was almost unbearable.

'How long was I out?' he asked.

'Why? Of what importance is that?'

'It just is. Trust me, Marie. How long?'

'Fifteen minutes, I suppose.'

'Too long... I have to get you out of here. Now.'

'I'm not leaving. And neither are you. I've locked the door.'

'Ha!' It was a harsh sound in the room, a laugh without humour despite his appreciation of the situation. 'What a joy you are to me, Marie-Claude. I must remember to give you a few lessons for the future. If you're to tangle with smugglers, it's not sensible to lock yourself in the room with the prisoner!'

Colour rose in her cheeks as she realised what she'd done.

'I…'

'No, you didn't think, did you? Now give me the key.'

'I will not. I won't let you help D'Acre.'

Zan advanced, keeping a wary eye on the pistol. He didn't think she would shoot him, but in a moment of panic—anything was possible. Nor did she look amenable to persuasion.

'Give me the pistol.' He gritted his teeth. 'I don't want to be shot by D'Acre, but by God I don't want to end my life at your pretty hands.'

He saw the moment his careless words made an impression.

'Why would D'Acre shoot you?'

'I should have lit the lamp.' He tried a shrug. 'The Captain doesn't like to be disobeyed.'

'Don't tell me you're not hand in glove with him!' she sneered.

'I won't tell you any such thing.' Another step. 'Now hand over the key.'

'No!' She retreated one step.

'Marie-Claude! In God's name—just do as I ask.' He stepped forwards again.

'I don't trust you.' Her back was against the door, the pistol clutched hard.

'You've no choice.' Frustration, impatience, began to war with a need not to frighten her any further—although perhaps a good dose of fear might have the desired effect, as long as she did not put a bullet through him first. He had to try it. He put a threat into his voice. 'Enough to say, madam, it's either me or the Fly-By-Nights. Who do you prefer to negotiate with?' He was so close to her that he could see the fear creep into her eyes and the leap of a pulse at the base of her throat, and prayed for a swift resolution. He kept up the pressure. 'We can't stay locked in here together. D'Acre will be on your doorstep any time soon to discover why the lamp is out. And if he finds that *you* are the culprit…' He let it hang in the air between them.

'And you would tell him that, of course,' she whispered. 'You would betray me to him!'

'Undoubtedly! You put out the lamp. Now unless you want me to strip that very pretty dress from you to find the key…' He saw her eyes widen in shock and pressed on. 'I've no time for niceties. Thanks to you my head aches far too much for me to be sensitive. So give me the key before I lose my patience.'

'You have no patience to lose!'

Zan held out his hand. 'And unless you really intend to pull that trigger—hand over the pistol.' On the edge of his consciousness, a faint sound registered.

He lifted his head, ears pricked—but nothing more. He breathed again. 'Wiggins won't come to your rescue. And I took the precaution of locking Venmore's man into his rooms. As I said, you really have no choice. Unless you'd really rather take your chances with D'Acre or Rackham?' He raised a brow.

'I...'

Zan waited no longer as her eyes darkened with fear of the fate that might await her. A sudden swoop. A hand around her wrist, pulling her towards him. He'd have to risk the pistol to force her to see sense.

'What's it to be, Marie-Claude?' he whispered against her mouth, snatching a hard, fast kiss. Again a faint noise, a scrape, perhaps the closing of a door, from somewhere distant in the house. He had not been mistaken. Zan tightened his grip in the urgency of it, until he felt her wince.

Whatever she read in his face had the desired effect. Marie-Claude handed over the pistol with distinct lack of grace.

'Take it! I think I'm too much of a coward to use it. Even against someone I detest.'

If his head did not ache so, if ruin did not stare him in the face, he would have laughed. As it was the bitterness twisted in his gut. He slid the weapon into his pocket. Success, but he'd only won half the battle.

'And now the key.'

He pinioned her against the wall with the weight of his body, one hand on either side so that she could not move. When she flinched from him, it twisted the knife even more. Couldn't be helped, he thought, steeling himself. He took her chin in his hand and forced her to look at him.

'Marie-Claude… We've no time for this.' He allowed the back of his fingers to slide down her throat to the lace edging of her gown. An unpleasantly overt threat that impugned his honour.

'Very well!' she hissed at him with true venom. 'I'll give it to you! Give me some space.'

He sighed with relief. And when he eased his body back, she stooped and took the key from inside her shoe.

'Ingenious! I must remember that! Now, listen to me. You carry the candle and no tricks. If you strike me again, you'll be at D'Acre's mercy. And he has far less than I might be willing to show you. We're going to go downstairs and, if I can, I'll find a horse for you in the stables. Otherwise you'll take my mare. You'll ride and join Meggie or Mistress Gadie. I'll tell you the route to take through the village. If it's too late for that…'

If it was too late, he had no idea.

Zan unlocked the Tower room door, stepped out on to the landing, pulling Marie-Claude with him.

* * *

They had expected to be engulfed by the darkness of the staircase. Instead the landing outside the Tower room was already illuminated by a sailor's unshuttered lamp.

'Good evening, Mr Ellerdine. And the Hallaston lady.' A feral grin in a dark, seamed face half-hidden by a grizzled red beard. 'Now I wouldn't have expected to see you two here together, but this, I think, is becoming a night of unexpected— and unsettling—surprises.'

The grating accents of Captain D'Acre. Full of disbelief. Full of suspicion. Not at all friendly, despite his choice of greeting. Would she wish to be at the mercy of either of them? Zan or D'Acre? Marie-Claude instinctively moved one step closer to Zan.

He won't save you! she admonished. *He'll put the blame for the Smugglers' Lamp on you and throw you to the dogs, to save his own worthless skin.* But still she felt an inexplicable comfort from his solid proximity. Still firm and warm around her wrist, his hand astonishingly gave her some comfort.

'D'Acre.' Zan inclined his head, as if they were in an elegant London withdrawing room. 'I did not expect you here yet.'

'No? Perhaps your attentions were fixed elsewhere.' An unpleasant leer. 'I can understand that. A tasty handful, no doubt.' The tone changed. Became biting. As D'Acre leaned towards Zan, Marie-Claude could see his hand clench into a fist. 'But not on my time. Not on one of my runs! You'll keep your mind on the job, Ellerdine.'

'Nothing has been overlooked, D'Acre,' Zan replied, magnificently unruffled. But Marie-Claude was aware of the tension in the fingers that held her still against his side. The hot grip did not mirror the confident delivery. 'To my knowledge everything's running smoothly. A fine night for a landing. I've arranged enough men and ponies to carry the goods from two vessels up the cliff path. All can safely be stowed in the double cellar until such time as you want to move such a large consignment further on. That's what you wanted. That's what I've provided for you.' Zan laughed softly. 'I see no problems. And what if I found time to snatch a few delightful minutes with the lady of the house? Your operation won't suffer for it.'

'Hmm!' There was no answering laugh. Rather a scowl. 'Then explain to me why the lamp's not lit, Ellerdine. I had to bring the cutters into the bay by fire-beacon on the cliff, and a poor show we made of it, given the time at our disposal when we saw there was no lamp in the Tower. Our crews don't know this coast as well as Rottingdean. They could've been aground on the headland.'

'Unlikely, if the captains are worth their pay. The visibility's good enough, even without a moon.' Zan clapped a friendly blow to D'Acre's shoulder. 'There was no danger, Captain, admit it, merely a minor inconvenience. As for the lamp here…' Zan gestured back into the room '…a problem lighting it after so many months—years, in fact—of disuse. A faulty wick. I admit I should have taken more care.' A lazy shrug. 'But the cutters are safe, I presume.' Zan turned as if he would usher D'Acre back down the staircase and Marie-Claude found herself shielded from D'Acre's direct gaze. A subtle little move on Zan's part, but she read it clearly despite the sudden confusion of her thoughts. He had protected her. He had shielded her from blame.

'Yes, they're safe,' D'Acre admitted. 'No thanks to you, I might say.' The smuggler was not persuaded to abandon his aggressive stance. 'Perhaps you'll explain the other *minor* inconvenience, as you put it, with the same ease. All the doors to this place were locked. Now why would that be?'

'I've no idea. I opened them—front and back—when I arrived.' Assured, unperturbed. An easy smile. Marie-Claude's throat was so dry she could barely swallow. No one would have guessed that

Zan, not half an hour before, had been unconscious with a blow to the head. The fluent explanation was perfectly reasonable. 'I came in by the kitchen door, then opened the front. I think Wiggins is your culprit here. He's old and forgetful. I expect he relocked them, as he has done every night for the past twenty years. How did you get in?'

'I broke a window,' D'Acre snarled, in no way mollified.

'You're an enterprising man, Captain,' Zan acknowledged cheerfully. 'I suppose I have to admit to my mistake. I should have kept an eye on Wiggins.'

'It's someone's mistake!' D'Acre's narrowed eyes gleamed. The suspicion was still there, as strong as ever. 'I don't like it. Something's not right. I haven't been a smuggler for nigh on forty years without having a nose for danger. And for betrayal. Double dealing, I'd call it. I can *smell* danger—like sulphur in the air.' He cocked his head. 'I can smell it now.'

The hand around Marie-Claude's wrist closed like a vice. She could feel the sinews tense in Zan's arm, and knew that the outcome here was very much in doubt. He was trying to deflect the blame from her, taking it on his own shoulders, playing the negligence card for all it was worth. But Zan was neither hapless nor irresponsible and D'Acre must have known that before agreeing to take him into the Fly-By-Nights.

Bewildered, she realised that he was not careless of her safety as she had thought, but was prepared to put himself in danger to shield her from D'Acre's wrath. She did not understand why he would do it. Then she felt an increased tension in him as if he had come to a crossroads in his own performance.

'Are you accusing me of double dealing, D'Acre?' No longer the easygoing acceptance of his mistakes. Zan's hackles had risen.

'Not yet, Ellerdine. Not yet.'

'I don't appreciate being accused of disloyalty,' Zan snarled.

'And I don't accuse you.' D'Acre continued to glare. 'But just so's you understand me, boy—if anything else goes wrong, I might consider the direction of your loyalties.'

'No danger of that.' At last Marie-Claude felt Zan's grip soften. 'Everything's in place.'

'You're more confident than I'm prepared to be,' D'Acre growled. 'Next thing we know there'll be Preventives on the cliff top—and then where will we be? I don't even know that this miraculous double cellar exists. Any more—mishaps—and I'll be looking to you for answers, Ellerdine. Now enough of this. The cutters'll be ashore by now.' He took on long last look between Marie-Claude and Zan, then nodded briefly. 'Come with me, Mr Ellerdine, if it's not too much trouble. I need you to unlock the doors and open up the cellar. I presume you have the keys?' A thick layer of cynicism. 'We don't want to waste time searching for them, do we?'

'I have them.'

'Then let's move it, man. I'd like you with me, at my side for the rest of this venture, if you take my meaning.'

As she felt a reaction in his body, Marie-Claude thought for a moment that Zan might have answered sharply. 'We should leave the woman here,' was all he said. 'She'll be in the way otherwise. I'll lock her in until we've finished.'

D'Acre hesitated, but not for long, his mind now on his profits of the night. When he grunted his assent, Zan turned to her at last, sliding his hands down her arms as if in memory of what had just passed between them in the Tower room, even though his expression was desperately stern, at odds with his words. 'Lovely mermaid. A shame we were interrupted. I'll come back when the shipment's safe stowed.' A sharp grin, with an edge to it. A quick kiss. 'You'll be safe here. Wait for me. We'll take up where we left off. How fortunate the room has a bed. Narrow and uncomfortable, but enough for me to take my pleasure…'

'Come on, man. She'll not run away. I might come

back for her later myself,' D'Acre added with a laugh as he set off down the stairs. 'If Ellerdine doesn't satisfy you, madam, I'll make compensation.' A coarse guffaw. 'Just one more gain from this night's operations.'

And Marie-Claude found herself pushed back into the room and the door locked against her. So she was alone, not knowing what would happen next. Nothing was as it seemed. For in her hand, shielded by the fall of her skirts, was Zan's pistol, passed to her under cover of his kiss.

Chapter Twelve

The footsteps died away. Marie-Claude looked around almost in a daze, finding herself standing in the centre of an empty room, the door locked at her back, preventing any escape, a candle in one hand and pistol in the other, with no clear idea of what she should do next. Not that there was anything she could do. For an age it seemed that she remained rooted to that same spot, listening for any creak or groan in the old house. Voices. Hoofbeats. Anything but this dreadful intimidating silence.

Any ability to make a decision had been shattered by the events of the past hour.

What is Zan doing now? Is he safe?

D'Acre had been so threatening, so suspicious—and rightly so. Marie-Claude had done her best to stop the use of the Pride, and Zan had deliberately deflected the blame. But D'Acre was still wary, and she knew deep within her heart that Zan's life was on the line. As he had said, D'Acre would not hesitate to remove those who worked against him.

Placing the candlestick on the nightstand as she sat on the edge of the bed, the pistol beside her, her heart raced, her skin felt icy cold, clammy to her own touch. The image of Zan at D'Acre's mercy simply refused to be buried. She forced herself to take a deep breath and apply cold logic to what she knew and what she could guess.

What was happening? Her first reaction was that she had been caught up in the smugglers' attempt to take possession of the Pride and make use of the cellars. Zan had obviously planned the run and the hiding of the contraband, and D'Acre and his gang were in the process of carrying it out. By remaining at the Pride against all advice and warnings, she had fallen into their hands, nothing short of a prisoner.

You are in danger! And it's your own fault! Why did you not leave when you could?

'Because I'm stubborn and wilful,' she announced to the empty room, unnerved when her voice caught on the words. 'I can't blame anyone but myself. And now I've put Zan in danger as well, by my intransigence.'

She studied her fingers, gripped tight, white-knuckled on her lap. She need have no fear for Alexander Ellerdine. He was just as unprincipled as the lot of them and would soon slither back into D'Acre's good books.

Then if that was so, why had he stood for her, allowing D'Acre to surmise that Zan had put the gang at risk by his own lack of attention?

Would D'Acre take his revenge for that?

She squeezed her hands together. And why did it matter to her anyway?

Because no matter what he had done, she loved him. Somewhere deep within her she believed he could not be as black as he was painted. He had tried to protect her. He had given her his pistol.

And there was the crux of it. He had given her the opportunity to protect herself. Or—fierce hands gripped her heart—if the worst came to the worst, she could take her own life. Would she do that? Could she bear to be thrown to D'Acre's men for their gratification? A fate worse than death. But then, if she pre-empted the smugglers in the only way possible, Raoul would be left alone. She could not do that either.

Marie-Claude stared at the weapon as if it might give her advice.

When Zan had slid the pistol from his pocket into her hand, had that been some kind of sign, a slide of his fingers against her wrist, a quick clench, then release? She had felt his intensity. His eyes had held hers. Such urgency there.

'You'll be safe here. Wait for me.'

Innocuous words. Was it more than a trite farewell? If so, she had put herself in Zan's debt and it was likely that he would have to pay the price for her mischief-making. What would that price be?

Such conflict.

The candle flickered. How long would she be kept here? The candle would soon burn down to leave her in the dark, which suddenly seemed entirely appropriate.

A sharp noise brought her to her feet, to the window. Obviously Zan had opened the doors. Was the contraband beginning to be delivered so soon? She had not expected it quite yet. But there was the sound of a horse ridden fast into the stable yard. Running feet. The opening and slam of doors. An exchange of words outside on the gravel. The horse and its rider departed. Then silence.

Probably just news that the contraband was on its way, loaded on to the backs of men and ponies alike. Marie-Claude paced the room. So all was going to plan. No reason why Zan should not be safe. D'Acre needed Zan for his organisation. Any differences would soon be patched up over a glass of brandy.

Why would she worry about him? He was quite capable of fending for himself.

A thud. A slam of a door. Booted feet, a heavy dragging sound. Muttered curses that grew louder. Savage instructions.

Marie-Claude hurried to the door, hands pressed hard against the wood, listening. They were approaching. Yes, the boots were coming up the stairs.

She leapt back with the presence of mind to push the pistol beneath the coverlet on the bed as the key was thrust in the lock and the door slammed back to crash against the wall, sending up a cloud of dust.

There was Zan, flanked by D'Acre and Rackham. She saw immediately what had happened, even in the flickering candlelight. Zan was unable to walk unaided. Eyes wide, breath shallow, she watched as Zan was dragged forwards by the two men and thrust into the room, to fall heavily and lie face down at her feet. He did not move. His jacket was gone, his breeches filthy and his shirt, what there was left of it, bloodstained and torn.

'What have you done to him?'

D'Acre, red-faced from the exertion, bared his teeth. 'Here's Ellerdine to keep you company—until we've finished.'

'What have you done to him?' she repeated.

'He's not dead. Not yet at any rate. Just a little difference of opinion.'

'He's bleeding.'

'That's the least of his worries. And when we've finished the landing, I'll come and collect you both. Those who betray me, pay dearly. Enjoy the rest of the night. Perhaps you should pray for a successful outcome, lady. I promise you—it'll be a warm ending for both of you, if we're caught.' D'Acre turned and stomped from the room.

'What do you mean?' Marie-Claude demanded.

'Ask your lover here, when he finds his voice,' Rackham replied, nudging Zan none too gently with his boot. 'So just pray it all goes well for us.' He slammed and relocked the door.

Marie-Claude promptly sank to her knees. The words of warning had made little sense—but that was not her priority. She turned all her concentration to the state of the man who lay broken and bloody. She could immediately see why he had fallen so heavily. His hands were tied behind him, cruelly tight, from wrist to elbow.

Was he dead? Fatally hurt? There was so much blood.

'Zan,' she murmured tentatively, terrified of what she might discover. Then more urgently, 'Zan!' She closed her hand gently over his shoulder.

'I'm not dead,' he croaked, voice raw. 'Not yet, by God! Untie the ropes so I can move.'

Without a word she set to worrying at the knots with her fingers. Impossible. They were tight and complex, tied by a master sailor, the rope unfrayed, of good quality.

'I can't move them.' She dared not think about Zan's injuries or the already discolouring patches she could see on his ribs through the remnants of his shirt.

He turned his head on the floor, dark waves of hair falling away so that she could see his face. What she saw made her draw in her breath. It was brutally clear how D'Acre and Rackham had spent the last ten minutes.

'Have you nothing sharp?' he asked.

'No. Nothing.'

'Not even a hair pin?' The ghost of a laugh on a sigh of pain as he tried to move his shoulders.

She saw what he meant. 'Too fragile for these knots.'

'Then use the candle.'

Marie-Claude felt the blood drain from her face. Horror and instant refusal. 'I can't do that. Your wrists—'

'Will be singed—but better that than lying trussed up here like a fowl prepared for the pot, for D'Acre to come back and haul me over the cliff! I'm not going to lie here and wait for him to finish us off.'

'Zan!' His words forced her to accept the truth. She could not deny it or argue against it. Their lives would probably be forfeit now, whether the run went well or not.

'Sorry!' he groaned instantly. 'I wasn't thinking. It won't come to that!'

But she knew it would. And knew he was trying to protect her.

'Get the candle, Marie.' The command was harsh, brooking no refusal. 'You've got to do this. I can't. And we don't know how much time we have.'

If she thought about it she would weep. Instead she set herself to carry out his instructions. If he could stand the pain, then so could she inflict it on him. She would set her heart and her mind and just do it with as little damage as she could encompass.

'You need to sit up.' She was impressed by the brisk matter of factness she managed to achieve even though her belly lurched with nausea at what she must do.

'You'll have to help me there too.'

Carefully she grasped his shoulders and used all her weight to lift him until he could sit. Then for a long moment, giving him time to catch his breath, she simply knelt and looked at him with horror, at what D'Acre had done to him. His shirt hung in bloody strips. He had been beaten, that was quite evident. Ugly red weals ran along his ribs, abrasions from frenzied fists to his jaw, his cheekbone. His lip was cut and still bled sluggishly. His knuckles, she had already noticed, were broken and bleeding— he'd obviously done what he could to defend himself before he'd been tied up. A knife had been used against him, slicing through the flesh of his arm. Heavy boots had done the rest. Rackham and D'Acre had kicked him when he had been helpless on the floor. There would be heavy bruises. Already his handsome face was marred by livid discolour- ing, one eye swelling.

So they had not settled their differences after all.

Was she the cause of this? Yes. Her meddling had forced Zan to make a choice. He had chosen to stand for her—and in doing so he'd thrown himself to D'Acre's dogs.

It was Marie-Claude's initial instinct to smother him with care and apologies. Soft hands to soothe, words of restitution and gratitude, tears of regret. Such womanly desires to heal and cherish. He had been hurt for her. Instead she clenched her hands in her lap. That was no good. If she were to allow her emotions free rein, she would be of no value at all. Nor would he want her tears or her compassion. She was not even sure he deserved them. If he chose to live his life by the precepts of vicious smugglers, then he could expect no quarter when deals and ventures went awry. It was his own fault in throwing in his lot with the Fly-By-Nights in the first place. He deserved no compassion from her.

No. I can't believe that.

All Marie-Claude's instincts cried out against her harsh judgement when she saw the lines of pain engraved deep between nose and mouth. When she saw the cruel marks on his flesh.

I love him, I love him still. I don't care what he is, what he has done. He came to my rescue and no man of vicious character would have done that. There is honour here, and integrity, a sense of decency. I don't know why he has lived the life he has, but he's not as black as he would like me to believe.

It was as if a light had been lit in her heart. A little flame that grew until it burned steadily. It gave her strength. She would do what needed to be done and weep later—if she—if Zan—were still alive.

'Well, Madame Mermaid?' he asked with a travesty of a smile, breaking into her decision. 'Behold a common, disreputable smuggler before you. Now you see what happens to a man who abandons the tenets of his upbringing and throws in his lot with criminals who have no sense of morality or rightness.'

Marie-Claude's eyes widened in shock. She knew

he had seen compassion in her face. And once again he would make every effort to destroy it.

'Did I not warn you that I was not a man for you to associate with?' The smile had become a hard line. 'Now you see it for reality. Smuggling is not pretty, nor is it romantic. I don't doubt I deserve everything handed out to me and you should damn me for my lifestyle and my chosen companions. I don't suppose D'Acre's improved my appearance any.'

So he would continue to decry his own character, would he? Well, for a little while she would let him. But when this was over she would force him to tell her the truth. She would accept this lie he was perpetuating for now, but not for much longer.

'No, he hasn't,' she replied caustically, deliberately smothering any pity she felt for him or it would swamp them both. Without another word she rose to her feet and brought the candle, set it between them. 'Are you sure about this?'

'Have you any better ideas? I'd rather not be helpless when D'Acre or Rackham returns.'

'Then I'll do what I can.' How cold her voice seemed even to her own ears. 'I'll try not to hurt you too much.'

'Just do it.'

'Then turn round.'

He shuffled so that his back was to her and he could lean his shoulder against the bed for support.

'If you can lift your arms up, away from your body…'

She lifted the candle with fingers that trembled and applied the candle flame to the rope.

They were the most excruciating of minutes she had ever lived through. It seemed more like hours, trying to get the dry hemp to catch without exploding into fire, to smoulder and weaken without burning Zan's wrists beyond what could be withstood. At first he bore it all without a sound, merely turning his face into the edge of the mattress. She felt his shallow breathing, the moments when he held his breath against the agony. She felt the suppressed grunt of searing pain echo in her own body when the flame licked along his flesh. His fingers clenched and stretched, but he would not cry out. She used her own skirts to protect him as much as she could, but feared she would set the flimsy material alight and consume them both. It was not without pain for her, but she set her teeth and continued to apply the flame.

Zan gasped on an intake of breath as the fire licked round the rope.

It was too much. Her courage almost gave out, her heart refusing to continue the torture.

'Zan. I can't.'

Zan heard her words as if from a distance. He

turned his head to look at her, his face grey and ravaged on a fresh flood of pain, eyes impossibly dark and shadowed with it. Such agony when she applied the candle flame. It was a monster with jagged teeth and sharp claws to bite and tear. He clenched his jaw as he rode the fierce full wash of suffering. But then he felt her cool hand on his. Saw the tears in her eyes that she had not, would not shed. Such strength she had. He would never have got through it without her. And there was still so far to go. Love for her, intense admiration and respect, burned far stronger than the pain. She would do it and he would be released and they would survive. She had to do it. Zan summoned all the authority he could into his voice, even though it seemed little more than a harsh croak to his ears.

'You can do it, Marie-Claude. A braver woman I've never met. There's nothing you are not capable of. You've got to release me. It could make all the difference in the world.'

Marie-Claude leaned forwards. With the ruffle of her skirt she wiped the beads of sweat from his forehead. And because she could no longer hide her fear and her compassion, she pressed her lips gently against his damaged cheek.

'I'll do it. I too feel the pain. Forgive me, forgive me...'

She set to it again. It was excruciating, unbearable. Tears ran down her cheeks when the skin of his wrists blistered and he wept. When he could no longer remain silent against the agony of it. But she stuck to the task, wiping the tears away with her forearm, working as fast and as efficiently as she could.

At last the strands of hemp began to give way with blackened edges. She put the candle aside.

'Pull now, if you can.'

His shoulders strained as he pulled his arms apart, unable any longer to stifle a hoarse cry as the rope dug into his burnt flesh. But the rope parted.

'We've done it!'

He did not respond, but turned his face once more against the linen on the bed.

Marie-Claire unwrapped the remains of the binding. Slowly Zan sat up, flexed his arms, his clenched fingers, breath hissing between his teeth. For a moment his head fell back, eyes closed. Then, cautiously, he stretched out his hand to touch her cheek.

'I said you could do it.' His eyes were blurred and without focus, his skin as white as the candle wax.

'So much pain. How could you bear it?' Marie-Claude forced herself to remain severely practical. 'I've no water to bathe your wounds. Or your wrists. I'll cover them with what's left of your shirt.' She tore at it to make a pad to dab at the blood on his mouth. Wrapped and tied loose cuffs around his wrists, conscious of every movement she made that caused him further pain. Never had she felt so helpless or so culpable. When it was done, gently she pushed him to lean back against the bed.

'Rest a while. I've nothing to give you. I can't even wash the blood away. You must be so thirsty.'

His eyes, barely open, glinted indigo. 'No brandy? Amazing in a house designed as a smuggler's paradise. And I recall you threw the water over me.'

His deliberate levity touched her heart, but she knew he was suffering, his breathing shallow, face still ashen. He closed his eyes again and she had the impression that he was harnessing what strength he had. All she could do was to sit silently beside him, waiting helplessly, conscious of every breath he took. She did not touch him again. She wanted to, would have taken him in her arms and let his head rest on her shoulder, but she gave him the space to conquer the pain and regain his self-control.

She knew the moment his eyes opened again, felt them resting on her and raised her head to find him looking at her, more focused now, but still shadowed.

'That's better,' he said. Sitting up with exaggerated care, he flexed his arms and hands again. 'Everything seems to work pretty well.'

'Your ribs might be cracked.'

He moved and grimaced. 'So they might, but I can deal with that.'

She leaned forwards and touched the back of his hand, the merest touch, not resisting when Zan turned his hand and enclosed her own.

'Thank you,' he said.

She could not read his expression. Quizzical. Regretful. A little sad.

'For what?' she found herself asking as her own guilt took hold. 'I put out the lamp. I relocked the doors. I lit D'Acre's suspicions. I brought this on you.'

'So you did—all of those things. But it was not your fault and you must not take any of the blame, Marie. Do you hear me? The blame is mine. I can carry it.' His attempt at a laugh nearly broke her heart. 'I thought we'd got away with it. D'Acre'd written me off as a careless bastard hardly worthy of a place in the Fly-By-Nights, but nothing worse than that. I'd expected a fist or two to the jaw, but nothing more. And then…'

Suddenly his hand tightened around hers. Taken by surprise she cried out, before catching her lower lip in her teeth. She watched as he turned her hand over in his, then snatched up the other. There was no hope of hiding it from him.

'Marie…I didn't know,' he said, horrified.

'It's nothing. I just tried to stop the rope burning

too fast, too dangerously, so I used my skirts and my fingers to crush the flames…'

'And burnt them.' He pressed his mouth very softly against the fingertips. 'You suffered because of me. I should be whipped for that, if for nothing else in this unholy mess I've landed you in. It was never my intention, I swear it. I would have saved you all of this, but circumstances conspired against us.'

Carefully he pulled her close and folded her into his arms. Palms against his chest, she let herself savour the heat and strength of him despite his injuries. For a little while she allowed herself to rest there. It was Zan who finally pushed her away.

'I should not have done that. Forgive me.' He let his arms fall and rested his head back against the bed as if he were very weary.

Which stirred Marie-Claude from her despair. She took his hand and held tight when he would have pulled it away.

'What was it that went wrong?' she demanded. 'Why did D'Acre turn against you?'

She saw him hesitate for the length of a breath as he decided what to tell her. Was it the truth or some version of it? Then he shrugged and she knew he would not lie.

'It was Rackham. He rode up from the beach to warn D'Acre. A rumour of a large body of excise-men mustering on the cliff top. He hadn't seen them himself, but couldn't afford to ignore the possibility. The word was that they were a substantial force, making their way in this direction.'

'So D'Acre accused you of laying information about the run to the authorities.'

'You can't blame him, can you? So much had gone wrong tonight. And then the final straw—the Excise threatening to appear on the doorstep. I was the newest member of the gang with the most to prove in the loyalty stakes. It had to be me. I couldn't argue my way out of it.'

'Why did he beat you?'

'To make me tell what I knew. A bit of gentle per-suasion,' he added. 'D'Acre wanted to know if we were to be trapped like rats in a barrel, here at the Pride, and what I might know about it. He thought to extract a confession from me. And enjoyed every bloody minute of it! His tolerance of me was always thin.'

'Did you deny it?'

'Of course. If I'd admitted anything, he'd have killed me on the spot and disposed of my body later. As it was—and there's still an element of doubt in his devious mind—he postponed the pleasure. At least we now have a fighting chance to survive.' He took a deep breath. 'By God, he has hard fists!'

'And vicious boots!' Marie-Claude considered. A chance. Perhaps. But when the run was finished, D'Acre would return to finish them off. They might never be together again. This might be the one time left to bridge the divide between them—and it was up to her to force Zan to tell her the truth. Not an easy task to set herself, but she was sure of her ground. She would not allow him to continue this ridiculous charade. She turned her mind against his battered body and compromised senses and went for the attack.

'Why did you work with him, with D'Acre? Why would you join so malignant a crew as the Fly-By-Nights? You have your own cutter, your own organisation working out of Old Wincomlee. Why do it?'

'Why not? You know my reputation.' Suddenly the focus was back. He had recognised the attack for what it was. His voice became clipped and very cold. 'It brings a healthy profit, far higher than my own operation out of Old Wincomlee. D'Acre has so many strings he can pull, so many contacts. That's what brings the gold in. That's what I'm in it for.' Savagely cynical, rebuilding the barrier between them.

She would not have it!

'A healthy profit? And what do you spend the money on? Not Ellerdine Manor for sure.'

'You know nothing about it.'

'I know enough. I'm not stupid.' She fixed him with a stern stare at odds with her delicate features, but not at odds with the lift of her chin. 'I have to say—I don't believe you, Zan. If you are going to continue to lie to me, you'll have to make a better job of it than this!'

A line dug between his brows, but he did not look away. 'What's not to believe? Venmore and Harriette have told you all my past sins. My bloody crimes. I've never denied them.'

'I don't know about your past sins.' She kept her voice level, unemotional. 'I expect Luke and Harriette have told me the truth as you allowed them to see it. All I know is what *I've* seen. I hadn't the sense to realise it at first. I was hurt and so believed what I was told—that you used me either for your own pleasure or to make use of the Pride. Or to hurt Luke. And you encouraged me to believe the worst of you. How could you do that? But now I've had time to think.'

His brows rose with magnificent arrogance, but she detected a wary look in his eye. 'How can you doubt I'm working with D'Acre? You know I came here tonight to open up the house for his contraband.'

'Stop!' Marie-Claude shook her head, entirely frustrated. 'You're not in league with D'Acre. You never have been. I think it's time you told me what you're really doing.'

The shadows that chased across his eyes deepened from far more than pain. 'You are wrong. Just accept what anyone will tell you. What point is there in building me up as a martyr for the cause? It will only bring you more pain and heartache.' His eye softened for a moment and he raised her damaged hand to his lips. 'You're a lovely girl. You burnt your hands for me. But I am not a man you should love, Marie-Claude. No matter how hard you try to make a good case for me. It's not fitting that you should.'

'No? I think it's very fitting. Listen to me, Zan. This is what I know. And I've had time to think about it whilst I waited to discover whether you were living or dead. This is what I know, what I see. A man who rescues me from a drenching, or worse, from a high tide. A man who creates an escape for me from D'Acre's embrace and the attentions of his gang. A man who tries to get me to leave the Pride when he knows it would be under attack—and don't even try to tell me you didn't write that letter from *A Friend*! A man who takes the blame for the careful planning I wrecked and accepts D'Acre's punishment. A man who gives me a pistol to defend myself if need be. How does the image of a man lacking all honour fit with that?'

'I'm no hero,' he muttered sullenly.

'No, I don't suppose you are. I don't know about the wrecking. Nor the attempt to kill Luke and destroy his marriage to Harriette. Nor what prompted your liaison with a man of D'Acre's stamp. I think that for your own reasons you made yourself into a villain so that I would not love you. Well—it didn't work. I do love you. And I think you love me too.'

His eyes were wide with shock. As if a kitten had leapt to maul his throat. 'No!'

'Yes, Zan. You made me believe you were a rake.'

Zan closed his eyes. 'Marie-Claude! This is not the time—'

'This is *exactly* the time!' She would not be swayed by the plea or the terrible weariness in his voice. 'I think it's time you told me the truth and answered to your conscience. There may never be another time. We could both be dead before this night's out.' She held up her hand when she saw him prepared to deny it. 'You know D'Acre is capable of cold-blooded murder, and I give as little for our chances as you. I don't want to die knowing you've gone out of your way to fool me, from some ridiculous sense of honour and decency. I want to know the truth behind the man I love. The man who loves me.' She leaned forwards, eyes bright, alive with conviction. 'You felt that instant, magical connection between us all those weeks ago. You still do. So do I. So tell me the truth, Zan. If it's the last thing you do.'

'I can't…'

'You can. You will. And if you do not believe that I love you…' Marie-Claude leaned forwards and pressed her lips gently to his. 'There. Shocking. Inappropriate. Unmaidenly. All of those. And I'll do it again…'

She did.

With the taste of her on his mouth, the drift of lavender from her hair weaving through his stunned senses like a drug, Zan found himself pinned under that beautiful but cruelly direct stare. All his carefully constructed life—or what passed for it—demolished under a deluge of honest knowledge from the woman he loved more than life, when it was clearer to him than it had ever been that they had no future together. All his carefully argued reasoning that he should drive her away because she was worthy of a man without blemish in the eyes of society, without a past of bad choices and disreputable actions, all his hard-won acceptance of the necessity of their parting, had just been cut away from under his feet. Her hands on his were strong, unrelenting. When they tightened they raised the level of his pain to near-excruciating, but he would not flinch. In that moment, with painful death a real threat, he was forced to face his past and his future. Should he continue to live the lie, the shady deceits, the half-truths? Or should he lay it before her and let her judge him?

She filled all his vision. Dishevelled, blood-stained—his blood ruining the pretty blue silk—she was more precious to him than the most valuable cargo of jewels and perfumes from the East Indies. He had known of her past, her brave escape from Jean-Jacques Noir. That was not even half of the inner strength she had shown in her facing of the smugglers, or her releasing of his hands.

Her fingers were sore and blistered, yet she had made not one sound of distress.

He owed her the truth. How could he not? A misplaced sense of honour and decency, she had said. It had seemed the right thing to do at the time, but times had changed and were probably running out for both of them.

'Tell me,' she demanded again.

Why not?

If everything worked out as he still hoped, even if it were not against all the odds, she would learn the truth soon enough. They would still part. The truth would reinstate him in her mind to some extent, but would not fully wipe out the sins of the past. She would return, grateful for her escape, to London and her life there.

And if they did not come out of this deadly mess alive—well, he would rather not go to his death— and hers—with her thinking he had tricked her and used her. Was that selfish, with death staring them in the face? To want to clear his name with her? A sudden urgency swept through him to tell her the truth. For someone to believe the best of him even though she must also see the worst.

Yes, it was selfish, but he desired it above anything.

'I'll tell you, Marie-Claude,' he relented. 'It's not pretty, but it's the truth.'

So he told her with the candle guttering at their side. With pain ebbing and flowing as he changed his position to ease his screaming ribs. With her eyes wide and watchful. With her hands clasped gently within his with a care for her singed fingers. How impossibly dear she was to him. So he set himself to be economical with his words. No emotion. A plain telling of what he had planned— and almost carried out to perfection. But he didn't look at her, instead focusing on the unlit lamp, not wanting to see the contempt in her face if she could not believe him, could not forgive him.

'It was all a conspiracy to catch the Fly-By-

Nights. They've terrorised the coast for too long. The landing here in the bay—two cutters bringing in a large consignment of silk and brandy. Some lace and tea. Worth a fortune. D'Acre negotiated the shipment. I organised the landing. I offered the use of Lydyard's Pride with the Smugglers' Lamp to guide them home, and the use of the double cellar. It was too good a deal for D'Acre to refuse—it would be hard to disperse so much contraband safely in one simple exercise without a good hiding place. So we set it up.'

'That's what you were doing with D'Acre at the Silver Boat.'

'Yes. The final arrangements.'

'And Captain Rodmell knew about it,' Marie-Claude prompted as he frowned at the darkened lamp, recalling the meeting she had witnessed.

'Yes.' Zan blinked and continued. 'He was in the planning from the beginning. When all the contraband had been delivered here and the smugglers engaged in stowing it—that's when the Excise would swoop and take them and the goods together. The whole shipment and all the evidence against them complete in one place, with no chance of their sliding out of it. That's why I offered the Pride as bait. Too easy for the gang to run and scatter if the capture was arranged on the beach. If they were here and surrounded on all sides—impossible for them to get away unless they're willing to shoot their way out. Which we know they'll try—but Rodmell knows the risks and will be well armed. And the result?' He set his jaw. 'What should have been done years ago in Rottingdean. The whole gang rounded up, taken prisoner, wiped out. D'Acre and Rackham to face justice at last.' He lifted his head, sensing the silence that surrounded them. 'The Excise should already be surrounding the house, lying in wait until the given signal.'

'That you would give?'

'Yes.'

'You were working against them, all the time. To lure them in and then betray them.'

'If you put it like that—yes.'

'I thought you were one of them.' She sighed.

'So did they. They had to. I had to make a solid case for my own inclusion in the gang. They had to trust me to be just as ambitious and hard-headed as they. So I've been working with them for… well, for some months.'

'You could not tell me.' A statement rather than a question.

'The fewer that knew, the better. I dared not risk discovery—or the whole enterprise would be put in jeopardy.' He paused. Lifted his eyes to hers. 'Do you believe me?' It mattered. It mattered so much.

'Yes. It explains why I saw you talking to Captain Rodmell on the cliff top. I thought you were passing him misleading information. You weren't, were you?'

'No.' He watched as she studied their linked hands. 'What are you thinking?'

'I destroyed all your careful planning, didn't I?'

'Well, you helped.' He tried a smile, but had to acknowledge it was a poor effort. 'You certainly made life difficult for me. I had to think on my feet. But the final nail in the coffin...' he winced at the unfortunate analogy '...was the bloody Excise. Rodmell's a good man, but his troops lack something in skill and discretion. Why could they not get into position without alerting the whole neighbourhood? Without that I think I could have carried it off.'

'I'm so sorry.'

'Why should you be? I made a good case for myself as a smuggler of D'Acre's ilk. Why should you not do what you could to stop us taking over the Pride? I would have done exactly the same, in the same circumstances.'

'You tried to make me leave.'

'Yes. I wanted you out of the way for your own safety.'

She was silent again. Then, 'What now? What

will happen to us?' And she lifted her eyes directly to his, demanding that he did not dissemble.

'D'Acre's nervous—but it could still all come right if Rodmell keeps his wits about him and his men are up for a fight.'

She tilted her head. 'What did D'Acre mean—a warm ending for us if the Preventives arrived to intercept the contraband?'

'Is that what he said? I don't recall very clearly. I've no idea what he meant.'

But Zan knew exactly what D'Acre had meant. And had no intention of telling her. That would be too hard a burden for her to bear. Better to wait and hope against hope that the pieces fell into place. When he drew her into his arms she did not resist, but leaned against him with a deep sigh.

'Tell me why you decided to do it, Zan,' she asked against his chest. 'I know D'Acre's evil—but why set yourself up against a fellow smuggler?'

'You mean he's not much worse than I am,' he said wryly.

'No, I did not mean that…I meant what persuaded you to put your life on the line to arrange an ambush of this magnitude?'

'Marie-Claude…'

The silence was broken by the fast clip of ponies' hooves. The heavy fall of booted feet. How sure the

Fly-By-Nights were of their success. They had not even spent the time to muffle the ponies' feet. Despite the rumours, they still envisaged no threat to their stowing of the contraband. Perhaps D'Acre had become careless in his old age. Zan's lip curled. Perhaps there was hope for their rescue yet.

'Listen…' he whispered. 'The contraband's arrived.'

Chapter Thirteen

'So it begins.'

Zan closed his arms strongly around Marie-Claude, acknowledging that he would give his life to protect her. The next hour would be crucial. His eyes narrowed on the locked door as if he might see through the barriers to the events that unfolded below them. Events that would determine either their ultimate escape or their death. He faced the latter possibility head on. Imprisoned as they were, his own strength drained and his physical abilities constrained, he could think of nothing he could do to determine the outcome in their favour if Rodmell was not there to deal the winning hand.

There was no way of knowing. Any number of mishaps could have kept Rodmell from the rendezvous. And even if the Preventive Officer was now in position, excise-men ready with their rifles trained on the doors of the Pride, who was to say that his Majesty's forces would come off best? D'Acre's men were always well armed and D'Acre was better than most at determining the outcome through iron-handed control. Few were prepared to disobey their Captain. If they did, their lives were brought to a quick and bloody end.

Which presented him with a problem of vast proportions as a tremor ran through the woman held so close against his chest. To paint for Marie-Claude the possibility of death—or for her a worse ending—at D'Acre's hands? Or to soothe and reassure with false assertions of rescue? He felt the tension in her small frame, fragile as a bird's, in the curl of her fingers against his skin. It made the decision for him. She would, he knew, face the future unflinchingly, but he could not lay this fear on her. All they could do was wait. Whilst he brooded over his lack of freedom to dictate any outcome, they sat unmoving and listened, Zan conscious of Marie-Claude's heightened breathing beneath his hands as the minutes ticked past. He lowered his head to press his lips against her hair.

'What's happening?' Marie-Claude asked.

There was nothing here that he could not tell her. 'The bales and barrels are arriving—that's the noise from outside—carried on the backs of ponies or tied back and front to the smugglers and tubmen I arranged for D'Acre. The contraband will be taken down into the cellar. We won't hear that from up here in the Tower. Gadie's with them. He'll open up the trapdoor to get into the lower level.'

'Will it take long?'

'No. Fast and efficient. Like all D'Acre's operations.'

A pause.

'So George Gadie knew? He too was part of this plot to bring D'Acre down?'

Zan gave a little laugh. How typical of her to pick up on this one salient point. That Gadie was not entirely ignorant of what had gone on in Old Wincomlee.

'I'd no desire to put Gadie's life on the line,' he admitted. 'But I needed another pair of trustworthy hands with this—in case there was some hitch in the operation or I was waylaid. I needed someone to open the cellar and so keep the gang fully engaged within the Pride.'

'And he agreed.'

'The Fly-By-Nights are not popular in this locality,' Zan observed drily.

'And I think George has always had a soft spot for you. I think he has never been convinced that you were as wicked as you attempted to make the world believe.'

'Perhaps. I think it was loyalty to my mother rather than to me. He had a lot of respect for my mother.'

The clip of more ponies' hooves outside. One voice raised, then stilled.

'I'm afraid, Zan.' He felt her sigh as Marie-Claude turned her face against his shoulder. Her breath was warm on his skin, teasing his senses. How foolish that her proximity should pull at him so strongly when they were faced with such danger. But it was so and he must accept it.

'No need for fear,' he replied, raising her chin so that he could see her face as she could see his. Her eyes were stark with a riot of emotions. But so trusting. He would not let her down, and he would trust her with his life. He might have to.

'You wouldn't lie to me, would you?' Her lips trembled.

'No. Not now. What would be the use? You know all the black corners in my soul.' He smiled and trailed his fingers down the soft bloom of her cheek. Nor would he willingly deceive her. Merely tell her what had been planned and how, in a perfect world, it should work itself out. 'Rodmell should be here, in place, by now. Too early and the Excise might spring the trap by being seen and their movement reported back to D'Acre. Easy enough then for the smugglers to scatter the ponies, hide the cargo in temporary caches, and D'Acre's pack will find enough holes to hide in. If Rodmell's too late— then the birds will have flown and all the planning's for nothing. Our efficient Riding Officer won't risk that. He has an ambition to effect D'Acre's capture. A real feather in his cap.' He stroked her hair to soothe the fears that raced beneath her skin, praying that she would accept what he said without question. 'We should hear the attack any minute, once all the cargo is delivered.'

'No one, apart from D'Acre, knows we're here,' she stated.

'No.' It was the thought uppermost in his mind. How quick she was to see the danger in this. 'No matter. If Rodmell does his job—and he's the best there is along this coast—we'll get out of here.'

The rattle of ponies' hooves disturbed them again, departing at a fast trot, fading into the distance.

'They've unloaded.' Marie-Claude's fingers dug into his forearm.

'Yes.' Unable to stop it, his breath hissed between his teeth as her hand slid down to grasp his burned wrist.

'Zan—forgive me…' And he knew she meant more than the sharp pain she had inadvertently inflicted.

'It doesn't matter. There's nothing to forgive,' he replied, knowing she would understand. He became aware of the shine of tears on her cheeks and brushed them away with his fingers. 'Don't weep, Marie-Claude.' He touched his lips softly to hers, and when she returned the pressure of his lips so sweetly, with such trust, his heart shivered.

'It can't be much longer, can it?' Her voice faltered.

'No…'

A shout from somewhere outside the house. A shot fired. Another shout, a voice of authority, although they could hear nothing of the words.

'There it is! Rodmell! Thank God! Go and look.'

Released, Marie-Claude sprang to her feet and ran to the window. 'I can't see—it's too dark and the angle's all wrong.'

'Help me up, Marie. My damned ribs…'

With a hand from Marie-Claude and an elbow against the bed, Zan struggled to his feet with a string of lurid oaths as pain and nausea gripped hard. Then, as it receded, he stood to his full height and took a breath. Not as bad as it might have been. At least he'd be able to stand on his two feet if he had to face D'Acre at the end.

Outside on the cliff top the noise of violent confrontation bloomed. Shouts grew into a crescendo of orders, cries and shrieks of pain now that there was no need for secrecy on either side. Battle had commenced, full of fury, attack and counter-attack.

The smugglers would, as D'Acre had so accurately predicted, fight for their lives like rats in a barrel. Zan could distinguish the military rifle fire from the answering crack of pistols. Racing feet, followed by more gunfire. All a muddle of clash and counterclash that gave him no indication of the outcome.

He made his way to stand beside Marie-Claude at the window. 'It's impossible to see,' she fretted.

'But we know Rodmell's here.' He took her hand in his.

A door below slammed, followed by more shots. Lights moved within their vision, then just as quickly disappeared.

'What if Captain Rodmell does not have enough men?' Marie-Claude demanded, turning her ashen face to his. He could see her struggling to control the tide of panic that threatened. She pressed her lips together to keep her fear locked tight.

'We must trust that he will. Stay here.' Zan left her to limp across the room and listen, head bent, at the locked door.

'What is it?'

'Nothing yet.' He looked up sharply, suddenly remembering. Why had he not remembered before? So much to take his mind from it, but it might prove to be the key to their survival in the end. 'What did you do with the pistol, Marie?'

'Here. I hid it from D'Acre.' Darting to the bed, she pulled it from beneath the covers. 'What will you do?'

'We must just wait.' He checked the priming. Not that one pistol would be of much use if D'Acre held his own against Rodmell, and came to take his revenge on the traitor in his nest—but it would be better than nothing.

'Zan…'

He looked up, suddenly alerted by the anxiety that was sharper than before.

'Will you promise me one thing, Zan? If D'Acre wins…'

Her accent was suddenly very pronounced. He dared not ask her to put into words what she wanted him to promise. He knew what it would be. His blood turned to ice.

'No, Marie-Claude…not that.'

But Marie-Claude in candid clear-sightedness spelled it out for him. 'If D'Acre wins…*if* he does…and if he comes for us to punish us for setting the trap… Well, I'm not afraid to die, you understand.' Her eyes did not flinch from his for one moment. 'But I am afraid of… Promise me, Zan. Promise me you won't let him take me prisoner. I couldn't bear that.'

'Marie…' He knew what she meant, what she could not in the end put into words. It broke his heart.

She continued quite calmly. 'I know what my fate would be if he comes for us. Promise me you won't let it happen. I would fight, but…'

'You must not talk like that.' The harshness in his voice surprised him.

'I must. Raoul will be cared for by Harriette and Luke. I've no fear for his future if I'm not with him. But I don't want to become a smugglers' whore. I could not bear that. Promise me, Zan. If you love me, promise me.'

And she stretched out her hand to touch the hand that held the pistol.

'Promise me. On your honour.'

And because he could do no other, Zan took her in his arms. 'I promise, Marie. I'll not let them hurt you or harm you in any way or humiliate you.' He would make the promise. But whether he could ever keep it, he doubted. Still he would reassure her and if it came to the making of that choice—he would give his own life first if it would save her hurt and pain. 'Whatever happens, I'll be with you.'

'On your honour?'

'On the honour that I've spent much of my life denying. On my honour, I'll not let them harm you.'

'Thank you,' she replied simply. 'You see, I am not very courageous at all.'

'You are magnificent. You have all my admiration.

Remember that—whatever happens. Now…' His head snapped round. 'Hush!' Scuffles. Booted feet close below the Tower on the paved terrace. A shouted order followed by a sharp reply. 'That's Rodmell.'

'Have they won?'

'I'm not sure.' He strode to the window, shading the reflections with his hand. 'As you said, the angle's wrong. I can't… By God!' A sharp explosion. 'I can see that.'

'What?'

There was no mistaking the faint glow of light that had begun down to their left, and was now growing. Soundless from their enclosed distance, it was still unmistakable as it danced and flickered, growing in intensity, throwing shadows across the terrace and gardens. Smoke, thick and acrid, began to billow from the burning straw.

'Fire!' Marie-Claude breathed.

'Yes,' Zan confirmed. 'He's fired the stables. D'Acre's fired the stables and the house.'

'That's what he meant, isn't it. A warm ending for us…'

Zan could only nod. That's exactly what he'd meant. Retribution was the name of the game. D'Acre would fire the Pride and fry anyone within the four walls who could not escape. That was exactly what he had threatened to do.

'And no one knows we're here.' Marie-Claude turned her head slowly to look at him. 'How do we get out? Or do we just wait here until the flames reach us and reduce us to ash?'

His eyes touched on hers, marvelling at what he saw. Before, she had been afraid. Of course she had. But now faced with the imminence of a painful death she had gathered all her spirit around her like a velvet cloak. Her shoulders were firm, her spine straight, her chin raised. She would face whatever came to them. He thought he had never loved her more.

But he was damned if he'd give in too easily.

To his amazement, overriding the pain from every part of his body, Zan felt the old excitement begin to race beneath his skin, the intoxicating thrill of facing overwhelming odds and defeating them. It was as heady as a glass of champagne and far more satisfying. Was this not one of the attractions of Free Trading—the main attraction—pitting his skill and talent against wind and wave to carry the goods from France to England, to evade the fast Revenue cutters and unload the cargo under the noses of the Excise? It was what he had done all his adult life. And, if he were honest, to him the sheer adventure was more important than the resulting wealth. The matching of mind and body against the dangers filled his blood with fire.

He turned to face Marie-Claude, confidence leaping along his veins. Ridiculous it might be, but better a fight than a cowardly retreat.

'We'll escape. You'll see.' His smile widened to a grin. 'It's a long way down—too far to jump—so we'll try this instead. Fetch the candle and light the lamp, Madame Mermaid. We're going to make a bid for rescue. We're going to signal danger—as if a smuggling run was under threat. Today you're going to play your part in destroying the worst gang of cutthroats on the south coast. So light the lamp, Marie-Claude!'

'I think I've just been given an order and should reply *Aye, aye, sir!*' Her breath caught.

Unshed tears shone in her eyes as her lips trembled, but she moved swiftly to collect the candle whilst Zan manhandled the shutters back into place. By the time this was complete with severe strain on his ribs, and every other part of his body that seemed to have been dragged through the fires of hell, she had applied the candle to the wick so that the lamp was lit and burning steadily.

'Now what?' She surveyed him, hands on hips.

'This is what we do. We open and close the shutters six times, counting to ten—slowly—between each closure. And then we wait—and repeat the signal again.

As he explained the old well-recognised warning, he began to carry out the procedure, sending the signal beaming out across the bay. 'This spells out danger. Anyone who sees it will know. And we hope that someone on land—in the village or even better George Gadie—will see and let us out.'

'And if they don't?'

'They will—have you no faith in me?'

Hands braced on the shutters, looking back over his shoulder, his eyes were fierce and bright on hers.

'I have. I have every faith. Have I not told you that I love you?'

'No more than I love you. How can I deny it? Then come, my love, let us work for our escape.'

Together they opened and closed the shutters in rhythmic sequence, sending out a signal that all was not right for the return of the smugglers to Old Wincomlee. Their only hope. When Zan's ill-used muscles trembled, Marie-Claude took the strain, giving him a moment to catch his breath. It should bring them aid. The problem as Zan saw it was that no one would have their attention on the Tower room. Would anyone even look up? All eyes would be on the fire that was clearly growing in strength, the glow strengthening into actual flames that leapt and caught in the gusting breeze. The old house would go up like a beacon, like an old timber vessel.

He wiped the sweat from his upper lip, wincing as he forgot his burnt wrists. They would continue to signal until all hope had gone.

'Stop!' He lifted his hand.

They froze, breath held, listening.

Footsteps. Climbing the stairs. Rapid. Clumsy.

'It's Captain Rodmell,' Marie-Claude whispered, releasing the shutter.

Or it might not be. Until the door opened, there was no way of knowing. And until he did, Zan picked up the pistol and moved to put Marie-Claude behind him. As an afterthought, seeing a faint possibility, he clasped his hands behind him.

The door opened on the turn of a key. A curl of smoke, a faint but rank smell of burning preceded the figure into the room.

Captain D'Acre stood on the threshold. His boots and breeches were encrusted with mud and dust. There was a smear of blood on his face from a cut along his cheek, but otherwise he was unharmed. In his hand, held loosely at his side but no less threatening for that, was a pistol. He showed his stained teeth in a snarl, his face contorted with fury.

'A neat plot in spite of all your denials, Mr Ellerdine, to sell me out to the Excise.' He spat the words, barely controlling his rage. 'It nearly worked. I've lost a complete cargo and the Fly-By-

Nights have suffered badly. I've lost good men because of you. But some of us still live…' he took a step forwards '…unfortunately for you. I trusted you and you betrayed me and The Gentlemen. You'll pay for the blood you've shed tonight.'

'So you're still alive, D'Acre,' Zan observed. No point in trying to mollify him, only to buy some time in useless conversation. 'A pity Rodmell didn't manage to send you to hell with the rest of your rabble. Did Rackham manage to save his skin?'

'Oh, yes. You'll get to hell before Rack or I do, Ellerdine. And you with your hands bound and no weapon can't do a thing to stop me.' D'Acre nodded with some satisfaction. 'But I might just keep the girl—' now the snarl turned feral and chilling '—for a little amusement. It'll be some weeks before I can rebuild my authority and put to sea again. I'll have to lie low and lick my wounds—I'll need some entertainment. So will the men who escaped.' He raised his pistol until it pointed at Zan's chest. 'I deserve some compensation for my losses, don't I? As for your punishment, Ellerdine, I'd like to make it long and painful, but time's pressing and Rodmell is too well organised, damn him. So for you—a fast descent into hell with my bullet through your heart. Then the girl is mine.' He took a step into the room. 'I suppose I should offer you a last request.'

'No request, D'Acre—except that you meet the justice you deserve.'

'Not even that I treat your mistress generously?'

'Your word's worth nothing.'

D'Acre laughed harshly. 'True. And I'd make you no such promise.' The smile vanished from his face and he held out a hand. 'We're wasting time. Come here, girl.'

As he felt Marie-Claude stiffen at his side, the urgency of the situation clamoured in Zan's head. There was no rescue. The signal had not been seen, no one would come to their aid. Zan knew his choices were narrowing by the second. There was only one left.

'I will not go with you,' Marie-Claude stated in a clear voice that shook Zan to the core. 'You'll have to shoot me as well.'

'Don't be so quick to refuse. If you show me your gratitude for sparing your life, I might be persuaded to make it a less painful death for your lover. A bullet to the heart is better than a bullet to the gut.' D'Acre beckoned with his fingers. 'Now come here to me.'

'I'll never come to you. I'll never belong to you.' Zan felt her hand close on his arm as she stepped to his side. 'I'll die with my lover rather than spend even one minute in your company.'

'A vixen!' D'Acre laughed harshly. 'I'll enjoy

that. I like a woman with spirit, in bed and out. We'll deal well together. And when Ellerdine's dead, who else will care for you? You've no reputation left. I doubt the Hallastons will want to know you.' Suddenly he lunged, surprisingly agile for so heavy a man, and gripped her arm. 'Your time's run out, girl.'

'Never!' Marie-Claude responded, and pushed against him with all her weight.

Taken by surprise, he staggered back. 'You vixen!' D'Acre spat and lunged, hand raised to strike.

But Zan was there. 'Time has run out for *you*, D'Acre!' And without a second thought Zan raised and fired his own pistol at the smuggler's chest.

D'Acre fell like a tree at his feet, the breast of his jacket red with blood. There was no doubt of the outcome.

'He's dead.' Marie Claude was white with shock, but her voice was clear and calm. There was no panic.

'It was my intention.' Zan's eyes were ablaze. 'Did I not promise that I would not allow him to humiliate you? Now, let's get out of here whilst we still can.'

He stripped the covering from the bed and shrouded it round Marie-Claude's head and shoulders, the only protection he could think of against smoke and flames. At least they now had a chance. Closing his hand around hers, he pulled her towards the door that stood open to their freedom. Barely had they reached it than a clatter of feet on the stairs announced another figure emerging from the smoke. Zan raised the useless pistol as a threat and held Marie-Claude against this side. Rackham might still be on the loose.

George Gadie's smoke-streaked face split into a grin as his brows rose.

'Well, y'r honour, you didn't need saving then. As it happens.'

Zan lowered his arm, relief flooding like a balm through his veins. 'By God! I'm pleased to see you, Gadie. I thought you might be one of D'Acre's crew.'

'No. Most are dead—those we missed have run for it. Don't know about D'Acre.'

'D'Acre's dead.' Zan stood aside to indicate the figure on the floor.

'Good riddance.' George spat on the floor next to the body. 'Gabriel was bringing some reinforcements from the village—in case the Excise needed more muscle. He saw the beam, so we knew someone was up here who knew the signal for danger. It had to be you, y'r honour. Seems you dealt with D'Acre without our help. And you, mistress.'

'Zan saved my life,' Marie-Claude explained, as if explanation was necessary.

'Well, he would, wouldn't he, mistress.' George

turned his head at a noise on the stairs. 'That'll be Rodmell.'

'Ellerdine.' The Riding Officer ran up the final steps and cast a rapid hard-eyed glance round the chamber. 'Thank God you're safe. We weren't sure…'

'Better late than never, Captain,' Zan said in dry welcome.

'We've been a bit hard pressed for the last half-hour, but it's done now.' Rodmell surveyed the body on the floor. 'I see you've saved me one job. Some of them escaped, but the gang's broken beyond repair.'

'A good night's work, I think, Captain.' For Zan, the danger receding, the pain that had been kept at bay with the need for action flooded back. All he needed was to sit—or lie—on the floor, or even better, a bed. It seemed as if the events that swirled round him had no reference for him. The only reality was the pressure of Marie-Claude's fingers around his arm. He felt her take the pistol from him and he allowed it because his brain did not seem to be functioning.

Only one thought stayed in his mind. It was over, and she was safe.

'I owe you a debt, Ellerdine,' he heard Rodmell say as if at a great distance. 'The whole of Sussex owes you a debt that can't easily be paid. Too many have died or have suffered at D'Acre's orders. There are many who'll sleep easier in their beds now he's gone. Now let's get you all out of here before the whole house goes up in flames.'

Which seemed a good idea.

Gathering all the strength that remained to him, he took Marie-Claude's hand and led her from the room.

Chapter Fourteen

A night of terrible, unimaginable anxieties. Heart-wrenching fear mingled with a desperate compassion. A night of terror at being consumed in flames, or killed by a bullet from D'Acre's pistol or thrown to the mercy of the Fly-By-Nights, layered over by a pain so intense in her heart that it matched Zan's physical suffering as his flesh scorched and blistered beneath her own hands. How could the mind face such emotion all in one night, how could her courage and control stand against it?

But she had withstood it all. She had rejected the hopelessness of tears, the weakness of doing nothing because her mind and her limbs almost refused to obey her. And now it was over. The storm had passed. The danger was gone. Zan and Captain Rodmell had it all in hand. Suddenly all Marie-Claude needed to do was to sit on the straight-

backed chair in the hall and watch the unfolding of
Zan's plot to its end. What a strange anticlimax it
was. Marie-Claude sat in a world of insubstantial
images, divorced from reality whilst the ultimate destruction of the smugglers continued around her.
With only minor interest she watched and listened,
feeling no relief, but a continuing nagging anxiety.

She knew its source. There was one more barrier
for her to scale if Zan would allow it. But for now
the events of the night must be tied up.

Lydyard's Pride was, it seemed to her blurred
senses, to be in no danger of being destroyed by fire.
Under increasingly deadly attack from the enthu-
siastic excise-men, the smugglers had made a ham-
fisted job of firing the whole structure of the house.
The stable block would need rebuilding, that was
true enough, and the storage rooms adjoining the
kitchen would need some attention to repair the
effects of smoke and water. Other than that, there
was no major damage and all the horses in the
stables had been safely rescued.

Marie-Claude sat and watched the final playing
out of the drama. The Fly-By-Nights, who were
still on their feet, were rounded up and taken off
with callous lack of sympathy for those who had
been wounded; with wrists bound they were hauled
to the nearest gaol in Hastings. From there they

would be transferred to Lewes and a court of justice. The bodies of those slain were loaded ignominiously on to the backs of ponies. Marie-Claude noted it all in passing, senses still frozen from the experiences she had lived through. Even when D'Acre's body was brought down from the Tower room, she was astonished at how inconsequential it all seemed.

She was aware of Zan in conversation with Captain Rodmell. He had recovered his coat from somewhere and now wore it to cover the evidence of D'Acre's fury. It failed, she thought. The clumsy bandaging round his wrists showed below his cuffs. Prints of fists bloomed livid on cheekbone and jaw. The shocking evidence of the contact of boots told its own tale when his coat swung open as he stooped to pick up a discarded pistol. Yet, dishevelled and weary, there was still a light in his eye, a heated simmer of exhilaration, of achievement. It was fading rapidly and she could see reaction begin to set in, but the energy still fuelled his blood, still drove him on to complete the task.

How she loved him, the heat of the emotion wrapping her around, a comfort in the bleak, battle-stained hall. She would never deny it again. No matter what he did, no matter what she had to face about his past. She loved him and would for ever.

His first concern had been for her. After leading her down from the Tower room, he had pushed her gently to the seat where she still sat.

'Stay there.'

'Surely I can do something…' Weary as she was, it was still difficult to sit and do nothing.

'You have done all that any could ask of you, Marie-Claude. More than enough. Let others take the weight now. The night is not over and you'll still have need of your strength.' He smiled and gently kissed her palm, folding her damaged fingers close over the caress. 'There is nothing more for you to fear.'

So now she was free to watch him and think about what she had learned of him that night. His courage, his selflessness in his care of her. The driving force to bring D'Acre to justice. Whatever she had still to uncover, to lay bare in the light of day, Alexander Ellerdine was not a man of dishonour. She would stake her heart on it. At the thought, as if he had sensed it, he turned his head and looked across the ravages in the hall to capture and hold her gaze.

He smiled.

The warmth in her blood erupted into flame.

Zan went outside with Rodmell, leaving her alone in a little space. She knew that George and Gabriel Gadie were busy ordering the closing up of the double cellar with its illicit cargo. She knew the slabs would soon fit perfectly with no trace of what was hidden beneath the flooring, a sweeping of sand to cover any tell-tale marks or joints. The contraband would remain there in the cellar until its collection could be arranged, and Excise paid on it. Meanwhile Wiggins, dazed from the noise and confusion, emerged from his room and applied port liberally to his recovery. Released from captivity, Mr Temple was justifiably angry at his incarceration—for which no one was prepared to take the blame—but was relieved that he did not have to report more damage to his noble employers. He willingly washed his hands of the proceedings and retired again to his rooms.

Marie-Claude sat, head laid back against the uncomfortable carving of the chair as the excise-men marched off, proud of their victory and their captives. At last silence fell around her. What now? What was expected of her now? Zan had told her to stay where he had put her, and so because she could not bend her mind to any more useful occupation, she obeyed and waited for him. She knew he would come to her. What she did not know was what would happen then. Anxiety began to trip again beneath her heart.

She would have recognised the confident clip of footsteps anywhere. Zan came back into the hall. Where did he find the energy to keep going after all he'd been through? They were alone. He came to stand before her, offering his hand to raise her to her feet. For a moment they looked at each other and said nothing. The lines were deeply marked, the corners of his firm mouth tucked in, but his eyes were still on fire.

'Well?' she asked. 'Is it finished?' Suddenly realising how cold and final that sounded. No, it would not be finished. She would not allow it.

'It is.' He inclined his head in a formal little bow. 'All complete, the ends neatly tied up in a magnificent bow by Captain Rodmell. Some few escaped—unfortunately Rackham's one of them—but the Captain's sent out a troop to scour the countryside. He's every hope of picking them up by dawn. The Fly-By-Nights will fly no more. Your adventure is over at last.' His lips curved infinitesimally into what might be a smile.

'And D'Acre is dead.'

'Yes.' The smile remained, but his voice acquired a hard edge. 'I promised I would keep you safe from him.'

Yes, he had. He had promised. Had she really asked him to put the pistol to her own breast if there was no other way? She shivered. He had promised on his honour that he would not leave her or allow her to suffer. And he had kept his word. Now it was time she swept away all his secrets, whether he wished it or not.

'You're safe now. You can continue your life without fear or harm.' Zan turned away from her.

'Zan!' The passion had drained from his face to be replaced with cold exhaustion. Marie-Claude blinked when he abruptly released her hand and walked towards the door. 'Where are you going?' she demanded.

'Home.' It was little more than a sigh. He stopped, but did not turn back. 'To Ellerdine Manor.'

'You saved my life and you would walk away and leave me here alone?'

'You are not alone. Rodmell has left some of his men on guard outside in case of trouble, but there will be none.' He hesitated, his voice raw. 'Better so, Marie. You know it is.' He turned his head at last. The fire had completely gone out. Dark blue hardened to flat grey. 'We can't be together.'

He was tired and in pain. Perhaps she should let him be alone if that is what he wished—but she would not retreat. She would not allow him to reject her.

'I know no such thing.'

'You know that I was not in collusion with D'Acre, but all the rest stands between us still. That has not changed.'

'Then it *must* be changed. I know what Luke and

Harriette told me. I know what you allowed me to believe. I know now that you did everything in your power to push me away, playing the cold-blooded smuggler and heartless rake to make me hate you. Why did I not see it at the time?' She shook her head, a little gesture of bewilderment. 'I should have seen through it. But you were horribly convincing and I think I was too hurt to see the truth. Now I want the truth from you. All of it.' She shook out her lamentable skirts and covered the distance between them. Walking round to confront him and block his escape, she rose on her toes to press her lips to his. 'Tell me that you can leave me.'

'Marie-Claude...'

'If you love me, you will tell me the truth. It would be cruel not to. It would be dishonest. I don't care what it is—I want to know.'

She kissed him again.

'Unfair,' he murmured. 'Unfair. You know I cannot resist you even though I know I should.'

So he kissed her. No soft caress this time, but a fierce meeting of mouths, a hot branding, a leap of flame to scorch them both.

'I love you, Marie-Claude.' It was wrenched from him, like an oath against her lips.

'I love you, Zan Ellerdine.' It soothed, assured. Healed.

Zan raised his head, but did not release her, so that they stood together in the ruins of the hall, Marie-Claude resting her forehead against his shoulder as he turned his face into her hair.

'I can't stay here,' he whispered.

'You can. If nothing else, I can do something about your wrists. Wash the wound, the blood from your hair, that I caused. I can put a proper binding on your ribs…'

'George Gadie's wife can sort that out.'

'I swear I can make a better fist of it than Mistress Gadie.'

'Are you sure you want me to stay? If you say yes, there's no turning back. I can't guarantee my self-control if I stay. I can hardly claim to act as a gentleman, but I'll not take advantage of you, Marie…'

Placing her fingers against his lips, she knew exactly what he was saying. And it was what she wanted more than anything. 'I am certain.'

'You are as beautiful as you are generous. And so desirable.' He kissed her again, the lightest brush of mouth against mouth. 'No. I can't leave you.'

'Good. Wait here.'

She left him, detoured into the kitchen with rapid orders for Wiggins. Then reappeared—to find him still standing in the same place as if he could not find the energy to move—with a decanter of brandy and two glasses in her hands. She gave the decanter to Zan.

'Carry that.'

'I think I am capable.' A wry smile. 'A managing female.'

'Sometimes. Tonight definitely.'

Because Marie-Claude felt that her future rested in the balance. He would resist. He would impress her with his disreputable past. He would live up to the reputation men had given him. Was he worth fighting for? Yes! So she would fight and she would win. She took his hand in hers and led him up the stairs to her own room.

Marie-Claude's brisk instructions in an unusually acerbic tone had clearly galvanised Wiggins into astonishing action. She took the tray with the bowl and ewer of hot water, the linen and scissors and two pots of salve and closed the door on him. Locked it. Then lit the kindling in the fire-grate. Sluggish at first, she persisted until the flames began to lick and burn.

That, she thought as she turned to look at her reluctant guest, would be the easy part. How to get a determined man to go against the whole pattern of his life and bare his soul? Her heart ached for him, but she would lavish care and sympathy on him later. Now she would play the shrew.

'Sit there, Zan.'

She pushed a low stool forwards in front of the fire and knelt beside him when he sat. It was important that she remain practical. How easy it would be to throw herself into his arms and weep on his shoulder. But he was damaged, hurt. First she would care for his physical needs, then he would tell her the truth. After that… If he wished to leave her she supposed she must allow it. It was his choice after all. He had been making difficult choices all his life and would do so even if he thought abandoning her was still in her best interests.

Damn her best interests! She loved him. She had no intention of being a sacrifice on the altar of Zan Ellerdine's resurrected sense of honour!

She saw the pain in his eyes and her strength of will—how could he think her to be brave when her heart fluttered uncontrollably?—almost deserted her. Instead she stood, walked behind him and took the collar of his coat to ease it from his shoulders, down his arms. He helped as much as he could, but it was an anguished affair. He made no word of complaint, but she felt the abused muscles in his back tense and strain.

Once more she knelt before him. 'Hold up your hands.'

When he did she unwound the rough bandaging

on his wrists, wincing, as he did. The flesh was red and sore, blistered in places.

'I made a mess of this,' she remarked.

A ghost of a laugh. 'You set me free. You probably saved our lives.'

'After putting them in danger in the first place! This will probably hurt you. Meggie's salve is good, but applying it will not be painless.'

He leaned and kissed her on her brow. 'I absolve you of all intent to punish me.' He wrinkled his nose. 'Except that it smells disgusting.'

Marie-Claude sniffed cautiously. 'Dreadful! Ivy boiled in wine, it says on the jar. But we'll try it.'

She did what she could, anointing, rebinding with clean linen, tucking in the ends neatly, conscious only that he let his head fall back, his teeth clenched when she smoothed the salve over the weeping blisters. When a white shade crept around his mouth, she stopped and poured him a glass of brandy. He did not refuse it.

At last it was done. 'I think it may scar,' she told him.

'It doesn't matter.'

She longed to touch his face, to press her lips against his temple, but instead she stood and, gentle as she could, parted his hair with her fingers.

'I broke the skin.'

'I know. I thought you'd cracked my skull.'

'You're far too hard-headed for that!' she teased gently.

It had stopped bleeding. Dipping a cloth in the warm water, she soaked away the dried blood from his scalp and his hair, feeling unaccountably tearful. When it was done, kneeling again at his side, she dipped another piece of linen in the ewer and stroked the cloth over his face, his lips, holding back when he flinched.

'Good God, woman! You've a heavy hand.'

'No, I haven't!' But compassion welled despite all her intentions. 'Oh, Zan. He hurt you!' The bruising, the raw abrasions where knuckles had made contact.

'I've no desire to look in a mirror. And I expect I've had worse injuries falling from a horse or being washed against the side planking of the *Spectre* in a gale.' But he could not smile.

So for him she blinked away the tears. 'You'll live.'

'I expect I shall.'

'Let me look at your ribs.'

'If you must…'

Bruising, scrapes from contact with heavy boots, but no broken skin. She pressed the flat of her hand softly along his ribs where the dark discolouration was worst.

'Does that hurt?'

He dragged in a breath on a whispered oath. 'Hell and the devil! Yes.'

'Cracked, probably, but I'm not sure.' Her voice was as raw as his, but she stuck to her allotted task. 'I could bind them for you.'

'No. Let them be…'

She resisted smoothing his hair away from his forehead. His eyes were closed as he rode the pain. She gave him a moment to recover, to collect himself.

'Let me finish. Soon now. I've a salve that will ease the pain here. I'll not hurt you again. Let me…' She stood, walked behind him, moving the branch of candles to cast more light. 'I don't think… Lean forwards a little.'

Her words froze on her lips, her skin suddenly chill as she let her fingers move softly over the skin of his back. Smooth, hard and taut where there were no abrasions. Tanned from working without a shirt in the warm days on board the cutter. Muscles hard and fluid beneath the skin. Satin smooth—except for the silvered marks of a whip, old and very faint, but still visible in the direct light, running across from shoulder to waist. She had had no idea. Despite their intimacy, she had no warning of this. She touched him, could barely sense them beneath her fingertips.

And felt him stiffen beneath her touch. Felt his instant resistance to what she saw. So here was another strand to be unravelled if she were ever to understand the complex man who was Alexander Ellerdine.

'What's this?'

He looked up and back over his shoulder, and she read under the pain a quick irritation as he prepared to deny any importance. He shrugged his shoulder under her hand.

'Nothing.'

'Someone has beaten you.'

'I probably deserved it. I was a wild enough boy. A long time ago now.'

'Yes, I can see.' A very long time ago, so long that the marks were almost invisible. But someone had taken a switch to him, or a riding crop, and she thought more than once. This was no casual beating. In places the lines overlapped, criss-crossed. Someone had seriously whipped him.

'Zan…' She placed her palms against the scars for one long moment, then moved to kneel before him, looking up into his face. 'Zan, who dared—?'

'Leave it, Marie. It's not important. I'm not proud of the scars and they have no bearing on my life now.' The hardness in his voice touched her. The bleak acceptance of whatever had caused them. And the refusal to compromise.

'You're hiding the truth from me again. So many secrets and lies.' Touching her lips against his cheekbone. 'So you don't want my pity, my compassion. Very well. I swear you won't get it. I'll remain hard-hearted and unmoved, whatever you tell me, if that's what you want.' She captured one of his hands and pressed her mouth against his fingers. 'Will you still not accept that I love you?' She did not wait for his reply. 'Who did this to you?'

The resistance remained, she felt his fingers tense and flex within hers, but she refused to let go. Calmly she sat and waited, tension snapping between them. Until he raised his head at last and breathed out, long and slow.

'I see there's no stopping you tonight, and I don't think I have the will to withstand you. It was my father who did it. As I said, I was a wild youth and not the son he wanted.'

'Your father?' Marie-Claude knew little about the previous owner of the Ellerdine acres, but she had thought, from Harriette's brief explanation, that he had been a mild-mannered ineffectual man who had failed to control his wayward son. Would such a man cause his son pain? 'But why?' she repeated. 'What could a boy do that was so bad that his father took a whip to him in this manner?' Her eye glinted in indignation. 'And why are you smiling?'

'Because your accent becomes most pronounced when you are angry. It is very attractive.' The smile faded. 'Ah, Marie-Claude, it is not worth your anger on my behalf. It is many years ago now—so many that I had forgotten. And my father—well, we didn't see eye to eye exactly.'

'But to beat you so harshly… Why did he do it?'

'It's simple enough.' He would brush it aside, to divert her away from sensitive ground. She could almost see him do it—except that he took another mouthful of brandy as if he needed it to help him face the unpalatable memory, whatever he claimed to the contrary. 'My father wanted his only son to toe his particular line, the straight and narrow and insufferably dull. The sort of life that he enjoyed—even if he proved not to be particularly effective at any of it. Master of the Hunt. A Justice of the Peace. A landowner. Part of the local social scene with balls and dances at the assembly rooms or with family friends. And do you know the saddest part? He shone at none of it. He had the worst seat in the county when he rode to hounds. The farmed land went to rack and ruin, as did the house. He had few friends who cared for anything but his deep pockets when buying a glass of brandy or a tankard of ale. He wasted money with no recompense to the family or our land. He went near to ruining the Ellerdines. And he wanted me to step into his oh-so-worthy shoes. At the same time he would give me no authority, no freedom to try my own hand at running the estates. I begged him. And he laughed at me. Damned me for a fool. Why would he waste money on investment when it was there to be spent? There was no moving him—and at last I stopped trying.'

Zan's hands clenched around hers, his nostrils narrowed on a sharp intake of breath. Now she understood. This was the reason he had adopted a life that led him into dangerous paths.

'He took every chance to ridicule my dreams of making Ellerdine Manor prosperous again. It could have been done, I know it. He said I was an ignorant lout and no son of his if I wanted to take the money from his pockets and squander it with no recompense. He just could not see…'

'That was a wicked thing to do.'

'All he wanted was a son in his own image.'

'And you did not fit the warped vision he had.'

'By God, I could not do it!' he continued as if she had not spoken, lost in the past with all its broken dreams and dashed hopes. 'I would not. What did I want with the withdrawing rooms of my father's so-called friends? The drunken wenching and drinking with his hunting cronies? He could not even be trusted to give fair justice as a J.P.' Forgetting his injuries, he shrugged and then winced as the pain arrowed to his ribs. 'I had no other guidance. My mother shut herself away into her own world of books and letter-writing and dreams. So, being young and full of defiance, I did what any lad of high temper and hot blood would do. I took the opposite path. There it was at my feet, already well developed in Old Wincomlee. It beckoned me, almost begging me to tread that path and don the mantle. Smuggling with all its excitement and ex-hilaration, bringing me adventure, danger, a way to challenge authority. So I did. Fell in with the Gadies. Lydyards had always smuggled. My mother was a Lydyard, so I told myself it was in my blood and I enjoyed it. It was like discovering a new life that gave me fulfilment and satisfaction beyond anything I could imagine. It allowed me to escape from Ellerdine Manor so that I need not see its dev-astation…' His words dried at last.

'And your father, of course, did not approve.'

His focus came back to her. He blinked as if he had not realised she was still sitting there, listening. 'No. He did not.'

'Didn't your mother try to protect you?'

'I doubt she knew. My father hardly broadcast that he took a riding crop to his son to break him of the habit of joining the Brotherhood of the Free Traders.'

'So he beat you.'

'Yes.'

'And it did no good.'

'It drove me to even greater excess. I can't deny it, can I?' Now he straightened and stood, stretching his spine. 'I need to walk or I shall stiffen.' He began to pace slowly up and down the room. 'I enjoyed it. Every minute of it. Don't mistake me. I was no martyr for my father's punishments. What lad would not enjoy the thrill of running the gauntlet of the Preventives? I should thank him for driving me into the arms of the Brotherhood. The excitement. The freedom. The sheer joy of sailing a cutter across the Channel under the eyes of the Revenue, a joy for its own sake, but also because I knew my father would hate it with every bone in his body. I revelled in defying him, as boys will.'

So that was it. Bored, lonely, left without sail or tiller to find his own way. As he had said, what lad would not embrace the charms of running contraband and thumbing his nose at his Majesty's forces? She understood and felt bitterly for him.

'And it threw you into D'Acre's path.'

'Sometimes. I kept out of it as much as I could. Even though I was young I could see that D'Acre was not a man I wished my name to be coupled with. His reputation was as black ten, twenty years ago as it is today. And, of course, he always did have a lively connection with the wreckers hereabouts. He never cared how he made his profits.'

'So he was interested in the ship that came aground in the bay,' she prompted, feeling her way, listening to what he did not say, suddenly alert.

'Yes. The *Lion D'Or*.'

'And was that how you became involved with the *Lion D'Or*?' she asked innocently.

'Yes. D'Acre said that I must—' His eyes snapped to hers. 'I didn't mean to say that.'

'I know you didn't. It wasn't you who arranged the wreck of the ship, was it? It was D'Acre.'

For a long moment their eyes held across the room, everything unspoken but clear between them.

'No,' he admitted as he continued to walk, 'it wasn't me. Except that I did nothing to stop it. I complied with what I knew would happen when I suppose I could have raised the Preventives. But it all happened so fast and… No, I'll not make excuses. I'm not innocent in all this, Marie.'

She stood, moved to stop him in mid-pace.

'What was so bad that you allowed D'Acre to lure the vessel into the bay?'

'He used threats. Even then so many years ago he was ambitious enough to consider extending his influence along the coast. For a man with wrecking in mind the bay here is perfect—and the use of the

Tower here at the Pride, of course, the Smugglers' Lamp. So he used threats. And not subtle ones either. Not against me, but...' He hesitated, the skin over his cheekbones taut. 'He demanded the use of the Tower and if I refused—which I did at first—he threatened Harriette's safety—and the responsibility if she were hurt would of course be mine. If I did not go along with his scheme to bring the ship to ground, Harriette would pay. So I did it. D'Acre made use of Tom—who was too young to know what he was doing—to carry the word to Wiggins to light the lamp. I didn't help him, but neither did I stop him.'

'How old were you?'

'What does that matter? Eighteen or thereabout? Old enough to judge right from wrong. You can't absolve me, Marie, however much you try.'

'I can make a case for vicious blackmail against you from a hardened criminal, threatening your cousin's life.'

'I could have stopped them—should have stopped them, gone to the authorities—to Sir Wallace even—anyone...'

'And risked Harriette's life? It's easy to know that in hindsight. But then—we all know what D'Acre's capable of. Who's to say he wouldn't have carried out his threat? I think you had no choice.' And he had lived with the guilt ever since. 'Oh, Zan!'

Marie-Claude covered her face with her hands and wept slow tears for him.

'You must not…' He reached for her, but she stepped back.

'How can I not weep for a boy dragged under a vicious current, out of his depth? And you never told Harriette, did you?'

'No.' His hands were gentle on her shoulders, but rigidly implacable. 'And neither must you. She does not need to know that her life was in danger from such scum as D'Acre or be made to feel guilty that a ship was wrecked to save her life. As for being dragged below my depth, I soon swam again! There was no nobility there.'

'Yet tonight you finally brought him to justice.'

'I did. I had to.' He walked away from her to pour two glasses of brandy, handed one to her. 'Usually there's a strong element of live and let live within the Brotherhood. We keep our mouths shut about the affairs of others. Our safety depends on it, so the least said the better. But I couldn't any longer. D'Acre had become a monster.'

He shook his head. He could not tell her of the more recent obscenities that had come to his ears. She had faced enough horror this night and he would not burden her with more. She did not deserve to have the images fixed in her mind to trouble her dreams, the horrors that, even though none of his doing, brought him to waking dread, dry mouthed, breathless, streaming with sweat. An unsuspecting excise-man lured from an inn and a quiet tankard of ale, D'Acre's ruffians moving the way-markers to lead the man over the cliff edge in the dark, stamping on his fingers where they'd grasped the edge, so he fell over to his death on the rocks below. The crew of a trading vessel taken captive, the captain and his officers manacled together with a heavy chain and thrown overboard to a certain death. The women of a neighbouring smuggling village, held to ransom so that their menfolk would co-operate and hand over their contraband to the Fly-By-Nights. The contraband was not the only thing D'Acre's crew stole that night. Wives were raped. Virgins defiled. No one had been safe.

Vile. Abominable. Tarnishing the name of the Free Traders who did no more than circumvent the paying of duty on brandy and tea.

'What had he done?' Marie-Claude broke into his unpalatable thoughts.

'You don't need to know. It doesn't make pretty telling. How could I be a party to that, allowing such obscenities to continue and flourish? How could I have my name linked to such foul deeds even though I was present at none of them, had no part in them?

It was time to end it.' His mouth softened, curved a little. 'And perhaps I saw a need to turn my life in a different direction. More is due to the Ellerdine name than a man who does nothing but thwart the law of the land. It was time to make a change.'

He tossed back the brandy, replaced the glass gently.

'So I decided it was time to make a stand. I would bring D'Acre to justice—and bow out with a fanfare. I set the trap and lured D'Acre into it. Rodmell would be here to take them in the act and the Fly-By-Nights wouldn't see the outside of gaol for a good number of years. D'Acre's rule would be over. I did not intend that he should die, though many would say he deserved it. It was enough that he face the weight of the law. But when he would have taken you...'

When he cupped her cheek in his palm, Marie-Claude held it there and turned her head to kiss his bandaged wrist. 'Why did you let yourself be accused without standing up for yourself?'

'I was guilty of so much. Why not add one more sin? I couldn't prove my innocence, so why torture myself trying to argue out of an impossible corner? I tried to stop Harriette's marriage—that was true. It was my bullet that wounded her. True, I aimed at Venmore—but only to frighten him off. It's difficult to exonerate myself from those acts. So one more stain on my soul didn't seem to matter too much.'

'Did you love her?' Marie-Claude asked, surprised by the sudden bite of jealousy.

'No.' Zan laughed softly. 'Did she tell you I offered her marriage? Well, no, she wouldn't. She never spoke of me, did she? But, no…I had an affection for her. My offer of marriage was hardly altruistic. I wanted to keep Harriette as Captain Harry—and the Pride as a base for smuggling—and so I tried to stop her wedding Venmore.'

'That was not well done.'

'No. It wasn't. In my own defence I thought it was a marriage of convenience. It was to start with, so I had no guilt over what I did. I tried to drive a wedge between her and Venmore. I'm not proud of it and it didn't work out as I hoped. They were in love, you see. I should have known—I like to think I would never have done it if I had known. Although perhaps I would. I think I had fewer scruples in those days… As for attempting to shoot Venmore—if I had meant to, I would have done it. How they could believe I was so bad a shot even on a moonless beach? He was an easy enough target against the light off the sea. But things went awry and Harriette was hit. That's the one true burden on my conscience. I could have killed her…'

'So you accepted the accusations.'

'It was difficult not to when guilt ran like fire through my blood. All that evidence stacked against me and I was not innocent. That's the man you see before you, Marie. Not a wrecker. Not a murderer. Not a traitor to his class and birth. But I'm not spotless.'

'No. You were young and headstrong and misguided—and I'd say you did the wrong things for the right reasons.'

'You are more generous than I deserve,' he acknowledged with a sigh.

Marie-Claude let her gaze travel over the smooth skin of Zan's shoulders and chest, the glimmer of candlelight enhancing the sleek definition despite the bruising, his scars hidden from her view.

'What now?' she asked. 'What road does your life take now?'

'The end of smuggling for me. And I need to put things right with those who matter to me. With Harriette, of course. And to make my peace with Venmore if I can. I'm tired of playing the villain.'

'What about me?' Her heart throbbed as she waited for his answer.

'I love you,' he said simply. 'I've loved you since you frowned at me and complained of losing your parasol, as if it were my fault, when I'd just saved your life. But there's no future for us, Marie. Your family would never support you. They would make it impossible for you. Would you truly want to be with me if it meant that you were shunned by Harriette and Venmore?'

'I can't believe that Harriette would shun me. Not if she knew the truth.'

'You have more faith in human nature than I. It's still my word only, and that stands for nothing.'

'So you'll turn your back on me,' she stated more calmly than she felt.

'I'm not worthy of you. Let it go, Marie.' He tunnelled his fingers through his hair, wishing he hadn't when the wound throbbed. 'I'm too tired to argue with you. You too must be so very tired and need to sleep.' Fleetingly he touched his hand to hers, his expression raw and wretched as he begged for her understanding.

But Marie-Claude tightened her fingers around his. 'I'll not let you go.'

'Marie, I can't—'

'One night.' Despair that he would still leave her made her bold. 'Just one more night together, if you can't promise me anything more. Stay with me.' Releasing his hand, she opened her arms to him. 'Even if we just sleep in each other's arms and I can give your hurts some comfort. But don't leave me.'

How could he turn his back on her? His heart thudded slow and hard as she offered herself. There was her embrace, inviting, alluring, waiting for him to step into it.

'You can't reject me now, Zan,' she said.

'No, I can't,' he admitted. 'I should, but I can't.'

Zan took her offered hands, did not resist when she pushed him to sit on the edge of the bed, helping him, ignoring his curses of frustration, to remove breeches and boots. When she stepped back to remove her gown, and bent to roll down her stockings, the bright memory slammed into him and made him laugh softly.

'What?' Still rolling the fragile silk, she looked up. Her eyes shone. She knew what he was thinking.

'Once I removed your stockings. When I was able to bend with some degree of success.'

'So you did. Now I'll remove them for you.'

She dropped them to the floor, followed by her shift, to stand before him with a shy smile.

'Look at me, Zan,' she invited.

'How can I not? Marie-Claude, my love. You fill all my vision.' He was trapped, he acknowledged, held fast for ever in her eyes. Then she was close, so close that she seemed to melt against him and they sank back together on to the old linen. If he had feared that pain and exhaustion would drag him under, he could not have been more wrong. His body responded immediately when Marie-Claude stretched along his side, all supple curves of breast and thigh against him, her lips drifting over his shoulder, his chest, only to return to stroke against his mouth. Her taste, her perfume was in his head, his heart, his mouth. Inside him. He could no more have rejected her than he could have stopped breathing.

She was every breath he took, every beat of his heart.

He wanted her. Marie-Claude's blood raced, her skin heated. In spite of the damage inflicted by D'Acre, his desire was strong, and it took her breath. How amazing that she could make so vital a man's control stretch to snapping point. With victory sparkling through her veins she proceeded to stretch it even further with a soft assault.

Pain retreated as his breath quickened, thickened. Need began to race and Zan felt his body respond. Within a heartbeat he was hard and ready.

'I want you,' he whispered into her hair. 'But agility is another matter. I'll apologise for my poor efforts before I have to.'

'No need. I can be agile for both of us.'

Her hands took over control, gentle but competent, strikingly confident. Lips and tongue moved and dipped, tasted, soothed and at the same time demanded, a steadily encroaching greed that took him over like fire on dry heathland. Any final thought of sleep or exhaustion vanished as his body and mind became drenched with desire.

He struggled to push himself up, to lift her.

'Don't move!' Marie-Claude admonished, shocked by her own audacity, but undeterred.

She must be careful. His wrists and ribs, his jaw and cheekbone. All sources of intense agony if she allowed the madness that seemed to have invaded her mind to make her clumsy. He wanted her and so she would overcome her shyness and lavish all the love of which she was capable on his abused body. Heat bloomed between her thighs, obliterating any diffidence, urging her into a heart-stopping voyage of discovery. The hollow below his collarbone where his pulse rioted against her tongue, the flat nipples that grew hard beneath her fingertips, the shiver of flesh as she drew the tip of her tongue down to his flat belly, blowing softly on the swirls of dark hair. It was impossible not to wonder at the extravagant beauty of his body, and when he quivered and drew in a breath, and not from pain, she could not but revel in his helplessness under her touch.

And so she blew out the candle. Before bracing herself, then rising swiftly, elegantly, to straddle him with her thighs.

'Is this a cherishing?' he asked breathlessly, mindlessly, saturated with sensation as she leaned down to brush his lips with hers, her hair falling softly against his cheeks. His mind wallowed, engulfed by the pleasure from her exploring hands.

'It is indeed.' She smiled against his mouth, outlining his lips with her tongue, feeling his response. 'How did you guess?'

Zan's breath caught. Cherishing, yes, and outrageously flirtatious. How sensuously soft her lips were, combining the tender with the seductive. How sleekly muscled her thighs that gripped him. 'You are always a surprise to me, Madame Mermaid.'

'Sometimes I surprise myself.' She laughed softly. 'I have little experience. Merely an intent…'

'And what would that be?'

'This.' Her hand enclosed him, holding, stroking from root to tip. Slowly she lowered herself, with such grace, and took him in until he was surrounded by her, deep within her, her hips beginning to move gently, rhythmically. It drew him down into a deep, dark place where nothing existed but his craving for her. Stunned again by her generosity, he let her set the pace as she desired.

But then he had no choice but to respond to it.

'My love. *Mon amour.* My dearest love,' Marie-Claude murmured when he arched his body on an intake of breath to meet hers. And then again as she gave him no respite.

Zan could not speak. The intense, outrageous pleasure submerged him as he thrust to bury himself deep within her. Dark, silent, soft, a world within a world, one of pure sensation that he must accept. That he must endure as the fierce talons of desire gripped him. Any command over his own response to the slide of her fingers from groin to shoulder, and back again, a tortuous caress, any control at all vanished like a iridescent bubble below the waves.

'Wait!' he gasped, clinging to the final edge of a precipice.

'No. Let go. I'll give you this release.'

She leaned and took his mouth with hers as he held her firm, hands splayed on her hips, as the need built until he could wait no longer. There was the edge approaching, sharp and dangerous, his body drenched and demanding.

'Now,' he growled, thrusting hard with her, all sense and thought overturned.

And he fell into the void.

In shattering delight, Marie-Claude fell too.

The room closed silently around them, silent except for their heightened breathing. Then, bone-lessly, Marie-Claude slid down Zan's body, releasing him with utmost care, to lie with her head on his breastbone.

'Sleep now,' she said.

As the thought came to him that she deserved more from him than he had been able to give, Zan fell under into blackness.

Thoroughly satisfied—how could she not be, having just brought a strong man to his knees?— Marie-Claude curled beside him as her heart settled and her blood cooled. She kissed his closed eyes, the corner of his mouth. What was he dreaming? It was nothing very pleasant, she decided as he moved restlessly against her. Some nightmare chasing him, dogging his steps even in sleep. Stroking his hair back from his forehead, she hummed a French lullaby as she might to her son when bad dreams made him wakeful. And eventually, with a sigh Zan settled, turning his face against her throat.

Sleep did not immediately come to her. She thought she had set herself a hard task to win Zan Ellerdine. But when had she ever given in before a superior force? She would beat the demons that tormented her lover. And she would beat down his resistance to her. Certain that he was now deeply asleep, Marie-Claude closed her eyes and let herself sink into oblivion.

Tomorrow would be soon enough to make decisions.

*   *   *

Zan woke again to broad daylight, sunshine streaming in, his muscles complaining, ribs tender to every movement, not helped by the fact that Marie-Claude's head was pillowed on his chest, one arm thrown protectively over him. Hardly the most comfortable of positions for him, but he would not change it for the world. Except to fold his arms around her, enjoying her soft murmur of contentment. For a time he lay quietly with her locked tight, savouring the one clear conviction.

He loved her. She was his centre. Marie-Claude was simply *there*. He knew it and acknowledged it because he could do no other. She had written her name on his heart in letters of pure gold.

And even more indisputable, even more miraculous, he had laid out his past before her and still Marie-Claude loved him. Here she lay, her head in the hollow of his shoulder, trusting, loving, after all he had put her through by turning her home into a battleground.

In an ideal world he would ask her to marry him, to live with him, to make a life with him. So that he might wake every morning like this, with her in his arms.

He sensed the moment when she awoke and turned carefully on to his side. The pain was not as bad as he thought. Desire was far more urgent than discomfort. Lifting her thigh over his, he drew her against him, to slide smoothly into her. On a long sigh she turned her face against this throat.

'I should ask you if you're in pain.'

'Don't ask.'

'Love me again.'

'It is my pleasure and my delight.'

He smiled against her hair, moving only as much as necessary, sinking slowly into the wet heat, soft as satin, smooth as silk, as the stroke of her lips along his jaw warmed his blood. It was enough. A rise and fall of breath, the glide of flesh, the flex of muscles. Long, slow kisses. A brush of fingers against welcoming flesh, soft, velvet soft to cushion them, and bring them both to heightened awareness. Slow, miraculously slow, to prolong every pleasure-soaked minute into a quiet ecstasy.

Marie-Claude linked her fingers with his, seeing her reflection in his eyes. There she was. Linked to him, within his sight, as he was locked deep within her.

Still he kept to that same steady peace of thrust and withdrawal, torturing her as the demand for release built, tightened its grip.

She felt his muscles tense at the end, and shudder uncontrollably, as she clung to him, helpless to resist the eruption of fire in her veins.

For a lifetime they lay, sharing each other's breath, then Zan stroked his hand down her back, along her spine from the nape of her neck.

'Marie?'

The words leapt to his lips. *Marry me!*

Only to be crushed by doubt. How could a man ask a woman to marry him when the public accusation of wrecking still stood against him? When his name was blackened with the stain of leading innocent men to their deaths?

'What is it?' she murmured, her breath warm against his skin.

He couldn't ask her to marry him. He would live with the dishonour, but he would not tarnish her name. If he wanted her he would have to be worthy of her. In that moment Zan resolved to work to reinstate himself in the eyes of the world. To put the Manor to rights and take up the role in local society that the name of Ellerdine demanded. To clear his name, if it were at all possible.

Much as his father would have wanted. His lips twisted against Marie-Claude's temple at the irony of it. And then perhaps there would be a chance for him with Marie-Claude.

'You're very quiet! What are you thinking?' she asked sleepily.

He could not tell her.

'I must leave you—go back to Ellerdine Manor.' He pressed his lips against her hair. 'I arranged to meet Rodmell there. And then it's over. D'Acre, the smuggling—everything.' And then on impulse he asked, because he really did not want to leave her, 'Will you come with me? Will you come to the Manor with me?'

Strangely his future, even though he had denied that they could have one together, seemed to hang on this question. He held his breath for her reply.

So, Marie-Claude considered. Zan might love her, but he resisted taking the next step. In her heart she wept for him, knowing why he would never ask her to marry him. Turning her face into his shoulder, she smiled sadly. Once she had accused him of being a man without honour. But now it was that honour that stood between them. Well, she could not force him into a decision, but she would make it impossible for him to put her out of his mind, and she had no intention of letting him go back to the Manor alone.

'Yes. I will come with you.'

Chapter Fifteen

It was a ruin. A rank, smouldering mess of scorched, tumbled stonework and burnt-out timber. The lovely manor house with its sweep of steps and elegant terrace was no more. Zan and Marie-Claude stood on the drive beside their horses and stared helplessly at what remained of Ellerdine Manor. Two wings of the house had been completely destroyed, whilst the rest, its roof gone and windows smashed, repelled with its sour reek of vicious vengeance on the part of the fleeing Fly-By-Nights. What the smugglers had singularly failed to do at the Pride in the heat of Rodmell's efficient attack, they had succeeded in achieving here at the Manor with all the time in the world to set the fire, light the flames and watch the house burn. Only when they were satisfied did they make a run for it, west towards their lair. The fire had been well under way before it was discovered and no fortunate shower of rain had blown in off the sea to douse it.

There would be no living at Ellerdine Manor.

Zan could imagine the brutal instincts of the remnants of the gang, their savage delight imprinting their faces as they had plotted this revenge against him. It held the taint of Rackham's vindictiveness.

Marie-Claude stood at his shoulder, eyes wide in distress, but dry and furiously angry. She would not weep for him. Instead her virulence made him smile a little.

'*Mon Dieu!* How dare they!' Her hands curled into fists. 'They deserve every punishment.'

'I expect they'll answer for every one of their crimes. Rodmell won't rest until they're caught.'

'But they've destroyed your home. All you possess.'

Now the tears came to glitter on her cheeks in the bright light that cast the ruins of his home into such terrible relief. When Marie-Claude turned her face into his shoulder, Zan held her, cradling her against the destruction of their future together. Even if he had asked her to wed him, how could he possibly ask her to make a new life with him when he had nothing— absolutely nothing—to offer her? No home, no comfort. Not even a bed. He had nothing but the clothes he stood up in and his mare. He felt surprisingly numb as the full horror hit him. He prayed silently that Mrs Shaw had escaped. His horses and dogs. Had they survived? He had no idea…

He was silent, his chin resting on Marie-Claude's hair. Although his eyes could take in what he saw, the whole terrible devastation, Zan could not find words or thoughts to match it. He had not loved the place, had found no love there during his childhood, but it had been his, his home, his inheritance to pass on to his own sons. Neglected, shabby, in need of care and investment it might have been, but it was his and it had figured in his new, hopeful vision of the future since he had woken with Marie-Claude in his arms. But now it was gone, replaced by an ugly smoking pile of stone and plaster and wood.

Beside him, fighting to hold back tears as she silently admitted to pure selfishness, Marie-Claude saw the destruction of all her hopes. If Zan would not take her as his bride because of the smear on his name, nothing would persuade him to do so now. All hope of happiness together was gone.

As they walked forwards to pick their way through some of the debris from what had once been Zan's library, George Gadie emerged from the ruined coach house, beating ashes from his breeches and jacket, followed by Tom, who had Bess securely tied on a short length of rope.

'Well, y'r honour. Mistress. Glad to see you both

in one piece.' He raised his chin towards the debris. 'A nasty business—but no lives lost. Your testy woman's gone to stay with her sister over in the village. She's a tongue an' a half on her. Callin' down the devil on all smugglers...' He grinned. 'And Tom 'ere got out.' Tom nodded, releasing the spaniel when she struggled for freedom. 'Could've been worse, I expect...'

And Zan felt a slackening in the grip around his heart as he bent to scratch Bess's ears, reducing her to ecstasy. 'What about the livestock, George?'

'Tom got the horses out. We took 'em over to Sir Wallace.'

A laugh was dragged from him. 'I can't imagine what he said to that.'

'He's content enough. The end of the Fly-By-Nights's good news for everyone. Sir Wallace says to tell you he'll look after the beasts as long as you need.'

'I seem to have suddenly gained popularity!' Zan remarked drily.

'Aye, sir, that you 'ave. The dogs are there too, y'r honour.'

At least there was some good news. But Zan's mind seemed to be caught in a loop that circled again and again to the woman at his side, to whom he could not offer a life. As they turned to retrace their steps, a hoof-fall announced Captain Rodmell and a troop of Excise.

'Bad news this, Mr Ellerdine.' Scowling, Rodmell swung down from his horse and stared down his long nose. 'I feel some responsibility. I never thought to send some of my men here. Never thought they'd have retaliation against you in mind.' He bared his teeth in disgust. 'Thought they'd be too busy saving their miserable skins.'

'Have you got them all now?' Zan asked.

'No. I was on my way to tell you when I heard about this… Some half-dozen still at large, we think. But we've had word they're making their way back to Rottingdean. We'll get them, sir, never fear. And at least without their leaders they'll just go to ground and we'll have some peace along this coast for a few weeks. Until the next gang steps into their shoes,' he added with jaundiced realism. 'D'Acre's death's the best thing that happened for many a year. I don't think you're in any danger of their return, but I can leave some men if you wish. I at least owe you that after all your work.'

'No. My thanks, but no.' For in all honesty there was nothing left to destroy. He put a hand up to Rodmell's bridle. 'Is Rackham still at large?'

'That's the good news,' Rodmell admitted, his lugubrious face settled in lines of satisfaction as he remounted. 'Rackham's under lock and key—and he's talking. Twenty to the dozen—anything to keep his head from the noose or his hide from a transportation ship. Putting all the blame on D'Acre as you'd expect. I doubt it will win him any sympathy with the justices, but it clears up a backlog of work for us. Rackham says D'Acre's behind every abomination, massacre, theft and smuggling run in this neck of the woods in the past two decades.'

'And that's not much of an exaggeration, I would think.' Zan acknowledged the relief that Rackham's future escapades need not trouble him.

Losing interest in the Fly-By-Nights, Zan turned away from Rodmell. There were more immediate concerns. Marie-Claude was beginning to shiver in the chill wind and, he suspected, in delayed shock. This was too terrible a prospect to subject her to any longer. He struggled to ward off a terrible sense of loss as he tucked her cold hand in his arm and led her back to where their horses were cropping the sward. What must he say to her now?

Go home, Madame Mermaid. Leave me, because it would be best for you. I spent a night in your bed, but I can't wed you. I have neither a home nor a good name to give you.

Well, as his father would have said, those who make their bed with the smuggling association must perforce lie down with them and share their noxious habits. He had paid for his fraternity with them and the debt was a heavy one.

'If you need me,' he said over his shoulder to the Riding Officer, 'I'll put up at the Silver Boat for the next few nights and then we'll see…'

But Rodmell urged his mount forwards, leaned down. 'Rackham's saying one thing that might be of interest to you, sir.'

Zan looked up.

'He spoke of the wrecking of the *Lion D'Or*.' A speculative look. 'I'm sure you recall it…'

Zan turned his body slowly to face Rodmell, releasing Marie-Claude.

'And what is it that Rack says?' His eyes on Rodmell's face were keen.

'That it was all D'Acre's doing. His plan, his operation. The rest of the crew followed orders because they were given no choice if they wanted to stay alive. Not that I believe him particularly— he's intent on saving his own skin—but Rackham's denying all responsibility. D'Acre wanted it, he says, and made use of the Smugglers' Lamp here at the Pride. Rackham even admitted, in his desire to heap everything on D'Acre's shoulders, that you and the boy had no part in it. He says D'Acre sent the order. And it wasn't the only wreck Rackham laid at D'Acre's door. A good half-dozen, by Rackham's count.'

As Zan absorbed the words, he was aware of Marie-Claude's hand slipping into his, of her little gasp of surprise, of pleasure.

'*Grâce à Dieu!*' she whispered.

'I'd heard the rumours hereabouts, sir—' Rodmell's voice was stern '—that linked your name with the Old Wincomlee wreck. Of your complicity. Not that I gave any credence to them. You might have been a wild young lad, but not as wild as that. But this exonerates you, I think. I'll make sure it's known in the right quarters.' He cleared his throat. 'You'll be glad to shake that off your shoulders.'

'Yes. By God, I shall.'

George Gadie, an interested audience, cast a sharp glance at the Riding Officer. 'No man of sense'd think Mr Ellerdine would have it in him to join the Wreckers. Nor the rest of that rubbish I've heard tell of. I know what's been spread about his making his fortune on the back of D'Acre, but it's not true—'

'Gadie—leave it!' Zan ordered. 'It doesn't matter now.'

'Aye, it does. I think the Captain should know.'

'Let him speak, Zan,' Marie-Claude urged. 'It needs to be said.'

'Well, Captain, it's like this.' The old smuggler needed no urging. 'The money Mr Ellerdine made from the ventures with D'Acre. A tidy sum, I'll warrant. In fact, I know it was.' He scowled when Zan raised a hand to stop him. 'I'll say my piece, y'r honour. We've all heard what's bein' said. That Mr Ellerdine was feathering his nest in league with as chancy a set of blackguards as you'd ever come across. None of it was true. None of the ill-gotten gains from D'Acre's operations was spent on Ellerdine land or property. That's true, isn't it, y'r honour?' His old eyes were fierce.

'Yes,' Zan admitted sardonically. 'It's true. Even I couldn't stomach spending the ill-gotten gains, as you put it. But there's no need to—'

'*I'll* tell you where it all went,' George continued remorselessly. 'Into the hands of the fishermen's wives and the empty bellies of their children in Old Wincomlee when the days were too wild for their husbands to take a fishing boat out. When the wind and fog kept their men at home. Mr Ellerdine kept none of it for himself.' He nodded his head in affirmation. 'It kept us all from hardship. It's only right you know that.'

Marie-Claude had no need to question if it were true. She knew that's exactly what he would do. Just as he would never speak of it. And it brushed her memory. Had she not seen some of the money change hands in the stable at Lydyard's Pride?

'What an admirable man you are.'

The planes of Zan's face were hard, skin pulled taut over his cheekbones. 'I'm no saint. I ran some of the operations with them to gain their trust. I kept quiet about some despicable deeds. I don't deserve your praise. The money I made from their operations—it was only right that it should go to help those who could not work. I don't deserve any recognition for it.'

'I beg to differ,' Rodmell stated, gathering his reins and signalling to his men to make ready to depart. 'And so will my superiors. I can't name many men who would have taken on D'Acre and brought him to book. You've rid us of a scourge. So you're out of pocket, sir? No need to worry about that. There's a large reward on offer for information leading to D'Acre's arrest. And since you handed over to us the whole gang you'll not be out of pocket for long.' His mouth twitched in sour amusement as he turned his mount away. 'And if some of the contraband at present stored at the Pride goes missing between now and our collecting of it—then many would say you've earned it. Quite an amount, I understand. Almost a fortune, Rackham tells me. Some would say you're welcome to it, with the loss of the Manor.' He touched his hand to the brim of his hat. 'Good day to you, sir. Madam. Gadie. I'll be in touch.' He nodded as he rode away.

Zan laughed. Raw and ragged, but still a laugh.

'It seems I'm not penniless after all. I can rebuild the Manor with the reward for upholding the law, and at the same time from the illicit profits of smuggling. Even my father would not know whether to approve or damn me!'

'Is that what you wish to do?' Marie-Claude asked. 'Is that how you see your future?'

It was the question he must answer. There they were, standing in the ruins of his home. The day was bright, the sun warm on their heads despite the chill wind to flutter her fair curls. A lovely day, but they were surrounded by destruction. Marie-Claude walked a little way from him, turning to look out towards the sea as if she would give him some space in which to make his decision. Some time to think of the answer to her question. It had been a momentous hour. His home destroyed. His name cleared with no fuss, both Gadie and Rodmell sweeping aside the past as if it had never been. Rackham had done him a favour at the end.

What do you wish? How do you see your future?

There was no decision to be made. He had avoided it last night, even that morning, when he was still hedged in by reputation and disgrace, simply because he could see his life following no pattern. But now… To hell with honour and reputation. He knew what he wanted. He did not know what the future would hold for them, but he could not live without her. He would make no more excuses to her. Nor would he let her go. Would she have the strength of will to take a stand against Venmore and Harriette if they still stood in judgement against him? After last night, her strength in the face of imminent death, he thought that she might. And he would fight for her. He needed her as he had never needed anything in his life before.

Dare he ask her?

If she did not lack courage, neither would he.

'Here's how I see it. I've nothing to offer you, Marie-Claude.' He kept his distance, eyes fixed on the proud lift of her head, her firm spine and straight shoulders. He would say it and let her choose. 'You see what I have around you. Destruction, ruin. Nothing else, except my horses, my dogs and the *Spectre*. And a sharp-tongued housekeeper. To some extent my good name is restored. There will always be those who have little good to say about me—a matter of the proximity of smoke and fire—but some now know the truth. You know the truth and to me that's the most important.'

He hesitated, gave her chance to speak. She did not. Unnerving, he admitted, but he continued.

'I cannot offer you a home. I cannot give you shelter, a room of your own or even a bed. And yet still I would ask—will you do me the honour of wedding me?'

Still he waited. Now Marie-Claude turned, but she did not approach. Nor could he read her face.

'If Rodmell is correct,' he continued, nerves churning in his gut, 'I have the reward. And with that I can rebuild the Manor. I have the will to do that and make the house live again, to make it a home, which it never was in my own childhood. In some ways I'm glad it's gone. I can start again.' He took a step. *'We* can start again. That's what I want for my future— because I have such love for you in my heart. I thought it would be dishonourable of me to ask you since I can hardly provide for you—but I will do it. Will you marry me? Would you come and live with me here when it is rebuilt? Would you be willing to set yourself against your family if they will not forgive me for the past? I don't know what the future holds, but whatever it is, I don't want to face it without you. Will you marry me, Marie-Claude?'

Marie-Claude tilted her chin in solemn contemplation.

And Zan's patience tottered on an edge. 'For

God's sake, woman, will you give me your answer? I'm dying of fear that you'll send me to the devil and tell me you're hanging out for a husband who can cherish you in silk and diamonds—or at least provide a roof over your head!'

'I would expect the silk at the very least, since you know the market so well,' she replied calmly.

'Then I promise you the silk. But I can't guarantee much else.'

'Then how can I accept your offer?' Hands folded demurely in front of her, Marie-Claude faced him. 'Unless…'

'Damn you, Marie! You would hold a suffering man to ransom.'

'I would. I want a new parasol.'

So that was what she was about. Zan's eyes glinted. 'Do you deserve one? You have already lost two to my knowledge.'

'I know. I need another.' A little lift of her chin.

'Then you shall have one.' A rare smile of great sweetness touched his stern mouth as he read the mischief in her. 'The one I gave you will now be a sorry pile of ash.'

'So you kept it?'

'Of course. Since you rejected it, perhaps I might have found another lady to appreciate it. And I might still have to, if you decide to refuse me after all.'

'Nonsense! You know very well that I'll take your offer. Who else would have me, after I've consorted with the most notorious smugglers in the country? I need you to restore my good name, now that you've become the local hero!' And with a crow of laughter Marie-Claude covered the ground between them and flung herself into his open arms. 'Sorry... sorry—I forgot your ribs... Kiss, me, Zan, or I too shall die—of severe neglect!'

It began as a gentle embrace, a brush of lips, gossamer light. A soft promise of passion. Until the heat built, to scorch and burn away all doubts. Marie-Claude clung to him, helpless, as Zan ravished and claimed. And Zan knew he was lost when she breathed 'I love you' against his mouth.

'So you will marry me?' he pressed, lifting his head, his hands framing her face.

'Yes. I won't allow you to live without me. As soon as we can. Where will we live?'

'I've no idea. And for now you must go back to the Pride. You can't live here.'

'Neither can you. You must come back with me.'

Zan looked askance. 'And what do you suppose Venmore would have to say to that, to find me under his roof?'

Marie-Claude fought to control the bubble of victory that filled her chest. 'When he knows the truth, what can he say? Luke's a fair man, and I think the Hallastons have much to thank you for. You saved Harriette's precious house from falling into D'Acre's hands. You saved my life. And Harriette's too, all those years ago, if you'll allow me to tell her. I don't think we'll need to win either of them round. So you will return with me to the Pride.'

'I always said you were a managing female. Very well, we'll break the news to Venmore that I'm not quite as bad as he'd like to think. I suppose I have no choice until I can rebuild.'

'Is that what you want?'

'Yes. It surprises me, but that's exactly what I want. We'll live at the Manor. I'll forswear my previous interests and turn my hand to all those dull law-abiding activities my father wanted for me. Even if it means I'll have to pay duty calls on Wallace and Augusta.'

Marie-Claude chuckled at the prospect. 'Will it keep you satisfied?'

'Yes. It's in my mind to create a home, and manage the estate to make it a profitable concern, to pass to my children. To our children. But there's one thing…'

Marie-Claude saw the tightening of the muscles along his jaw and her heart fell.

'What is it?'

The words were torn from him. 'You once said that you would not willingly allow your son near me…'

'Oh, Zan.' She smiled, a touch of sadness at the memory. 'Said in a temper when you had persuaded me with great skill that you were not fit for my company.'

'I still have to ask,' he replied. 'Will you let me care for your son? As my own?'

It was so simple for her to answer. She took his hand and raised it to her lips. 'Of course. I can think of no one better.' Her smile trembled a little. 'You can teach him to skim stones over the waves.'

'I can?' A quirk of a brow.

'I'm sure you can.'

'Then I will, of course. Marie-Claude…' he turned her hand within his so that their fingers linked together '…your generosity unmans me.'

They walked towards their horses, where Marie-Claude grasped the pommel and lifted her foot to allow Zan to boost her into the saddle. Then lowered it to look over her shoulder at him.

'Would you have asked me to marry you if Rodmell had not cleared your name?' she asked.

'I'm not sure,' he replied honestly. 'I knew I should not. Had persuaded myself I must not. But I don't think that, in the end, I could have let you go. A good smuggler knows the value of his possessions.'

'Good. For I would have made myself a thorough nuisance and camped on your doorstep, ruined as it is, until you gave in.'

'Marie-Claude—I adore you.'

'I am so glad.' She released the pommel to slide her hands around his neck. 'Kiss me again, Zan.'

'In public? What of your reputation?'

'I don't have one. And there's no one to see. I love you, Alexander Ellerdine. I'll love you for ever.'

He grinned, the old Zan, full of unquenchable spirit. 'Then if you promise to watch my ribs, I'll kiss you again.'

* * * * *

HISTORICAL

Large Print

RAKE BEYOND REDEMPTION
Anne O'Brien

Alexander Ellerdine is instantly captivated by Marie-Claude's dauntless spirit – but, as a smuggler, Zan has nothing to offer such a woman. Marie-Claude is determined to unravel the mystery of her brooding rescuer. The integrity in his eyes indicates he's a gentleman…but the secrets and rumours say that he's a rake beyond redemption…

A THOROUGHLY COMPROMISED LADY
Bronwyn Scott

Has Incomparable Dulci Wycroft finally met her match? Jack, Viscount Wainsbridge, is an irresistible mystery. His dangerous work leaves no space for love – yet Dulci's sinfully innocent curves are impossibly tempting. Then Dulci and Jack are thrown together on a journey far from Society's whispers – and free of all constraints…

IN THE MASTER'S BED
Blythe Gifford

To live the life of independence she craves, Jane de Weston disguises herself as a young man. When Duncan discovers the truth he knows he should send her away – but Jane brings light into the dark corners of his heart. Instead, he decides to teach his willing pupil the exquisite pleasures of being a woman…

MILLS & BOON